Diamond D for Danger

Center Point
Large Print

Also by Arthur Henry Gooden and available from Center Point Large Print:

Call of the Range
Death Rides the Range
Valley of the Kings
Trouble in the Saddle
Trails Into Danger

Diamond D for Danger

ARTHUR HENRY GOODEN

CENTER POINT LARGE PRINT
THORNDIKE, MAINE

This Center Point Large Print edition
is published in the year 2025 by arrangement with
Golden West Inc.

The text of this Large Print edition is unabridged.
In other aspects, this book may vary
from the original edition.
Printed in the United States of America
on permanent paper sourced using
environmentally responsible foresting methods.
Set in 16-point Times New Roman type.

ISBN: 979-8-89164-727-5

The Library of Congress has cataloged this record
under Library of Congress Control Number: 2025941596

Chapter I

The little mules were blowing hard from the steep pull out of the pass, and the driver slid a booted foot to the brake, brought the stage, a two-seater buckboard, to a standstill.

"Over the hump," he said. Reins loose across his knees, he fingered a piece of plug tobacco from a pocket of his calfskin waistcoat. "If you look careful you can see La Cruz yonder—down thar in them trees other side of the crik." He glanced at his lone passenger, who shared the front seat, and a hint of wonder deepened the network of sun-wrinkles round his eyes. He gnawed reflectively at his piece of tobacco, returned the plug to his pocket. "Ain't growed much the past couple hundred years," he added with a dry chuckle.

The young man was silent for a moment, gaze intent on the blur of trees in the bend of the stream that made a serpentine of paler green across the valley. Directly south of the town was a mesa slashed with arroyos that sprawled down from bleak, desert hills. The sun was dipping low to the western peaks, laid shadows on the lower slopes, filled the canyons with blue mist.

Except for an added brightness in his eyes, the vast panorama apparently aroused no emotion in the young man, who at first glance seemed hardly more than a boy. He was of medium height, with smooth cheeks and a burnish of red-gold in the dark hair under the brown derby hat he wore, and there was an air of innocence about him, a pleasing amiability. A more careful look would have discovered a certain ruggedness in his firm-lipped face and resolute chin, a quiet fearlessness in his steady eyes. His attire, like his brown derby, was a far cry from this remote corner of southwest New Mexico, and it drew fascinated glances of mingled awe and amusement from the stage-driver. The high white collar, the silk cravat, the city clothes, were obviously in the latest New York mode.

He turned a calm look on the stage-driver. “La Cruz—” His tone was musing. “I suppose some pioneering Franciscan padre made camp here in the long ago when Mexico was a province of old Spain. He’d set up a cross—call the Indians to worship. The camp became a town, and it was just natural to call the place La Cruz.”

“Sounds reasonable, son.” The stage-driver chewed his cud reflectively, an odd respect in the look he gave his passenger. “Savvy Spanish, huh?”

“I specialized in Spanish at college.” The young man gave him a shy smile. “You see, I’m going to live out here in New Mexico, and it seemed a good idea to learn Spanish. Lot of Spanish-speaking people in the Territory.”

"Figger to teach school or somethin'?" wondered the stage-driver. He shook his head dubiously. "Plenty Mex kids in La Cruz, but they sure ain't needin' nobody to l'arn 'em Spanish."

The young man grinned, shook his head. "I'm going into the cattle business—" He broke off, gave the driver a startled look.

"Swallered my baccy," gasped the red-faced stageman. Another spasm of choking seized him. He spat a brown stream over the wheel. "Cattle business, huh?" His eyes had a dazed look in them.

A hint of a frown shadowed his passenger's face. He said coldly, "I don't see the joke."

The stage-driver fingered his drooping, grizzled mustache, studied him with shrewd eyes that now took in a certain disturbing formidableness under the innocent-appearing mask of his young passenger's face. A smile warmed his own weathered features and his hand went out.

"Shake, mister." His tone was apologetic, friendly. "Jim Ball's the name, only most folks call me Uncle Jim."

"Mark Destin," grinned the young man, "out of Boston. Glad to know you, Uncle Jim."

They gripped hands, and Jim Ball said in a chagrined voice, "Them city clothes sure fooled me, Mark. Had you figgered out for a school teacher or a professor or mebbe a lawyer shark."

"I've been too busy to think about clothes,"

Mark Destin told him. "It didn't seem important, and it's something I can soon remedy when I get to La Cruz."

"Only one store in La Cruz," Jim informed him. "And about all the clothes you can get at Ben Stock's Great Emporium is pants and shirts. The boys most always head over to Deming or Silver City for hats and boots and things."

His foot slid out to kick off the brake, was suddenly rigid as he heard a low whisper from Mark.

"Jim, that man!"

His two hands filled with leather reins, Jim Ball's head turned in a startled look. Dismay froze his face.

Rifle menacing, the bandit stepped from behind the clump of buckbrush, his eyes black holes under the mask he wore. He spoke in a curiously whispering voice.

"That's right, mister. Keep as you are."

"Ain't carryin' a thing that's any good to you," spluttered the stage-driver. "Lootin' the mail pouch won't get you a red cent."

"Shut your trap and keep awful still." There was the threat of death in the masked man's whispering voice. "Ain't wantin' the mail pouch. All I want is for the young dude feller to reach back of the seat and shove that trunk over the wheel."

Mark hesitated, an odd consternation on his face. The man waggled the rifle.

"Ain't askin' you a second time," he warned.

Mark squirmed round in the seat, leaned over and reached down to the trunk, a small, stoutly strapped affair. The movement momentarily hid the hand he slid inside his coat. He heaved the trunk on end with his other hand, steadied it against the side of the buckboard. It seemed surprisingly heavy, and he paused for a moment, glanced over the top of the trunk at the man with the rifle.

"Get a hustle on you," warned the bandit's whispering voice. "Shove it over the wheel."

The hand Mark had under his coat whipped out and flame spurted from the derringer grasped in his fingers.

The bandit staggered, dropped the rifle, clawed frantically at a wrist that flowered red sprouts of blood.

The derringer in Mark's hand barked again. A red streak appeared on the masked man's face, and with an agonized yell he was suddenly in panic-stricken flight.

Mark was down from the stage with the swiftness of a cat. He snatched up the fallen rifle and fired two quick shots as the bandit fled into the brush.

"That should keep him running," he said coolly to Jim Ball, who was fighting the startled mules to a standstill. He climbed back to his seat, laid the rifle across his knees. "New model .44 Winchester," he added, in a pleased voice. "I'm keeping this rifle, Jim. Just what I'll need when I get my cattle ranch."

The stage-driver seemed to be having difficulty with his breath. He sat there, big-framed body limp, incredulity and something like awe staring from his eyes. He said in a slow, admiring voice, "Never seen anything so fast in all my born days. You'll do, son. You belong in this man's country."

"I wasn't letting him get away with my trunk," Mark said with a faint smile.

"Beats any play I ever seen," declared Jim. He shook his head, added soberly, "You took an awful chance, savin' a little old trunk. You've got plenty nerve, son, standin' him off with a pocket-pistol and him with the drop on you."

Mark shrugged, said simply, "I've got twenty thousand dollars gold in that little old trunk."

Jim Ball gazed at him, mouth open, eyes bulging. "Twenty thousand gold—*in that trunk?*" His voice was a hoarse croak.

"My cattle-ranch money," Mark explained. "No Wells Fargo service to La Cruz, so I had to bring it in my trunk."

The stage-driver came out of his daze, was inclined to be indignant. "If I'd knowed I was carryin' a gold shipment I'd have fixed me up an armed guard to ride with us," he fumed. "Of all the goldurned fool tricks!"

Mark made an attempt to pacify him. "It

seemed safe enough. Nobody knew I had a lot of money in my trunk—" He was suddenly silent, his expression thoughtful.

Jim eyed him shrewdly. "Ain't so sartain nobody was knowin' about it, huh?"

"Only the man I've been writing to about the ranch," Mark said, a hint of a frown on his face.

"Whar does this land-shark feller live?" asked Jim.

"La Cruz," Mark told him. "You see, Jim, it's a cash deal, payment to be made in gold coin of the United States, and this man told me to bring the money with me. He said people out here in the Territory don't like cheques or paper money."

Jim nodded. "Folks out here don't like paper money for a fact," he agreed. "Only money we savvy is gold." He glanced nervously at the surrounding brush, kicked off the brake. "Let's get away from here. Mebbe thar's more wolves smellin' out your trail."

He sent the mules into a run down the winding grade, foot on the brake, steadying the careening buckboard round sharp turns. His scraggy face was grim, and now and again he darted sharp, speculative looks at his passenger.

He broke his silence. "Reckon the feller's name is Ab Matoon, huh?"

"That's right," admitted Mark.

"A smooth-talkin' hombre," Jim Ball said. He

slowed the mules to a walk. "How come you got mixed up with him in this cow-ranch deal?"

"I saw an advertisement in a Boston newspaper and wrote to him." He gave the stage-driver an uneasy look. "It seemed a good chance to get into the cattle business and that's what I wanted to do."

"An awful lot of Eastern fellers been headin' out here to get into the cow-business," grumbled Jim. "Lots of furriners too, Britishers an' such. Most of 'em get their eyeteeth skinned, doggone their innercent hides."

Mark offered no comment, kept a stony gaze on the road ahead.

Jim Ball looked at him, a brief, sideways glance. "Ain't carin' for my talk, huh?"

An oddly hard look wiped the boyishness from his young passenger's face. He said quietly, "I may look like a tenderfoot, Jim, but I'm not losing any skin off my eyeteeth."

Jim Ball suddenly kicked on the brake, reined the mules to a quick halt. "Now, you listen to me, young feller." His tone was gentle, almost pleading. "This here town of La Cruz comes close to bein' hell's back yard. Thar's more border thieves and cut-throats roostin' thar than you can shake a stick at. I ain't no friend of yours if I don't warn you proper that you're headin' for plenty trouble." He reached for his plug of tobacco, savagely bit off a quid.

The tenseness left Mark's face. He grinned. "I like you, Jim. I don't blame you for thinking I'm a fool tenderfoot, carting a lot of gold around in my trunk." His face sobered again. "It's possible I've been too trusting, and, after all, that's the sign of a *very* green tenderfoot."

"Sure is," Jim declared. "I'm cravin' a powwow with you, son. Seems like me and you should have a right good powwow before we hit town."

"Go ahead," invited Mark good-naturedly.

The stage-driver spat over the wheel, considered him thoughtfully. "You've got plenty guts," he announced. "You sure handled that low-down, sneakin' wolf back yonder as good as any man I ever knowed. Couldn't have done better myself." He nodded gravely. "You're sure long on nerve, son, but I'm thinkin' you're mighty short on know-how when it comes to a cow-ranch."

"I took a special course in animal husbandry," Mark told him shyly, "after I left college."

"Huh?" Jim looked puzzled, rubbed a beetling nose with his forefinger, decided to let the remark pass. "Runnin' a cow-ranch takes plenty savvy," he went on, "and right now, what with the price of beef so low, and dry seasons and border rustlers, it seems a mightly poor time to sink a lot of good gold money in a cow-ranch."

"I've been making a study of the markets," interposed Mark. "We'll see big prices two or three years from now." He shook his head, added firmly, "I'm out here to go into the cattle business, Jim."

The expression on the stageman's face showed that he was impressed. He sensed here a determination that won his respect.

"Mebbe you're right about beef prices takin' a jump," he grudgingly admitted. "Sure will if we can get Harrison elected next November."

"It won't matter who is President," Mark argued. "Cleveland or Harrison, the Southwest is in for a big time, especially the cattle business."

"Ain't no chance for Cleveland to be re-elected," insisted Jim Ball.

"Well," Mark grinned, "we don't vote for President here in the Territory. We'll have to take what we can get and mind our own business."

"You don't scare easy, once you get set on a notion." Jim's voice was gruffly admiring. "You talk like you got plenty savvy under that slick city hat."

"I'm not going to be scared out of the cattle business," Mark assured him. "It's going to be my job to have a nice big bunch of steers ready when the beef-market booms."

"Son," Jim gave him a kindly look, "I'm likin' your style." He was more and more drawn to this young tenderfoot, felt a consuming urge to help him.

He asked abruptly, "What's the name of this cow-outfit Ab Matoon figgers to sell you?"

"The Diamond D," Mark smiled faintly. "That's what caught my eye when I read the advertisement. Seemed like a good hunch to look into it. That brand is a natural—Mark Destin's *Diamond D*."

Jim seemed unimpressed. "Rick Dunbar's place," he said. "Only Rick ain't alive no more. Took a rustler's bullet in his back."

"I suppose that's why the place is for sale," surmised Mark. "This La Cruz man wrote that it was a forced sale to close an estate and was a bargain."

"Wasn't knowin' the Diamond D's for sale," Jim said dubiously. "There's a young gal, Janet—she's Rick's daughter and as fine as they come—and a young no-count feller name of Ray Wellerton, some sort of kin to her pa by marriage." Jim shook his head. "First time I've heard Janet figgers to sell Diamond D."

"I've got it in writing from Mr. Matoon," Mark said.

Jim's face darkened. "You say Ab Matoon told you to fetch the money in gold coin, huh?"

"That's right." Mark paused, added doubtfully, "I suppose there's a bank in La Cruz. Be safe enough in the bank."

"No bank in La Cruz," Jim told him bluntly. "You could have banked in Deming, closed the deal for the ranch in Deming, and Ab Matoon knowed it."

"I'm beginning to think you haven't much use for Mr. Matoon," accused Mark.

"Ab is so crooked his shadder makes snake tracks." Jim scowled. "Like as not he's the answer to that road agent you scotched up on the summit. You said Ab knowed you was bringing your money in cash-gold. He'd figger to get it before you hit town."

"Perhaps *he* was the road agent," suggested Mark.

Jim shook his head. "That feller was too tall, all of six feet. Ab Matoon is a little, fat hombre, and he ain't got the guts to pull off any job like that personal. He hires his killers, and they come awful cheap in La Cruz."

Mark nodded, his expression thoughtful. "I've an idea the man was somebody you would have recognized if you could have seen under the mask he wore. That explains his queer, whispering voice."

"You smashed his hand and marked his face plenty," chuckled Jim. "Won't be hard to spot him if we run into him ag'in."

"He'll need a doctor for that hand," Mark said. "Any doctors in La Cruz?"

"Doc. Bralen," Jim spoke doubtfully. "Doc.'s a good man when he's sober, only it ain't often you can ketch him sober. Reckon that's why he landed in La Cruz. Knows his business, though, sober or drunk."

"Our unknown road agent would go to him, you think?"

"I reckon he would, Mark. Fixin' up gunshot wounds and knife stabs is what the doc is best at. Plenty of gunplay and knife stabbin' in La Cruz."

"I'll have a talk with him," Mark said grimly.

"Won't get nothin' out of Doc. Bralen," grumbled the stageman. "Him and Ab Matoon is awful close friends." He paused, added with an obvious attempt to be fair, "Ain't claimin' the doc is a crook like Ab. His trouble is too much hard likker, and I've a notion Ab Matoon is to blame." Jim's frown deepened. "We've got to figger out what to do with the gold money in your trunk. Them border wolves that hang round in La Cruz will smell you out in no time at all."

Mark's young face took on a hard look. "I can take care of myself—and my money," he said.

"No sense talkin' big," Jim told him with some impatience. "You don't know that town like I do."

Mark forced a grin. "What do you suggest?"

"Cain't take it to the hotel. Might as well leave it lay in the street as in your room thar." Jim rubbed his nose thoughtfully. "Ben Stock's got a big safe in his store—"

"Fine!" interrupted Mark. "Just the place."

Jim shook his head. “It ain’t that I don’t trust Ben,” he said. “Ben is postmaster, and square as they come. Only trouble thar, his safe has been busted a couple of times.”

“I’ll stand guard all night.” Mark patted his rifle on his knees, his expression hard again.

“Leave me to do some more thinkin’,” grumbled the older man.

Mark waited, gaze on the little border town in the bend of the creek. It looked very peaceful down there in the deepening twilight. Vague thoughts came to him. Perhaps Jim Ball was unduly alarmed for the safety of his twenty thousand dollars. It was possible that the stageman was all wrong about Ab Matoon and his intentions towards the young Easterner who had answered his advertisement. Jim’s dislike of Matoon might derive from some personal grudge.

An odd chill suddenly stirred in him as he recalled the attempted holdup, the whispering-voiced bandit, the menacing rifle. Death had been very close during those tense moments up on the summit. No, Jim Ball was not unduly alarmed. Somebody had known that he was bringing twenty thousand dollars in gold on the stage. And Matoon was the only man supposed to know about it. Unless . . .

Mark broke his silence. “Jim, there’s a chance that Matoon may have unintentionally let out the news that I was arriving today and bringing the cash with me. It's quite possible that he said just enough to tip off somebody."

"Don't alter things none," Jim said laconically. "Leave me do some more studyin' on it, son." He fingered his plug of tobacco from calfskin waistcoat, gnawed meditatively.

Lights began to wink through the trees down across the creek. "Got it!" Jim exclaimed. He kicked off the brake, slapped the mules into a fast trot.

"Got *what?*" Mark held on to his derby as the buckboard careened wildly round a hairpin bend.

"Got it figgered whar you can cache your gold-money safe," yelled Jim.

"Where's that?"

"The *cantina* of Plácido Romero." The stage-man's voice lifted shrill above the clamor of rattling wheels and pounding hoofs. "We'll fool 'em, son—we'll sure fool 'em!"

Chapter 2

The road twisted up a deep arroyo. Sheer bluffs, hardly visible in that darkness, leaned so close that Mark could have touched the one on his side.

The mules came to a sudden standstill, and Jim said softly, "Waal, here's the place."

Mark peered ahead, saw that a high barricade or gate blocked the way, and now he heard a low voice.

"*Quién es*?"

"It's me, Rafael," Jim called out. "Open up quick. I'm wantin' a powwow with Plácido in a hurry."

"*Sí, señor*," answered the voice.

Bolts rasped, and Mark heard the scrape of heavy bars. The gate swung in. Jim kicked off the brake, and the mules lurched forward. Mark caught a glimpse of the man—a vague shape, motionless by the open gate, his face a dark blur under a steeple hat.

The gate closed behind them, and Jim halted the team, waited for the Mexican. He came up, soft-footed as a cat, peered at the occupants of the buckboard.

"*Cóm' están, señores*?" he greeted courteously. He flicked an interested glance at Mark.

"*Gracias, muy bien,*" responded Mark, his smile friendly.

Rafael's eyes widened a trifle, and a hint of pleased surprise showed in his quick, answering smile. He stood silent, while they climbed from the stage.

Jim waved at his vacated seat. "You set there and watch things for me, Rafael," he said.

"*Sí, señor.*" The Mexican slid into the seat.

"All right, Mark." Jim turned away. "Let's go find Plácido."

They moved through the darkness towards lamplight that glowed from windows some hundred yards away.

"Just what is this place?" queried Mark.

"Used to be a fort way back when all this country belonged to Spain," Jim informed him. "Them Spanish settlers had plenty trouble with the Comanches, I reckon. Right now it's Plácido's back yard. Them bluffs we drove through circle purty nigh all round, and whar they ain't bluffs thar's ten foot 'dobe walls, four foot thick. Was a natcheral stockade for them old settlers to hole up in when the Injuns got to raidin'."

They came to a gate and another voice challenged them from the darkness.

"*Quién es*?"

"It's me, Felipe," reiterated Jim.

A shape materialized, opened the gate, admitted them into a *patio*.

"Whar can I find Plácido?" Jim asked.

The Mexican peered at them, widened curious eyes at Mark. He jerked a thumb at a dimly lit doorway.

"Your friend keeps his place well-guarded," Mark commented as they moved on towards the beckoning light.

"Plácido ain't takin' chances with the no-count hombres that roost in La Cruz," explained Jim. "He's got to be keerful."

"Seems to be important for a man who runs a *cantina*," observed Mark.

"Waal—" Jim hesitated. "I reckon the *cantina* is only one of the irons he's got in the fire." He paused, added warningly, "He don't like it much for folks to get nosy."

"I won't get nosy," Mark promised, aware now of a mounting curiosity. It was possible that Plácido Romero had affairs across the not-far-distant border that he preferred to keep a jealously guarded secret.

They reached the wide entrance, and another man slid from one of the numerous doors that opened on the long *galería.* Some accident had happened to his nose, flattened it. He listened to Jim's request, motioned to them to follow him.

"Mule kicked his nose in one time," Jim told Mark. "That's why they call him Chato—means 'flat nose.' "

The Mexican led them through a maze of

corridors, halted, rapped on a door. A deep voice answered, and he gave them a grin, pushed the door open, and motioned to them to enter.

The room was small, the only furniture a wooden bench against the wall. A lantern stood on the bench, and its light played on the face of a man sitting on his heels in the middle of the mud floor. A red gamecock stood motionless between his hands. Their heads lifted in a stare at the intruders, in the eyes of man and bird an oddly similar look of untamable fierceness.

Pleased recognition warmed the man's tawny eyes. "Ha—it is you, my frien'!" His deep voice was cordial. "See my fine one—thees leetle dove of mine." He bounced the red cock on the mud floor. "W'at you theenk, my frien'? Splendeed bird, no?"

"Sure looks like a fightin' fool," admired the stageman.

"Thees bird 'ave 'eart of tiger," asserted Plácido Romero. He bounced the red cock again. "Tonight thees bird goes to Chihuahua and tomorrow night weel win me mooch *dinero*." He tucked the gamecock under an arm, was suddenly on his feet. "W'at ees on your mind, my frien'? You 'ave purpose for come 'ere, no?"

"You've guessed it." Jim grinned. "Want you to meet a friend of mine—Mark Destin."

Disturbing doubts chilled Mark as he felt the impact of appraising eyes that took him in from head to foot in one comprehensive glance. He was not so sure that he liked the idea of entrusting his gold to the care of this Mexican.

Plácido was suddenly smiling, hand outstretched, and the chilling doubts evaporated. "Señor Ball's frien's are my frien's," he said in his rich voice. "My 'ouse ees yours, Señor Destin."

"*Gracias*, *señor*." Mark shook the offered hand, felt steel-hard fingers clasp his own.

"You speak my language?" The Mexican beamed. He was a wide-shouldered man considerably past middle life, and there was a hint of Indian in his broad face and high cheekbones—the coarse mane of grey hair. The fierceness was gone from his eyes now. He looked kindly and singularly intelligent.

"Just got in with the stage from Deming," Jim said. "Mark fetched along a lot of gold-money in his trunk, figgered to bank it in La Cruz. Wasn't knowin' thar ain't no bank in this town."

Plácido pushed out mobile lips, looked grave, made no comment.

"The boy's got twenty thousand dollars in his trunk out thar in the stage," Jim said.

The Mexican narrowed his eyes in a quick look at Mark.

"You want me to be your banker?" he asked in Spanish.

"*Sí*." Mark shrugged. "Jim tells me that you are

the one man in La Cruz we can trust and that my money will be safe here."

"You speak very good Spanish," complimented Plácido. He looked at the stageman. "*Bueno*, my frien'. I keep thees *dinero* in safe place." He clapped his hands.

The door opened, revealed the *mozo* who had guided them to the room.

"Tell Felipe and Rafael to bring a trunk they will find in the stage," Plácido instructed in Spanish. He thrust the gamecock at him. "Make haste, Chato!"

The *mozo* vanished with the cock, and Plácido said courteously. "You weel 'ave food—a glass of wine, no?"

"Cain't stay no longer than to get this gold put away," demurred Jim. "Got to get the mail pouch over to the post office." He explained further. "Wasn't wantin' folks to know I come over this way, Plácido." He gave the Mexican a brief account of the attempted holdup. "I figgered it warn't safe for the boy to keep that gold-money in his trunk at the hotel."

Plácido Romero nodded. "I understan'." He looked with undisguised interest at Mark, lowered his eyes in a brief glance at the brown derby in the young Easterner's hand. "You have courage for one so young," he said admiringly in Spanish.

"There are times when a man must fight," Mark

told him with a shrug. He paused, added simply, "I am most grateful for your kindness."

Plácido's hand lifted in a lordly gesture. "You are my frien'," he said.

Felipe and Rafael came in with the trunk, left the room at a word from Plácido. He eyed the trunk thoughtfully. "You leave thees box just so, or only the gold?" he asked.

"Mark's got to have the trunk along when he shows up at the hotel," Jim said. "Don't want them wolves figgerin' he's mebbe cached the trunk some place."

Mark produced a key, opened the trunk. The gold was in ten canvas sacks, a hundred twenties to a sack. He stood the sacks against the wall, closed and relocked the trunk. He gave Plácido a troubled look.

The Mexican correctly interpreted the question in his eyes, smiled, shook his head. "The hiding place is my secret," he said. "Have no fear, my frien'."

"Let's get movin'," Jim said. "Ben Stock'll be yellin' his head off if I don't show up quick with the mail pouch."

Plácido summoned Chato, who shouldered the now-much-lighter trunk, and, with mutual cordial expressions, Jim and Mark followed him out to the yard. Felipe led the way to the buckboard, a lantern in his hand. Rafael swung open the high gate, and in a few moments they were again in the deep arroyo, heading back to the road.

The familiar sound of the approaching stage brought Ben Stock to the doorway of his store. He stood under the glare of the big lantern overhead, a round-shouldered, angular man in a black alpaca coat. He wore a stubby beard on his chin, grizzled black, like his thinning hair, and there was a disapproving look on his deeply lined face, with its long, clean-shaven upper lip.

The stage-driver was apparently making up for a lot of lost time and had the mules going all out, the buckboard swaying wildly at their scampering heels. He jammed on the brake, made a quick halt in front of the store, grinned through drifting dust at the glum-visaged postmaster.

"Reckon I'm some late, Ben," he said. "Run into plenty trouble back on the grade." He reached under his feet, dragged at the mail pouch, and tossed it over the wheel into Ben's hands. "She's kind of light today. Won't take you no time to get your letters sorted." He kicked off the brake and was rattling up the street before Ben could question him about the cause of his late arrival.

Two men emerged from a saloon, recognized the stage, and started across the street to the store into which the postmaster had vanished with his pouch. Another man appeared in a lighted doorway, and Mark had a glimpse of a moon face under a wide-brimmed black hat, a rotund figure in a black frock coat. Jim Ball said, "That's Ab Matoon, watchin' from his office."

In another minute the stage was at a standstill in front of the hotel. Mark was not able to see much of it in the darkness. The light of a big swing lamp showed a porch, with a bench on either side of the entrance. Two men occupied one of the benches, cigarettes between lips. Cowboys, from their attire, Mark's brief look told him as he climbed from the stage. One of the pair was, perhaps, in his early forties, lean, watchful-eyed, a touch of badger-grey in his temples and drooping mustache. His companion was younger, of an age with Mark, and he wore his Stetson pushed back on unruly red hair. Even under the dim light of the swing lamp his eyes were a startling blue against the deep tan of smooth-cheeked face, and there was a reckless devil-may-care manner about him that drew a second look from Mark.

Jim was swinging the trunk over the wheel. Mark seized it, dragged it on to the hotel porch. He said in a low voice to the stageman, "You keep the rifle for me, Jim."

"Sure will," promised Jim. He straightened up, gave the two men watching from the bench an amiable grin. "Hello, Buck," he rumbled. "Ain't seen you in town since fall roundup. How's things out at Diamond D?"

"You're wastin' breath, askin' *me,*" drawled the older of the cowboys. "I quit that outfit. Me and Red both."

The redhead nodded confirmation, his fascinated gaze on Mark's brown derby.

"Waal, I'll be doggoned." Jim gave him an astonished look, slid his gaze to Mark, added briskly, "Here's the rest of your stuff, mister." He heaved two leather portmanteaus over the buckboard's side, swung back to his seat.

"Thanks, driver." It was the agreed plan to keep their already close friendship a secret. Mark was just another stranger arriving in La Cruz on the stage.

Jim said, a double meaning in the words, "You can most always get word to me at the stage barn, mister. Stage makes the trip to Deming every three days."

"Thanks," Mark repeated. "I'll let you know when I want to book a seat."

Jim's hand lifted in a parting gesture as he drove away, and now Mark's brief sideways look discovered a rotund, black-coated shape emerging from the darkness down the street. He was reluctant for an encounter yet with Ab Matoon, pushed hastily into the little lobby, bag in either hand. It was a dingy place, smelled of dust and stale cigar smoke. Several wooden armchairs lined the wall, a brass spittoon between each. There was a narrow stairway leading to the second floor.

Mark went to the battered desk that faced the street door. The man behind the desk eyed him indifferently. Mark thought that he had never seen a more unprepossessing face, the skin drawn tight over high cheekbones, the eyes in their sunken sockets, unwinking, devoid of expression. He was tilted back in an ancient swivel-chair.

Mark felt impatience growing in him. He said curtly, "I suppose you have a room?"

The clerk nodded, leaned towards the desk, inked a pen and thrust it at him, pointed to the register, a dog-eared schoolroom copy-book.

Mark wrote his name, and the clerk leaned forward again, studied the signature, reached in a drawer, and fished out a key.

"Room 15." He pointed to the stairs. "Last door on your left."

"I've a trunk," Mark said.

The clerk's voice lifted in a shout. "Squint!"

Mark became aware of somebody pushing into the lobby, knew without looking it would be Ab Matoon. The clerk turned his head, showed something approaching animation.

"Hello, Ab," he said. He raised his voice again. "Oh, Squint, get a move on, you!"

The newcomer said, genial smile on Mark, "I've an idea this young man is a friend of mine, Louie." His glance slid over the register. "Ah, yes, Mark Destin." His hand went out. "Welcome to La Cruz, sir. I'm Ab Matoon."

They shook hands, and Matoon said to the clerk, "Make Mr. Destin comfortable, Louie—the best in the house."

"He has it," grunted Louie. He wrote the room number opposite Mark's name, spoke to the man who slouched in from the rear hall. "Trunk outside," he said. "Room 15, Squint."

The man rubbed an unshaven chin, looked doubtful. "I'll go get Joe to give me a hand—"

"It's only a little trunk," interrupted Mark. "You can handle it." He was vaguely aware of an odd surprise in Matoon's protuberant eyes as he spoke.

Squint shuffled out to the porch, and Matoon drew a cigar case from an inside pocket of his frock coat. "Cigar?" he invited.

"Don't smoke them," smiled Mark.

Matoon selected a cigar, returned the case to his pocket. "I trust you had a pleasant trip in from Deming?" His prominent eyes, a pale, cold blue, did not match his pleasantly sonorous voice, made Mark think of a shark.

He had no intention of telling Mr. Matoon about the attempted holdup, and his answer was purposely vague.

"Interesting scenery," he said. "Some splendid views, especially from the summit."

He saw that the paunchy man was looking

speculatively at the trunk that Squint brought in slung over a shoulder. He hid a grin. It was obvious that Mr. Matoon was puzzled at the ease with which the man carried the trunk up the stairs, was mentally calculating the weight of twenty thousand dollars in gold coin of the United States.

"Well," said Mark, picking up his bags and turning to follow the trunk, "I'll look you up in the morning, Mr. Matoon."

"Needn't wait for morning," Matoon told him with a gesture. "Drop in at my office when you've had a wash. We'll have a drink at the Horsehead."

Mark said he would, hurried up the stairs, and unlocked the door of Room 15. Squint was waiting. He carried the trunk inside, looked with surprise at the twenty-five-cent piece Mark put in his hand. He grinned, pocketed the coin, evidently decided that such unexpected liberality called for extra service.

"Best place to eat in this town is the Chinaman's," he advised. "Hotel don't serve food, but Ah Gee's most always open."

Mark thanked him, and, left alone, stood for a moment, gaze roving round the room. The hotel's "best" was less than attractive. Dust was thick, and the bed had a suspicious sag in the middle. A tin washbasin stood on a stand in one corner, but he could see nothing that contained water. A ragged towel hung on a hook over the washstand. There was another larger stand with a piece of cracked glass for a mirror, and two rickety-looking wooden chairs.

Mark heaved one of his bags up to the bed, heard a rap on the door. Squint reappeared, a bucket of water in his hand. He stood it by the washstand, stared interestedly for a moment at the derby hat Mark had tossed on a chair.

"Gents' room is down the hall," he informed Mark. "Mebbe Louie told you baths come two bits extry."

"Louie didn't tell me anything," Mark said a bit grimly.

"Room is a dollar a day, baths two bits extry," Squint said. "Ain't no hot water, 'less you call for it, and that comes another two bits."

The door closed behind him again. Mark went briskly to work, stripped to the waist, found a piece of soap in his bag, and had a hasty wash.

He put on a fresh shirt, retied the cravat with the aid of the cracked mirror, put on his derby, and took a look from the single window—found only the black night. It was his guess, though, that the window overlooked the back yard.

He blew out the light, left the room, and locked the door. It was a cheap lock, vulnerable to almost any key.

At the end of the dimly-lit hall he saw another door close to his room. He tried it, found that it opened, and took a look, saw a steep flight of steps that evidently went down to the yard. He closed the door. There was no key in the lock. The upper hall was open to any intruder.

His expression thoughtful, a bit grim, Mark headed for the front stairs. *Might as well leave it lay in the street as in your room.* It seemed that Jim Ball had told him the truth. Guests of the La Cruz Grand Palace Hotel were more than vulnerable to thieves.

Louie, hospitality apparently warmed by injunctions from Ab Matoon, managed a smile that reminded Mark of a grimacing skull. "Hope your room is comfortable, Mr. Destin. You'll find Ah Gee's Chop House the best place to get a meal in this town."

"Thanks," Mark said. He pushed through the door, halted abruptly, gaze on the girl dimly revealed under the soft glow of the swing lamp. She was apparently waiting for him, and he felt the impact of eyes that seemed black under that uncertain light. Angry, decidedly contemptuous eyes that looked him up and down.

"*Mister* Mark Destin?" The scorn in her voice put a flush on his face.

"Why—yes," Mark found himself stammering, "I'm Mark Destin."

The girl—she was of medium height, slim, and at this moment defiantly erect—slapped her short skirt with the riding whip in her hand, and her eyes took on angry fire from the lamplight.

"I'm warning you that Diamond D is not for sale, never has been for sale, and never will be for sale." Her words spilled out in breathless haste. "Understand, *Mister* Mark Destin?"

Mark managed to find his tongue. "No," he said, "I don't understand." Anger stirred in him, and curiosity. "May I ask who you are?" He paused, added a bit incoherently, "You—you see, I—I really *don't* understand." He was thinking that he had never laid eyes on a girl who so instantly held his attention. The lamplight showed deep-chestnut hair, an uplifted face that he felt was always to remain in his memory. There was a pride there, an undaunted spirit that fired his imagination.

She took a step towards him, motioned with her whip. "I'm telling you the truth." Her voice was low, vibrant with emotion. "Don't waste your time in La Cruz. Diamond D is not for sale." She swung away, ran down the porch steps.

Mark stood there, watched until she vanished into the blanketing night. He knew then that he had been talking to Janet Dunbar, daughter of the slain owner of Diamond D, the ranch that Ab Matoon was advertising for sale. He recalled the stage-driver's words. *Rick ain't alive no more. Took a rustler's bullet in his back . . . Wasn't knowin' the Diamond D's for sale.*

It seemed that Jim Ball's doubts were confirmed. The girl had made it very plain that the ranch was *not* for sale, had warned him away.

Mark went slowly down the porch steps, his mind in a whirl. Something was very wrong, and he could think of no answer that made sense.

Chapter 3

The restaurant was small and scrupulously clean, the tables clothless but well-scrubbed. Mark pulled out a chair, hung his hat on a hook, and sat down. The place was a pleasant contrast to the grimy, ill-kept hotel.

An elderly Chinese shuffled from the kitchen, gave him an inquiring look. Mark guessed that he was Ah Gee in person.

"What have you that's good?" he asked.

"Steak velly good." Ah Gee glanced obliquely at the derby hat, and something like a smile broke the impassivity of his face. "You flom Flisco?"

"Boston," Mark answered.

"Me flom Flisco," Ah Gee informed him, a hint of longing in his voice. He vanished into his kitchen.

Mark's glance lifted to the offending derby. He must get rid of the thing. It marked him as a tenderfoot. He should have done some shopping in Deming, provided himself with the garb of the country.

Ah Gee reappeared with water and a bowl of soup, gave him a benign smile, and shuffled back to his kitchen.

It was good soup. Mark's heart warmed to the

old Chinese proprietor of the Chop House. He was a culinary artist.

The steak came, sizzling and succulent, with fried potatoes and delicate, fresh string beans that Mark guessed must come from Ah Gee's own garden. A huge slab of apple pie followed the steak, a second and third cup of coffee—an appetizing meal that filled him with a comforting sense of well-being, restored the wavering confidence in himself.

He suddenly remembered his half-promise to drop in at Ab Matoon's office. Matoon had said something about a drink at the Horsehead, would be wondering what had become of him.

He got hurriedly out of his chair, reached for his hat, and handed Ah Gee a silver dollar. Ah Gee dropped the coin in a cigar box and fished out seventy-five cents in change.

Mark said, astonished, "Keep it. That dinner is worth any man's dollar."

The old Chinese shook his head, continued to hold out the change. "Twenty-five cen'," he said. "All time twenty-five cen'."

His expression warned Mark not to argue. He dropped the coins in a pocket, said warmly, "You're the best thing I've met here in La Cruz, Ah Gee. You'll be seeing a lot of me."

Ah Gee patted his neatly coiled queue with a thin hand, gave him an oddly concerned look. "You stay in La Cluz?"

"That's right," grinned Mark. "I'm going into the cattle business."

Ah Gee looked dubious. "La Cluz not good place," he warned. "More better you go back Boston."

Mark hid the annoyance he felt. He was tired of being warned away from La Cruz. "Thanks for the advice. I'm here to stay." He managed another grin. "When I get my ranch going I'll maybe offer you a job as cook. You're a grand cook."

"You clazy in head." The old Chinaman's gaze followed his customer into the night beyond the door, his expression wistful. In faraway China was a son he had never seen. He would be about Mark's age.

Mark crossed the street to Matoon's office. Lamplight glowed from the curtained window, but no response answered his knock. Apparently Matoon had given him up, was probably already having his drink at the Horsehead. The fact that he had left the lamp burning indicated that he expected to return.

Mark hesitated, gazed up and down the street, hating the darkness that hid the town. He could count the lighted windows on the fingers of one hand. He had gathered from Jim Ball that most of the inhabitants were Mexicans. It was probable that they had small liking for the *americanos* who ruled the town, wisely chose to avoid possible clashes with drunken cowboys. Those of them seeking the pleasures of the night would be at the *cantina* of Plácido Romero.

He came to a decision. There were questions he wanted to ask Ab Matoon. The chances were good that he would find the man at the Horsehead Bar.

The dim light of the smoke-blackened swing lantern above the door made vague shapes of the horses huddled at the hitch-rail in front of the saloon. Beyond them the black curtain of the night.

Mark slowed his step, came to a standstill, narrowed his eyes at the horses. Fifteen of them, not including the buckboard-team at the far end. It was obvious that a lot of cowboys were in town, enjoying the hospitality of the Horsehead Bar.

His look shifted to the door. A section about a foot square had been cut from the upper panel and the hole covered with a piece of dirt-encrusted fly-screen through which lamplight made a pale yellow smear. Peering in, he could dimly see faces under wide-brimmed hats lined raggedly in front of the bar and hands lifting glasses to lips.

Somebody was playing an accordion, a mournful tune vaguely familiar. A pleasant tenor voice took up the refrain and instantly the rumbling murmur of conversation hushed as the singer's companions gave appreciative attention. It was a sad song, something about a lone dying cowboy, and the ballad singer put plenty of pathos into it.

A man swore softly. “You sure sing that song good, Red. Gets me to cryin’.” A coin rang on the bar. “Set ’em up for the crowd, Pegleg.”

Mark pushed his way through the door, uncomfortably aware of a sudden stillness as it swung to behind him. Faces turned his way, like puppets pulled on a string. He forced his legs to keep moving, pressed close to the bar.

“I was expecting to find Mr. Matoon here,” he said to the bartender.”

“Huh?” The bartender stood rigid, the bottle in his beefy hand tilted over a glass, a dazed look in his pale, bulging eyes. “Ab ain’t been in yet,” he said. The glass under the bottle splashed over. He muttered an oath, snatched up a dirty rag, and began mopping the spilled liquor.

The man next to Mark said complainingly, “Watch out who you shovin’, mister.”

“I’m sorry.” Mark gave him a grin. “Didn’t know I shoved you.”

The man glowered at his untouched whisky. He was obviously a cowman—tall, wide-shouldered, dusty black Stetson framing a bony, high-nosed face that might have been carved from granite. He was not drunk, and Mark wondered what could have caused the smoldering anger in him. It was plain that he wanted an excuse to unload pent-up ill-humor.

The barman expertly spun a glass, gave Mark an inquiring look.

"I'll take a Scotch highball," Mark told him. He was wishing himself out of the place, realized that eyes were on him, that these men were wondering if the dude would show a yellow streak. "Matoon doesn't seem to be in his office," he added.

The barman said laconically, "Only just plain whisky here, mister."

The tall cowman's head turned in a menacing look. "I'm not liking Ab Matoon's friends. Make dust away from here, mister." His hand lowered to the gun in his holster.

Mark ignored him, refused to believe the threat in that gesture.

"Make it a highball with your plain whisky," he said pleasantly to the bartender.

"I'm not telling you again," loudly declared the gloomy-faced cowman. "Get away from here, fast!"

A drawling voice interrupted him. "Easy, Benton. You're makin' awful hard talk to a man that's friend to Ab Matoon. Ab won't like it."

"To hell with Ab Matoon!" Benton's rage was obviously aggravated by the mention of the name. He reached out a hand, crammed Mark's derby over his eyes.

Mark's fingers closed over his assailant's gun-hand. He twisted hard, and the gun clattered on the floor. Surprise held Benton momentarily rigid, and his eyes widened at the younger man.

Somebody swore softly, admiringly. Mark's quick look took in the tensely watching faces. Two of the men there he had seen before. One was the red-haired young cowboy he had noticed on the hotel porch. He was nursing an accordion on his knees. The other was the lean, competent-looking man Jim Ball had addressed as Buck and who had informed Jim that he had quit the Diamond D payroll. He guessed it was Buck who had warned Benton that Ab Matoon would resent his behavior.

Benton's hoarse, furious whisper broke the momentary stillness. "Ain't needin' a gun." He plunged forward, fists flailing.

Mark avoided the rush, and the cowman crashed into a table which overturned. He recovered his balance, charged again. He was a big, powerful man, inches taller and pounds heavier than Mark, who again side-stepped the rush. He felt a big fist graze his cheek, swung his own right in a short upper-cut to the jaw that drew a surprised grunt from his opponent.

Mark swung again—lefts and rights to the jaw that staggered the bigger man. He dropped his hands, a dazed look in his eyes.

Mark waited, a hope in him that Benton would come to his senses, realize that he was up against a trained boxer and drop the affair.

A voice yipped drunkenly, "Looks like Bill Benton's went and cotched hisself a clawin' bear-cat."

Benton shook his head angrily, sprang at Mark, long arms curved to draw him into a hug, and now Mark knew he would have to finish it. He drove a terrific smash to the body, another hard left and right to the jaw. Benton's eyes glazed. He went down.

Mark stared at him, conscious of an odd regret. He felt that he could have liked this man. There was character in his fine face, and this seemingly uncalled-for animosity was more than puzzling. It came to him vaguely that Ab Matoon was the answer. The seeds of this violence were nourished in the deadly soil of ill will between the two men.

A clamor of excited voices broke the momentary stillness. Mark hastily snatched up the fallen gun, a long-barreled Colt .45. He was not sure just how the saloon's patrons would react to the affair. He heard Buck's drawling, reassuring voice.

"Don't get on the prod for the rest of us, young feller. You give Benton what was comin' to him. We ain't grievin' none."

Mark saw grinning faces, friendly, approving—admiring. Pegleg pounded his bottle on the bar. "Here's your drink, mister. It's on the house."

"You sure pack a wallop," Buck said. He eyed the prostrate man. "Laid him out cold."

"I did some boxing at school," Mark said. "There's a lot in knowing how." He could have told them that he had been lightweight champion at Harvard. He was not feeling happy about the affair, found himself resenting the obvious satisfaction of these men. Their elation indicated that Bill Benton was not popular here.

The big cowman stirred, turned on his side and slowly lifted his head. Mark bent down, gave him a hand, helped him to his feet.

"Sorry!" He was at a loss for further words, could only grin, thrust the recovered gun into Benton's holster.

Perhaps the act of returning the gun was more significant than words. A hint of a grin broke the dazed look on Benton's face. He rubbed his bruised chin, stared wonderingly at the younger man's sober face. The insane rage had left his eyes, and Mark liked what he saw in them.

"I maybe acted hasty," Benton muttered. "Heard you tell Pegleg you were looking for Matoon. Got the wrong idea about you."

"Forget it," Mark said, uncomfortably aware of attentive ears.

"Been looking for Matoon myself," Benton continued. "Doesn't mean he's a friend of mine."

The street door swung open with a bang, and a man suddenly stood framed there, gun in hand.

"Get your hands up, Benton. Quick, or you're leavin' here on a shutter."

Benton hesitated the merest instant, lifted his hands, stared with bleak eyes at the man in the doorway. The badge pinned to his shirt told Mark that he was the town marshal.

A second man followed the town marshal into the barroom. Mark recognized the rotund, black-coated shape of Ab Matoon. He also read an unholy satisfaction in the land broker's eyes.

"I'm takin' you to gaol for disturbin' the peace, Benton." The marshal's voice was harsh, his gun steady. "I was watchin' when you tried to kill this young feller."

Mark interrupted him. "It's all a mistake. I'm making no charge." He was conscious of a quick, penetrating look from Benton, also of the sneer on the marshal's face. "A mistake," he repeated desperately.

"I ain't finished," the marshal said. "I'm arresting Benton for threatenin' the life of Mr. Matoon here. Was listenin' at the door—heard him say he was lookin' for Mr. Matoon. He's going to gaol."

He stepped warily behind the big cowman, snatched the .45 from its holster. "Get movin', Benton."

"I'm not giving you an excuse to shoot me in the back," Benton said. He gave Matoon a bitter smile. "Looks like you win this hand."

He stepped outside, the marshal at his back. Matoon turned an affable smile on Mark. "Sorry

I couldn't wait for you, Mr. Destin. Heard that Benton was looking for me with a gun. Had to keep out of sight until the marshal put him in gaol."

"He doesn't seem like a killer," Mark protested.

Matoon tapped his head with a pudgy forefinger. "Got crazy notions." He turned to the door. "See you in the morning, Destin. Too busy now to have that drink with you." His look went to the barman. "Set 'em up for the crowd, Pegleg, and treat Mr. Destin right. He's my guest here tonight. Anything he wants is on me." The door slammed.

Mark felt depressed. He wanted to get away from the place. He was not liking the way Benton had been hurried off to gaol, sensed that some hidden purpose had motivated the man's arrest.

Chapter 4

The bar was crowded now, and he went to a table where Buck and Red sat with their drinks. They gave him friendly grins. He pulled out a chair and sat down. It was possible he might glean some information from these two former Diamond D men.

"Name's Salten," the elder of the pair said in his drawling voice. "Buck Salten, and this younger feller is Red O'Malley." He chuckled. "Red is some taken with that shorthorn hat you wear."

The red-haired young cowboy gave Mark an embarrassed grin. "Ain't denyin' I'd admire to own one," he admitted.

An idea seized Mark. "I'll trade with you," he offered.

Red said quickly, "I'm callin' you on that."

They solemnly exchanged hats. Mirth convulsed Buck Salten. "You doggone kids! You watch out for this slick pardner of mine, Destin, or he'll be tradin' your dude clothes right off of your back."

Pegleg stumped over from his bar, set a bottle of whisky on the table, a glass in front of Mark. "On the house, Mr. Destin," he said affably. "Ab said you wasn't to spend no money here tonight."

He returned to the bar, wooden leg tapping briskly.

Buck's gaze followed him. "Sure gets around fast on that timber he uses for a leg," he admired. "A good hombre, if you don't get on the wrong side of him."

"Does he own the Horsehead?" Mark asked.

"Well—" Buck was suddenly cautious. "That's what the sign that hangs outside the door says."

Mark smiled, made no comment. It was in his mind that Pegleg had a silent partner whose name was Ab Matoon. The rotund little land broker's manner had plainly indicated proprietorship.

"Ain't knowin' much about Pegleg," Buck went on. "He showed up couple of years back when the feller that used to run the place got himself killed. The feller was owin' Ab Matoon a lot of money, and Pegleg took over. Seems like they was old friends back in the Panhandle."

Mark pointed to the bottle. "Help yourselves," he invited.

Red O'Malley shook his head. "Cain't handle my accordion good when I soak up too much of the stuff," he said.

"Same with me," smiled Mark, conscious of Red's appraising eyes covertly studying him. He thought he sensed what was in the red-haired cowboy's mind.

Buck splashed whisky into his glass, a tolerant grin on his lean, brown face. "You kids ain't growed your horns yet," he drawled. "Not meanin' the pair of you ain't got plenty guts. Red was never one to turn tail on old man Trouble, and there's a lot of folks here tonight that's goin' to talk awful soft to Mr. Destin after the way he handled Bill Benton."

"You can leave off the *mister,*" Mark told him. "My friends call me Mark."

The lean man gave him a steady look, said slowly, the drawl absent from his voice, "I'm right proud to be your friend, Mark."

Mark saw his opportunity. "Speaking of Benton, what has Matoon got against him?"

"Plenty, I reckon." Buck's face was suddenly an expressionless mask. It was plain that he was reluctant to discuss the subject, showed relief when Red O'Malley came out of his brooding silence.

"This shirt don't go so good with my new hat," he complained. "I should get me a coat and pants like Mark's got on him."

Buck said mirthfully, "Told you he'd wangle another trade out of you, Mark."

"We're the same build," argued Red. "This outfit of mine would look mighty good on you, Mark."

Mark pretended a hesitation he did not feel. He had been waiting for Red to suggest some more trading. "I don't know," he demurred. "Paid a Boston tailor a lot of money for this suit."

"Throw in that shirt and collar and the fancy tie, and I'll throw in my boots," offered Red. "Paid thirty dollars for them boots."

"Throw in the gun belt and the gun and I'll call it a trade," Mark bargained.

"Got any more of them high collars like the one that's on your neck now?" Red asked.

"Couple of dozen of them in my trunk over at the hotel," Mark assured him. "I'll throw them in, and half a dozen cravats."

Red got out of his chair. "It's a trade," he agreed. "Let's go back in the washroom and make the switch right now."

"What's the idea, you wanting my dude outfit," Mark asked curiously.

"Well, it's like this, Mark," Red's blue eyes were very bright. "I figger to go East and get on the stage with my accordion. Ain't wantin' to show up there in these cowpoke clothes."

Mark was aware of vague doubts, wanted to suggest that as a genuine cowboy entertainer Red would stand a better chance by appearing in character with his accordion and songs of the range. He knew it was too late and that any well-meant advice would be regarded as an attempt to squirm out of the deal. He threw the amused Buck a grin and followed the red-haired cowboy to the washroom.

Buck Salten's gaze followed them, a hint of grim speculation in his keen eyes. He rapped his glass on the table and after a moment Pegleg stumped over, a water jug in his hand. He set the jug on the table, a question in his eyes as he looked at the other man. The water jug was only camouflage. He knew there was something on Buck's mind.

"Seen Ray Wellerton today?" Buck asked in a low voice.

Pegleg shook his head. "Ain't seen Ray for a couple of days." He paused, his smile unpleasant. "Janet's lookin' for him too."

Buck nodded, gestured angrily. "She's on the warpath. Fired Red and me both."

"That girl's a damn' fool," snorted the barman.

"She's damn' smart," Buck said. "Don't fool yourself."

"She won't do no good for herself, telling Ab to his face he's a crook," prophesied Pegleg. "She's in town now," he added. "Louie Renn was in here, told me. She said she wasn't staying at the hotel. She wouldn't tell Louie where she was stayin'."

"Hope she won't run into young Destin," worried Buck.

Pegleg grinned. "She's already run into him and bawled him out plenty. Louie told me."

The quick scowl on Buck's face quite altered his expression, gave him a hard, ruthless look. "He's smart, too." His fingers pulled thoughtfully at drooping mustache. "Mebbe too smart."

“He can sure handle his fists,” admired Pegleg. His puzzled look was on the two clean glasses. “Seems like the kids is leavin’ you to do all the drinkin’. Where-all have they gone?”

“To the washroom,” Buck told him, a hint of a wintry smile on his face. “They’ll be back.”

“I’m fillin’ their glasses,” grumbled the barman. He tilted the bottle, splashed whisky into the glasses. “Ain’t polite for ’em to leave their glasses clean when it’s on the house.”

“Red figgers likker makes his fingers clumsy on his accordion,” chuckled Buck. “Reckon young Destin figgers the same way.”

“He don’t play no accordion,” argued the barman aggrievedly. “Looks like he’s got a weak head, huh?”

Buck shrugged, his expression skeptical. “I’m tellin’ you he’s smart.”

Pegleg snorted, went back to his bar. Buck reached for the bottle, filled his glass. He suddenly had the look of a man beset by troublesome misgivings.

His gaze went to the washroom, and now the darkness left his face. He grinned appreciatively. In that dimly lit room it was difficult to distinguish Mark from Red. Nobody there, except himself, would have readily recognized that the slim young cowboy was the tenderfoot.

Red O’Malley swaggered up, the derby hat at a rakish angle. “How do I look?” he asked.

"Like a doggone maverick dude." Buck wagged his head sadly.

Red smirked, seized his accordion, strutted between the tables, pleasant tenor voice lifted in song to the accompaniment of his music.

> "I was a young cowboy and I know
>   I done wrong . . ."

Mark resumed his chair, met Buck's appraising eyes with a satisfied grin. The cowboy garb had done something to him. He seemed harder, more mature—formidable

Buck said softly, almost wonderingly, "You sure look like you been eatin' range dust all your born days, Mark."

Mark's hand caressed the butt of the gun Red had thrown in to clinch the deal. "I've been eating range dust in my dreams ever since I was a kid in knee pants."

"Kid dreams, huh?" Buck eyed him curiously. "Maybe you're still dreamin'."

"It's past the dream stage," Mark said simply. He continued to caress the gun-butt. The feel of it was good.

Red O'Malley, the derby hat tilted on the back of his head, pranced past. He rolled triumphant eyes at them, voice and accordion making melody against the growly backwash of convivial voices.

“ ’Twas first to drinkin’ and then to
card-playing,
Got shot in the back, I’m dyin’ to-day—”

A gunshot crashed from somewhere outside in the street. Red’s step faltered. The gun roared again. He lurched, went down on his face. The accordion groaned dismally under his shuddering body.

Startled yells ripped the shocked stillness. The chair under Buck Salten hurtled to the floor. He leaped to the side of his prostrate friend. Mark’s horrified look glimpsed a red stain widening down the back of the Boston-tailored coat. The derby hat had slid over an ear, still clung to the red hair.

Mark was suddenly driving savagely through the excited, milling crowd. The quick thud of pounding hoofs warned him that the killer was already in flight. He was certain now that the bullets had been intended for himself and not for Red O’Malley. The change of clothes had deceived the killer. At best the dirty screen in the door could have offered only an indistinct view of the target he sought. The clothes, the derby hat, had been enough to draw the deadly gunfire.

The drumming hoofbeats were fast drawing into the night. Mark ran to the nearest horse at the hitch-rail, snatched at the tie-rope, and flung himself into the saddle. He reined the horse into the street and sent him into a dead run. The saloon door was slamming furiously now. Yells followed him into the blanketing darkness, told him that he would not be alone in the chase.

The horse under him was fast, but when the road suddenly forked he was compelled to halt. He had no idea in which direction the killer had fled; and now his ears could pick up no sound. Only the night wind sighing in the sagebrush, the sound of other riders closing in from behind.

Mark reluctantly kept his horse at a standstill. For him this was unknown country, and to attempt a blind search in the darkness would be senseless. The killer was already lost in the night-shrouded chaparral.

He waited gloomily for the approaching riders. The hope that one of them might suspect the identity of the man was too thin to cheer him. Not Red O'Malley, but himself had been the intended target. The thought sent chills down his spine. If he had not traded clothes with Red O'Malley he would be where Red was now, lying on that barroom floor, a dreadful stain spreading over his back. The thought sickened him. If he had suspected that he was marked for death he would not have placed young O'Malley in jeopardy, made him the target for an assassin's gun.

Horsemen drew up, halted. Dust drifted on the night wind. One of the riders swore softly. "Lost him, huh?" He was a lean, bearded man and his face swung for a close look at Mark. "You didn't see which way the feller went?"

"I've no idea," Mark answered.

His words, his voice, seemed to hold the bearded man's attention. He peered for a closer look. "Ain't knowin' who you are, mister."

"I'm Mark Destin."

"Huh!" There was a brief silence while the bearded rider absorbed the information. "What you say don't make sense." Bewilderment, growing suspicion, put a rasp in his voice. "That Destin hombre is layin' back there in the Horsehead, and we're out here lookin' for the feller that emptied his gun into him. How come you claim to be *him*."

Mark realized that these men had rushed to the pursuit believing that the victim was himself. Like the killer, they had been deceived by the clothes. They had not taken a second look at the assassin's victim, had made a rush for their horses.

"That wasn't Destin you saw lying on the floor." He was uncomfortably aware of eyes on him, unbelieving, suspicious. "The man you saw lying there was Red O'Malley."

The silence now was long, touched only by the creak of saddle leather as men stirred uneasily. Another rider pressed close, hard gaze on Mark's night-shadowed face. His gun was out, leveled at Mark's head.

"Your talk don't fool us none, mister." His

voice was rough with deepening suspicion. "You're the feller that shot the dude."

"You're wrong!" Mark kept his voice quiet. "I'm the dude, only I'm wearing Red's clothes. We made a trade."

A rider, hidden back in the darkness, chortled disbelievingly. "Hell!" he exclaimed. "Let's dangle him right now."

Another voice said dryly, "Ain't no tree handy."

"Soon find one," growled the bearded man.

Mark realized their ugly mood. These men had ridden in swift pursuit of a killer. They had overtaken him but did not recognize him because of the clothes he had traded from Red O'Malley. Rage at the cowardly shooting had quite blinded them to the truth. It was obvious that they were unaware of his own immediate dash to overtake the man who had shot Red O'Malley. They actually believed that the killer was in their hands. The possible outcome sent a shiver through him. These men were themselves the law in this primitive and lawless land. With them justice was swift and sure—a rope, the nearest tree. It was a time to use convincing words, adroitly cool the boiling anger in them.

He said quietly, "Buck Salten will tell you I was sitting with him when Red was shot."

"How come you're ridin' that Diamond D bronc?" queried the bearded man, head bent close to Mark's face.

"I took the first horse I saw handy." Mark fastened a chill look on his questioner. "Ask Buck Salten about me."

"Don't see you so good." The man's low mutter indicated doubt. "Ain't rememberin' seein' you in the Horsehead any time tonight."

"Let's go back to the Horsehead and ask Buck Salten," urged Mark. "Buck will tell you I was sitting with him when Red was shot, and the shots came from outside, through the screen in the door."

"We'll do that," the man finally agreed. "If Buck backs up your talk we ain't swingin' you for killin' the dude feller."

A rider on either side of him, they trailed towards town. Mark wondered unhappily if Buck Salten *would* back up his story. He had not quite made up his mind about Buck Salten. The man had plainly sided with Ab Matoon against Bill Benton. And as he rode through that black night he found himself thinking of Janet Dunbar. She had warned him that La Cruz was a good place to leave.

Don't waste your time in La Cruz. Diamond D is not for sale.

He wondered dully if Janet Dunbar could have sent a man to kill him, make certain that his stay in La Cruz was indeed short. The thought was too shocking. He was letting the affair wreck sane thinking.

His face lifted to the night wind. He must clear wild conjectures from his mind, think it out coolly. Somebody wanted him dead, but that somebody could not be Janet Dunbar. Nor could he suspect Bill Benton. The man was in gaol.

He continued to search his memory, and suddenly a picture took shape. A masked man, a curiously whispering voice, a new Winchester rifle dropped from a bullet-smashed hand as the bandit had fled.

It was a possible solution that left Mark dissatisfied. The bandit could have shot him at the time of the holdup. It was plain that only robbery was his motive. He had wanted the twenty thousand dollars in Mark's trunk.

Also he was reasonably certain that Matoon would not want him dead. Matoon merely regarded him as a fat pigeon ready for plucking. Mark could not see *murder* in the pot-stomached little land broker. It was possible that he had planned the attempted holdup on the mountain slope. The failure there was not a motive for murder.

Don't waste your time in La Cruz. Diamond D is not for sale.

The cool, scornful voice was back with him. Mark was suddenly sweating. *He was crazy—crazy.*

Dim lamplight glimmered. The horse under him halted. The long hitch-rail in front of the

Horsehead—the bearded man's gruff voice.

"Climb down from your saddle, feller. Too bad for you if Buck Salten ain't backin' your talk."

A buckboard rattled past them, heading out of town from the livery barn. For a moment the light of the swing lantern touched the driver's face. Mark recognized Janet Dunbar. She was alone.

Wordless, the heart in him heavy, he got down from the horse, obeyed the gesture of the bearded man's gun, and pushed through the swing door.

Chapter 5

The same glow of the swing lantern that had briefly glimmered on Janet Dunbar's face as she drove past the Horsehead had more fully lighted the faces of the dismounting riders. Janet had seen Mark Destin only once before, those few moments on the hotel porch. His face was not one she would soon forget, and despite the curious fact that he now wore the garb of a cowboy she had instantly recognized him.

She unconsciously pulled on her reins, slowed the team to a walk. There was a mystery here, one that might possibly involve herself.

She had good reason to be deeply puzzled. She had stopped at Ah Gee's for a cup of coffee before starting on the long drive back to the ranch. The old Chinese had told her with sad shakes of the head that there had been a shooting. His laconic description was unmistakable. The victim could be none other than Mark Destin. She recalled Ah Gee's grieved voice.

Me see men take him hotel. Too bad. Velly nice boy. Too bad!

The news had shocked her, naturally, but after all the man was practically only a name to her—a potential enemy involved in a ruthless conspiracy to steal the ranch that had always been her home.

The only thing she knew in his favor was Ah Gee's apparent liking for him. She tremendously respected the wise old Chinese, trusted him, valued his canny judgment.

She pulled harder on the reins, halted the team, sat there in the dusty buckboard, confused, bewildered. She refused to doubt her eyes. She knew that she had just seen Mark Destin entering the Horsehead Bar, and evidently a prisoner of the men with him. The recognition was positive, in fact, mutual. He had caught her startled look.

Janet leaned back in the seat, began a deliberate scrutiny of the scrambled picture. One thing was certain. The man Ah Gee had seen carried to the hotel was not Mark Destin. The victim of the shooting must have been somebody wearing Mark Destin's clothes. The tell-tale garb would easily deceive Ah Gee in that darkness.

She concentrated on the brief view of Mark Destin as he had climbed from his saddle. The light had been dim, and she had hardly more than caught a glimpse of the horse under him. In fact she had been more interested in the rider, completely astonished at his changed appearance. She was aware now that something about the horse had been vaguely familiar, and suddenly she remembered. The white blaze down the nose—Big Baldy, a Diamond D horse. Or, more correctly, *had* been a Diamond D. She had only the day before given Red O'Malley a bill-of-sale for Baldy as part payment of wages due when he quit the payroll in protest against the ousting of Buck Salten as foreman. Buck was Red's idol, and he had chosen to leave with the discharged foreman. His desertion had hurt. Red had grown up on Diamond D. He was a valuable hand, and the outfit liked his accordion and innumerable songs of the range. A bit wild, but nothing really wrong with him, unless it was his absurd ambition to become a professional singer of cowboy ballads. She wondered guiltily if she had been wrong, opposing his dreams. He really did have a way with his accordion, and his voice had an appeal that reached the heart.

Her fleeting thoughts of Red suddenly recalled something else she had vaguely noticed about Mark Destin when he got down from the bald-faced horse. The shirt on his back, its vivid red and green checks distinct even in the smoky light of the swing lantern. She remembered that shirt now. She had chosen it herself in Silver City—a gift for Red O'Malley on his recent birthday.

Janet's heart stood still. She was getting somewhere, and the answer was too shocking. Mark Destin in Red O'Malley's clothes, and over at the hotel a man wearing Mark Destin's clothes. She knew now that the victim of the shooting was Red O'Malley, lying there in the hotel—dead or dangerously wounded.

She made no attempt to delve further into the mysterious affair, swung the team in a sharp turn and headed back for town. Her whip stung the backs of the surprised horses. They broke into a gallop, the light buckboard bouncing and swaying at their flying heels.

She recognized Doc. Bralen's buggy at the hitch-rail in front of the hotel. Perhaps Red was still alive—a reassuring thought that instantly faded. The doctor was also the coroner. His presence might mean a grimmer duty than succoring a wounded man.

She sprang from the buckboard, hastily tied the team to a tooth-gnawed post, and ran up the porch steps.

Another man had replaced Louie Renn at the desk. He hastily slid a flask into a drawer, smirked surprised recognition. He was a former Diamond D rider her father had practically kicked off the ranch for drunkenness. The sight of him smirking behind the desk increased the contempt she felt for Ab Matoon. It seemed that he found such men useful. He was certainly on good terms with the town's border rascals.

She asked abruptly, "Where is he, Cooner?"

Cooner's smirk left his unshaved, purple-veined face. He was a burly, middle-aged man, and his shifty, murky eyes took on a glassy blankness.

"Meanin' who, Miss Dunbar?"

"Red O'Malley!" She wanted to hit him. "Where is he?"

Footsteps came sharply up the rear hall, and Buck Salten pushed into the lobby, halted abruptly as he saw the girl.

Janet ran to him. "Buck, how is he?"

Her tall ex-foreman's brown face was a stiff mask. He said, gruffly, "Red ain't dead—not yet. The doc's with him now."

She gazed at him miserably. There was good reason for his hostility. She had only recently discharged him with bitter words, accused him of treachery, of complicity in the ugly conspiracy to steal the ranch that her father's courage and fortitude had wrested from an inhospitable and grudging wilderness. He had not denied her accusations, simply asked for his time. Perhaps her stepbrother had lied. Ray had never got on well with Buck—had been jealous of his authority.

She asked a question that was troubling her. "Who—who shot him? Was it that Destin man?"

"Ain't knowing who shot him," Buck said.

Her expression showed disbelief. "You were there?"

"Yeah, I was there." Anger glinted in Buck's eyes. It was plain he resented the implication that he lied.

"I saw them taking Destin into the saloon with a gun at his back—" Janet paused, startled by the shocked dismay in his eyes. "Destin was wearing

Red's clothes. It's all dreadfully confusing."

"It's hell!" Buck spoke harshly, pushed past her, made for the door on the run. The screen slammed at his back and she heard the quick pound of his feet down the porch steps.

Cooner said speculatively from behind his desk, "Buck wasn't likin' what you said."

Janet ignored him, hurried along the dark hall. Cooner's hand went to the drawer, reappeared with the flask. He took a long drink, wiped his untidy mustache with the back of his hand, and replaced the flask in the drawer. He scowled, shook his head like a man annoyed by an unsatisfied curiosity.

Dr. Bralen heard the girl's quick, light step. He opened the door, gave her a keen look as if sizing up her possibilities. She pushed past him, went quickly to the bed, and gazed down at the slim red-haired cowboy. His stillness frightened her, and she turned an anxious look on the doctor.

He gave her a faint, reassuring nod. "There's a fighting chance," he said. His eyes continued to appraise her. "I've got to operate—get that bullet out of his back. I'm wondering if you can help me, Janet."

"I—I'll do anything," Janet whispered. She did not like Doc. Bralen much. He was too friendly with Ab Matoon, and he drank too much. There were whispered rumors that it was drink that had ruined a fine career—brought him to the little border town of La Cruz. She also knew that he was a skillful surgeon when sober. He seemed sober enough now.

"A fighting chance," repeated Doc. Bralen. He was a tall, craggy-faced man with a rough mane of iron-grey hair. "You're a godsend, Janet. Usually have Mrs. Dorn help me when I operate. Unfortunately she's visiting in Silver City."

"I'll do anything," Janet said again. Her gaze returned to the wounded cowboy, went briefly to the blood-stained coat and shirt lying on the floor. She repressed a shudder, forced herself to listen attentively to the doctor's instructions. She had a job to do—must keep her mind cool—do all she humanly could to help Doc. Bralen give Red O'Malley his one fighting chance.

He sensed the resolution hardening in her, smiled approval. "We'll do it," he promised grimly.

She lost all track of time, knew only that she was fighting for the life of a man, was suddenly amazed to hear the doctor's low, contented voice.

"We've done it, Janet."

She stared at the piece of flattened lead in the palm of his hand, lifted her eyes in an oddly awed look at the craggy face, read weariness there and the quiet satisfaction of a man who knows he has done a good job.

"He—he'll be all right?" She asked the question timidly.

Doc. Bralen nodded. "Young—tough as rawhide. Good as ever inside of a couple of weeks. He'll need some nursing though."

It was a question almost, and Janet said simply, "I'll nurse him."

"Fine!" The doctor's smile was warm on her. "You make a mighty good nurse, Janet." He jiggled the flattened bullet in his palm, eyed it with professional interest. "Lodged right up against his spine. A successful operation, if I do say so."

"You were wonderful," Janet said. "You're a great surgeon, doctor."

He was very still for a moment, a hint of a shadow darkening his face as if her words stirred unpleasant thoughts in him. And now Janet was aware of the two men watching from the open doorway. She wondered how long Mark Destin and Buck Salten had been standing there. She had been too oblivious of outside things to notice.

Her low exclamation drew Doc. Bralen from his momentary abstraction. His head turned in a look. "He's fine, Buck." The cloud lifted from his face. "Got that damn' piece of lead out, and everything's fine—thanks to Miss Dunbar's help."

"Sure good news," muttered Buck Salten, and there was no hint of hostility now in the look he gave the girl, only gratitude and warm admiration.

Mark Destin was staring at the still form on the bed. The hot anger in his eyes startled Janet. The change of clothes quite altered him. He looked hard, competent, and at this moment decidedly dangerous, as he stood there, grim, silent, bleak gaze on their bandaged patient.

"Janet's going to stay on the job, play nurse at least until Mrs. Dorn gets back," Doc. Bralen told Buck in a pleased voice. "No need to worry, Buck."

Janet found her voice. "Can he be moved?" She glanced round the untidy little room, distaste in her eyes.

Doc. Bralen shook his head. "Not advisable for a day or two."

"I'd like to have him out at the ranch," Janet said; and she added in a low voice, not looking at Buck Salten, "After all, the ranch is about the only home he's ever known."

"We'll see—we'll see," smiled the doctor. "I couldn't wish him in better hands, my girl."

Buck's face had hardened. "I ain't sure Red would like it," he demurred. His look defied her. "Red ain't callin' the ranch his home no more."

Quick tears smarted in her eyes. She could only look at him, helpless, unable to find words. It was Mark Destin whose quiet voice broke the momentary uncomfortable silence. "I think Miss Dunbar is right, Buck," he said. "She can do a lot more for him out at the ranch than here in La Cruz."

"Quite right!" gruffed the doctor. "You can't object, Buck. Not after what Janet has done tonight. Couldn't have managed without her—" He broke off, bent hastily over his patient. "Coming out of it," he added in a satisfied voice.

Red's eyes were open, and after a tense moment Janet heard his voice, hardly audible in that sudden stillness, the whispered hum of a ballad that she recognized with a choke in her throat.

> "Put bunches of roses all over my
>   coffin,
> Put roses to deaden the clods as they
>   fall. . . ."

"No, no!" She went on her knees by the bed, placed a hand over his. "No roses yet, Red! Not this time!"

His eyes took on a puzzled look. "Where-all did *you* come from, Janet?" His gaze shifted in a wondering look round the room. "How come I'm layin' here?" His whispering hum began again.

> "Take me to the green valley and
>   lay the sod o'er me,
> For I'm a young cowboy and know
>   I done wrong."

"No, Red," Janet said in a clear, firm voice. "You're not that poor cowboy in the streets of Laredo. You're all right now, and you haven't done wrong." She placed a cool hand over his brow. "Go to sleep, Red."

"He was singing that song when he was shot," Buck muttered softly.

Red spoke again in the same feverish whisper. "I want my accordion. Where-all is my accordion?"

Mark said quickly, with a warning look at Buck, "It's all right, Red. I'll get it for you."

"*Gracias*, Mark. You're a good hombre." The cowboy's eyes closed.

"He's all right," Doc. Bralen said in a relieved voice. He smiled at Mark. "Be a good idea to get that accordion so he can see it next time he wakes up."

"It's smashed," Mark said in a low voice. "He fell on top of it."

Buck Salten's gloomy nod confirmed him. "Reckon there ain't another accordion in La Cruz," he mourned.

"Plácido Romero has one," remembered Janet.

"I'll go ask him to lend it," volunteered Buck.

Janet was on her feet now. She looked at him doubtfully. "I don't know, Buck—" She hesitated, embarrassed. "I think the best way is to send Pedro Ortega, have him tell Plácido that I want to borrow the accordion for a few days."

"Where can I find Pedro?" Mark asked, quick to observe growing anger darken Buck's face.

"He works at the livery barn," directed Janet. She was suddenly keenly aware of him and wondered how Buck Salten had managed to get him away from the men who were holding him a prisoner in the saloon. It was quite apparent that he was not the man who had shot Red O'Malley. His anxiety about Red almost won her liking. It was plain that Red liked him. Red had called him Mark, said he was a good hombre. She felt a shiver of doubt run through her. Ah Gee liked him too, and yet she knew that he was mixed up in Ab Matoon's sly schemes. And Buck Salten. She must continue to harden her heart, be wary of these two men.

Buck said curtly to Mark, "Come on, let's go find Pedro."

Mark followed him into the hall, came to a standstill. Doc. Bralen was speaking, his voice jocular. "Fixed up another gunshot wound this evening, Janet. That stepbrother of yours. A fool accident cleaning his gun. Sent a bullet smashing through his hand. Cut his face, too."

He heard the girl's startled ejaculation, waited to hear no more, hurried to overtake Buck. He felt a bit sick. The lone bandit on the mountain slope was Janet Dunbar's stepbrother.

You smashed his hand and marked his face plenty. Won't be hard to spot him.

Jim Ball had spoken prophetic words. The bullet-smashed hand, the cut face—damning proof that Ray Wellerton was the guilty man.

Mark wondered unhappily if Janet Dunbar could possibly be involved in the affair. It could explain her strange antagonism.

Chapter 6

He came up with Buck in the lobby, sensed from the puzzled frown on the man's face that he had overheard Doc. Bralen's gossip.

Cooner was grinning at them, avid curiosity in his eyes. Mark repressed the question he was about to ask, and followed Buck out to the porch, conscious of Cooner's disappointed gaze.

Moonlight was flooding over the mountains now, made a silver lane between the huddle of buildings. Mark halted, spoke softly.

"You heard him, Buck?"

"Yeah, I heard him."

Mark asked another question, although he already knew the answer. He wanted Buck's reaction. "Who is this stepbrother?"

"Name of Ray Wellerton, a son of her dad's second wife by her first husband and no decent skunk would claim him for kin." Buck's tone was bitter. "A plumb no-good hombre, only you cain't make Janet believe it. No good trying to make her think that Ray ain't all right."

Mark said gloomily, "Lot of hell going on here I don't understand." He paused, looked steadily at the other man. "You were sitting on the hotel porch when I climbed from the stage. I heard you tell Jim Ball that you had quit Diamond D.

I'm all confused, Buck. I've an idea that Janet Dunbar is in trouble. Why would a man like you quit the job when she's needing help?"

Moonlight lay cold and bright on Buck's face, and Mark was aware of a quick, searching look from him, and when he finally spoke his voice held a curiously troubled note.

"Let's get Pedro started for the *cantina*," he said, and moved down the porch steps.

Mark halted again. "Listen, Buck. Have you any idea who shot Red?"

Buck said laconically, "I've done some figgerin', and it don't add up sensible."

Mark said quietly, "I'd like to hear how it adds up."

"Red was wearin' your clothes," Buck reminded. "I reckon you can figger it out."

"Yes," Mark said. "I've figured it out. You mean those bullets were intended for me."

"That's right." Buck's puzzled eyes were on him. "Only I cain't figger why them bullets *was* intended for you. The thing don't make sense. Who in hell should want to kill you, and you in town less than six hours."

"I could make a guess." Mark's smile was thin. "Only I don't like to guess. I like to *know*."

"I reckon you know more than I do," grumbled Buck. His sideways glance held a hint of suspicion.

"I don't know enough to make any sense out

of it." Mark hesitated. "I like you, Buck, and something in me tells me you're playing a game. A man like you must have some good reason for quitting Diamond D, and I don't think that reason means you can possibly be a friend of Ab Matoon."

"You've got me guessin' your own self," drawled Buck. "For a tenderfoot dude you sure have plenty savvy. I'll take a chance and say that *you're* playing a game—makin' out you're a shorthorn fresh from Boston."

"Tenderfoot is not another word for fool," Mark retorted. "I came out here to buy a cattle ranch, and it's my first trip west." His quiet voice hardened. "If that makes me a tenderfoot then I'm a tenderfoot, but I'm no fool."

"Was just saying you've plenty savvy." Buck's grin was apologetic. "Got plenty nerve too. I liked the way you handled Bill Benton."

"I'm sorry for him," Mark said. "I don't like the way he was hustled off to gaol."

They were moving down the street again. The moon made lights and shadows on the rugged slopes beyond the town. They turned into the livery yard, halted as if by mutual consent in the deeper blackness of a giant chinaberry tree. The sweet smell of hay came to them from the big barn. They could hear voices, the stamp of hoofs. A man appeared with a lighted lantern. An eight-mule hitch followed at his heels, trailed him to a lone freight wagon that stood on the far side of the yard. The man set the lantern down, began with low-voiced profanities to hook up the team. A second man stood watching from the dimly lit doorway.

"Looks like Jim Ball standin' there," Buck remarked. He continued before Mark could comment, his voice low, thoughtful. "I'm mighty sorry, too, for Bill Benton. Wasn't likin' it myself, the way they throwed him in gaol."

Mark said, surprised, "I wouldn't have guessed it."

"Well"—Buck's tone was cautious, as if he were feeling his way over dangerous ground—"you're maybe right about me, Mark. You guessed it. I *am* playing a game, like you figgered, and I've got to walk soft—watch myself close. That's why I acted the way I did over in the Horsehead, made out I was runnin' with the pack that's after Benton."

"I think," Mark said, "it's about time for you and me to do some trading."

"That's what I'm thinkin'," agreed Buck. His look went to the motionless figure in the yawning entrance of the barn. "Be a good idea to get Pedro started for the *cantina* before we make any more palaver."

Mark nodded, and they left the darkness of the chinaberry tree, heard Jim Ball's surprised voice. "Doggone—seen shadders thar under the tree. Was gettin' some narvous and ready to line up my shotgun on you. What's on your mind, Buck?"

"Got a job for Pedro—if you can spare him," explained Buck.

"Sure I can spare him—if it don't take him too far," assented the stageman. He peered curiously at Mark, his expression puzzled. "Seems like I've seen you some place—" He broke off, slapped a thigh. "Doggone! I wasn't knowin' you in that rig, Mr. Destin." He was suddenly cautious, evidently mindful of their agreement not to let their already warm friendship be known even to Buck Salten. "What for you want Pedro?"

"Looks like you ain't heard about the shootin'," Buck said.

"Just climbed out of my bunk," Jim Ball told them. "I most always stretch out for a couple of hours after I bring the stage in. Was gettin' set to head for Ah Gee's when I seen you two fellers kind of sinister-like under the chinaberry." He shook his head. "No, I ain't heard of no shootin'." Tobacco plug came out of his pocket. He bit off a quid. "Who's 'lected 'for Boothill this time?"

Buck gave him a terse account of the affair. "We've got Red over at the hotel now. Janet Dunbar's nursin' him. Looks like the kid will pull through, only he kind of got to ravin' about that accordion of his. We ain't told him it's busted, and Janet figgers we can maybe borrow one from

Plácido Romero. She wants Pedro to hightail it over to the *cantina* and get it."

"I savvy." The old stageman nodded. "Pedro's back in the stalls some place. I'll go get him." He turned a wide back on them, hurried at a stiff-legged gait up the tunneling passage. The expression on his face told Mark that he was a very puzzled man and that he did not *really* "savvy."

The mule driver came up, a lean, dusty-faced man, a black-snake whip coiled over an arm. He gave Buck a recognizing grin. "Hello, Buck. Long time no see you."

Buck gave him a preoccupied nod. "Hello, Pete. Pullin' out, huh?"

"Yeah. Want to make Wagon Mound Springs by sunup." He grinned. "Moonlight's good for night travel, and night travel's a damn' sight cooler than that blisterin' sun. Sleep all day at Wagon Mound and then hit the road ag'in for Silver City."

"That's right," agreed Buck. "Well, good luck on the road, Pete. Keep your eye peeled for Injuns . . ."

"I reckon Geronimo's made his last break," chuckled the mule-skinner. He hesitated, fiddled with his black snake. Mark guessed there was something on his mind.

"Waal, reckon I'll go settle my bill with Jim." Pete took a step, halted. "Say, Buck, run into

Ray Wellerton back on Coyote Wash. Was sure in bad shape, hand bleedin' bad. He rode out of the willows, stopped me, and got me to fix him a bandage." The mule driver paused, shook his head. "Ray said it was an accident, foolin' with his gun."

"Sure too bad," commented Buck in a flat, toneless voice.

The dim lamplight showed a hint of a skeptical grin on the freighter's face. "Ray's story didn't make hay with me," he said. "You see, Buck, that gun in his belt was a forty-five, and it wasn't no forty-five bullet that smashed his fingers. He wasn't foolin' me with his talk of an accident." He disappeared into the barn, and they heard his voice calling for Jim Ball.

Pedro Ortega appeared, pitchfork in hand. "*Sí, señores*. You wan' me, boss say."

Buck gave him Janet's message for Plácido Romero. "Make it fast, Pedro," he urged. "Get that accordion over to Miss Dunbar quick as you can."

"*Sí, señor*. I go *pronto*." The Mexican vanished into the barn.

They waited there for Jim Ball to finish his business with the mule driver. The voices of the pair reached them from the office, and Mark gathered they were discussing a shipment of grain the stageman wanted hauled from Silver City.

He glanced at Buck, met his eyes appraising, troubled and it came to him that the man was in a panic, wondering if he had admitted too much. Theirs was a brief friendship as yet. Each was taking the other on something bordering a perilous trust—a liking that one man feels for another on sight. He could not blame Buck for the doubts so visible in him. And, after all, he still had his own shred of doubt. He was no novice in sizing up men. He had learned a lot during his years at college, become familiar with all the signs that betrayed rotten spots, lack of character. His sober judgment told him that in Buck Salten there were no rotten spots. The character of the man was plain in his fine face. A fact that made the feud between him and Janet Dunbar all the more puzzling.

The thought of the girl decided Mark to ask the question that had been lurking in the back of his mind. Buck's answer would do a lot to clear away his last shred of doubt.

"Listen, Buck." He wondered at the thin edge to his voice. "You admitted you are playing a game so dangerous that you have to walk soft and watch yourself. I'm asking you as man to man—is your game against Janet Dunbar."

"I'm asking you the same question." The light of the big swing lantern glinted on Buck's eyes, fierce, diamond-hard. "I've played the game long enough to know you and Ab Matoon are in cahoots to get hold of Diamond D." Buck gestured savagely. "Was just thinkin' I was crazy, talking like I did."

"You're wrong!" Mark held his voice steady. "I'm not in cahoots with Ab Matoon, and I never heard of the girl until a few hours ago. You ask Jim Ball."

Buck's gun hand was down, fingers tight over butt. He said heavily, "If I thought you was lying I'd fill you with lead here and now."

"You haven't answered my question." Mark made no move to reach for the gun in his belt. He met the other man's threatening look without flinching. "I asked you if your game is against Janet Dunbar."

"No!" The word came explosively. "Ain't I just told you I'd kill you here and now if I really thought you mean her harm?"

A smile spread over Mark's face. "That's the talk I wanted from you." His hand went out. "Shake on it, Buck. I've never killed a man yet, but I'd feel the same way if I were in your boots. I'm in a maze—a fool tenderfoot who doesn't know what's going on in this town, and what's between you and Janet Dunbar has me guessing."

He felt Buck's hard fingers close over his hand, heard his soft drawl. "A *fightin'* tenderfoot, Mark, I reckon. That's what you are—a *fightin'* tenderfoot, and I'm sayin' out loud that I'm right proud to be ridin' stirrup to stirrup with you—"

He broke off, winced. "Some grip you've got. Nothin' tender about you, feller, 'cept the smooth look you wear on your face."

Mark grinned back at him. "Give me time to get weathered under your New Mexico sun." His face sobered. "What do you make of that teamster's story about Ray Wellerton?"

Buck shook his head. "You can search me. I'm gamblin' that Pete's right, though, and that means the crawlin' snake has been up to low-down business. Ray cain't tell the truth across a stack of Bibles."

Mark's smile widened. "You ask Jim Ball what *he* thinks about that smashed hand. I've an idea he can tell you a lot."

The old stageman followed Pete from the office. He leaned against the door, gaze following the freighter across the yard to his wagon. He looked disgruntled, and Buck said with a sly grin at Mark, "I'm bettin' Pete stuck you good for that load of feed-barley."

Jim chewed hard on his quid. "Jumped his price five dollars a ton," he admitted gloomily. "Claims he's riskin' his scalp every load he hauls."

Buck chuckled. "He was just tellin' me he figgered that Geronimo had made his last raid. Looks like Pete pulled a good one on you, Jim."

"Doggone his schemin' hide!" spluttered the stageman. "I'll fix him next time he comes. I'll put that extry five dollars a ton on his feed-bill."

The big freight wagon rumbled into the street, bells on the lead-team jingling softly. Jim Ball's look went to Mark. He said, with elaborate politeness, "You figger to stay long in La Cruz, Mr. Destin?"

Mark gave him an amused grin. "It's all right, Jim. We don't need to do any pretending in front of Buck."

"Huh?" The stageman seemed nettled. "Thought we'd fixed it not to let folks know that you and me is friends."

"A lot has happened since I climbed from your stage," Mark told him. "Buck's my friend too, now. We've thrown in together."

Buck nodded. "That's right," he confirmed. He shrugged, added grimly, "Looks like we'll be ridin' a lot of crooked trails together before we're done cleanin' up this cow-town."

Jim Ball was silent for a long moment, evidently digesting the import of Buck's words. He said solemnly to Mark, "You're the fightin'est tenderfoot I ever seen in all my born days. Dog-gone if you ain't! Knowed it ever since I seen the way you scotched that gun-totin' rattlesnake up on the grade." He pulled a fat silver watch from a pocket, looked at it, frowned. "Should be headin' over to the Chinaman's for chow," he grumbled. He thrust the watch back, shook his head annoyedly. "Cain't leave until Pedro gets back from Plácido's with that accordion."

Mark glanced at the little office. "We can do some talking while you wait," he suggested.

"Sure can," agreed the stageman, brightening. "I reckon the office is a right good place for us three to have a powwow."

He led the way into the office, lowered his ponderous frame into the big chair behind a battered, untidy desk. Mark and Buck found seats, and after a brief hesitation Jim drew a flask from a drawer. The two younger men shook their heads. He dropped the flask back in the drawer, beamed his approval.

"I reckon you sure mean business," he said dryly. "Waal, I'm listenin'."

Mark spoke briefly of the mule driver's encounter with Ray Wellerton in Coyote Wash. "I told Buck you might have an idea about that smashed hand."

"Sure do," chuckled Jim. "Fastest gunplay I ever seen, Buck." He described the attempted holdup. "Ain't no question in my mind," he finished. "The feller was Ray Wellerton. Him runnin' into Pete down in Coyote Wash sure pins it on the sneakin' wolf."

"Looks like a good bet," agreed Buck. He was looking intently at Mark, respect mingled with curiosity in his eyes. "I'm wondering why he was so set on getting hold of your trunk. Must have had some powerful good reason."

Mark hesitated, looked at Jim Ball. He was not

certain that it would be fair to Plácido Romero to divulge the whereabouts of the cached gold.

Jim nodded encouragement. "If you and Buck figger to ride the same trail you cain't hold nothin' out on him," he said. "You can trust Buck Salten from here to hell and back."

"I was thinking of Plácido," Mark frowned. "It's *his* secret now."

"Him and Buck are friends," Jim reassured. "Ain't nothin' Plácido wouldn't do for Buck. No call for worry *there,* son."

Mark's doubts vanished. "I was carrying twenty thousand dollars gold in that trunk," he told his new friend, with a rueful grin. "Crazy thing to do, but I thought there'd be a bank in La Cruz."

"Seems like that Ab Matoon wrote him to fetch his money along with him—in gold," Jim said, with a grim smile. "It's my bet him and Ray Wellerton figgered to get that gold before Mark got to town with it."

"Looks mighty suspicious," agreed Buck. "Sure is queer business."

"I'm not so certain that Matoon had any part in the holdup," demurred Mark. "He was in the hotel lobby when the porter carried the trunk in. Seemed surprised the man could sling it over his shoulder so easily. He knew twenty thousand dollars gold would make a lot heavier load."

They eyed him in respectful silence, and Jim

said admiringly, “You’ve got a smart head, son. I reckon you figgered it right, and that means Ab wasn’t knowin’ about the holdup.”

“Looks like Ray was playing a lone hand.” Buck glowered at the cigarette taking shape between his fingers.

“He couldn’t have known I was bringing the gold with me unless Matoon told him,” puzzled Mark. He looked at Buck. “You said you were playing a game. Perhaps I can think straighter if I know what your game is.”

Buck lit his cigarette, looked at him speculatively. “Maybe you ain’t knowing that Janet’s pa, Rick Dunbar, was shot a couple of months back.”

“Jim told me he was killed by rustlers,” answered Mark.

“That’s the story.” Buck scowled. “I’m thinking different. I’m thinking Rick was murdered—and the killer was no rustler.”

“You mean you can name the murderer?” guessed Mark.

Buck hesitated, his face troubled. “I reckon so, only I cain’t prove it—yet.” His hand lifted in an angry gesture. “Been prodding Janet to get rid of Ray—kick him off the ranch. She won’t listen to no talk against him. I’ve gone as far as I can until I get more proof.”

“You mean you’re accusing Ray Wellerton of the murder?” Mark’s tone was disbelieving.

"Doesn't seem likely that Ray would murder his own stepfather."

"You don't know Ray," Buck said grimly. "I reckon that hombre was spawned in hell." He paused, gave Mark a bitter smile. "You was wondering how come I quit Diamond D and Janet needing a man's help. The way things were shaping, there wasn't nothing for me to do but quit. Ray was fillin' her up with lies about me. She won't believe me, but his talk rings the bell with her. She's got a crazy notion that I'm mixed up in some crooked deal to get Diamond D away from her and that it was me that maybe shot her dad."

"Sure is bad business," muttered Jim Ball. He rubbed his beetling nose thoughtfully. "She's maybe got more reason than just Ray's lyin' talk."

Buck nodded soberly. "Something like that," he admitted. "She didn't like it that I used my homesteader's rights on that Borrego Creek strip south of our Pioche range. Kind of backed up Ray's talk about me, I reckon."

Mark looked puzzled. "Why should she object, if the land was open for homesteading?"

"The Borrego Creek strip's been Diamond D range ever since Rick Dunbar's been running cows here," explained Buck. "Rick had used up his own homestead rights, bought in a lot of rights that he'd got some of the outfit to use, only he never did get title to the Borrego that controls about all the water there is on the Pioche range." Buck shrugged. "Rick kind of slipped up on that Borrego strip, been running cows there so long he got to thinking he owned it."

Jim Ball studied him with worried eyes. "Ain't blamin' Janet for gettin' some suspicious," he observed.

"It was Rick Dunbar's idea." Buck gave the old stageman a resentful look. "Rick knew there was squatters nosin' 'round and got mighty worried. We talked it over, figgered the only thing we could do was for me to file on the land myself."

"I'm believin' you," Jim said in a relieved voice. "Would have hit Rick awful hard to lose that Borrego strip."

"That's right." Buck flipped cigarette stub into the brown earthenware pot the stageman used for a spittoon. "That Pioche range ain't worth a damn without the Borrego Creek strip." His fingers were busy shaping another cigarette. "Rick was killed before I got 'round to filing on the land. Clean slipped my mind until Red come in with a yarn about runnin' into a couple of strangers nosin' round over there. I was sure scared then and filed the next day."

"You didn't tell Janet Dunbar?" Mark asked the question thoughtfully.

"That's the trouble," grumbled Buck. "I didn't speak of it at the time, and that's how Ray

Wellerton got the jump on me. He learned about it and told her. She flew off the handle, tackled me like a wildcat, said I was in cahoots with Ab Matoon to ruin her, force her to sell Diamond D for next to nothing. She just wouldn't believe that it was her own pa got me to use my homestead rights on the strip."

"Would losing the Borrego Creek strip be so bad for the ranch?" Mark asked.

"Diamond D ain't much good without the Pioche range," Buck told him gloomily. "And the Pioche ain't no good without you've got control of the Borrego Creek water. Ain't hard to figger the answer."

There was a silence, their faces hard with grim speculations. Mark was aware of a growing dismay in him. He had walked all unwittingly into a dark mire of intrigue and treachery that promised unpleasant possibilities. If he had any sense he would say a prompt *adiós* to La Cruz, recover his gold from Plácido Romero, and take the first stage out. It was a solution he found displeasing. He was not turning his back on the dark face of danger, seeking safety in a coward's retreat. This called for courage and loyalty—a cool mind. He was already pledged to Buck Salten. No matter how perilous the trail ahead, he was resolved to keep that pledge.

The decision stiffened in him. For the present he must put aside his own personal plans, do what he could to make light where now there was only darkness.

He found himself thinking of his first meeting with Janet Dunbar on the hotel porch. The memory would always cling to him—the glint of lamplight on her chestnut hair, the pride and fearlessness that had animated her uplifted face. He knew then that she alone was reason enough to hold him in La Cruz, meet any challenge to the best that was in him.

He heard Buck Salten's voice—hard, grim with purpose. "I reckon that's enough to show you why I'm playing a game, Mark. You figgered back there in the Horsehead that I was sidin' with Ab Matoon against Bill Benton. It's what I want Matoon to think, get on his blind side, and maybe find out if he's backin' Ray Wellerton's play."

"It looks as if Matoon must have told Ray about my twenty thousand dollars," Mark said. "I'm willing to bet, though, that Matoon doesn't know about the attempted holdup."

Jim Ball snorted. "Only one answer," he told them. "Ray was pullin' a double-cross on Ab." He chuckled. "He would have got clean away with that gold if Mark hadn't been faster than greased lightnin'." He chuckled again. "Ab nor nobody would have suspected Ray was the road agent."

"Just the same, there's a tie-up between them,"

argued Mark. "Matoon was careless, let enough drop to give Ray the tip. We've got *that* much to do some thinking about." He paused, added worriedly, "Right now I'm thinking about Benton." His eyes questioned Buck. "Matoon claimed that Benton was looking for him with a gun and that's why he had him thrown in gaol. Why would Benton want to kill Matoon?"

"Bill Benton claims he had Matoon sell a bunch of beef-steers for him and that Matoon held back the money," Buck told him. "Bill needs the money bad, says he needs it to carry him along to next roundup."

Mark frowned. "What's Matoon's reason for holding back the money?"

"Ab says it's owing him on an overdue note." Buck's tone was skeptical. "Bill claims the note is ten times bigger than the one he signed and that Ab is all set to ruin him so he can get hold of his Bar B ranch."

Mark thought it over. "I don't like it." His smooth young face suddenly looked years older. "I don't like that town marshal either," he added.

Jim Ball broke his attentive silence, his voice a gruff rumble. "For a tenderfoot dude you sure can size a man up good. Teel Furner is one killin' gent if he *does* wear a law star."

Mark sensed an ugly significance in the old stageman's laconic summing up of the town marshal. He repeated uneasily, "I don't like it."

"Ain't likin' it my own self," Buck said, the drawl gone from his voice.

A shadow crossed the open doorway, and they saw Pedro Ortega peering in at them. Jim Ball lifted his bulk from the big chair, reached for the hat he had tossed on the desk. "You get that accordion, Pedro?"

"*Sí, señor*." The Mexican grinned. "Take heem to *señorita* at 'otel."

"*Bueno*!" Jim eyed his companions apologetically. "Got to get started for the Chinaman's, fellers. My belly's gettin' real on the prod."

"Nothin' more to keep us here." Buck got out of his chair. "Let's blow, Mark."

They accompanied the stageman towards the Chop House. Buck said, "Well, so long, Jim," and swung round the corner. Mark hesitated, hurried after him.

"Where are you going?" he asked.

Buck halted, looked at him, and the moonlight on his face showed a grimness there that made Mark wonder.

"I'm going to the gaol."

Mark continued to look at him, aware of an odd stir in the pit of his stomach. He believed he knew what would be the answer to his next question.

"Why?"

"I'm going to bust Bill Benton out of that damn gaol," Buck said in a fierce, low voice. "He won't be alive, come sunup, if he stays there."

Mark said, his voice so hard he almost failed to recognize it as his own, "I'm going along with you, Buck."

Chapter 7

They followed the wash of a brush-choked *barranca* that Mark guessed would lead them unobserved to the proximity of the gaol. What they would do when they got there he had not the glimmer of an idea.

Misgivings set in. He had amazingly committed himself to an enterprise that savored strongly of lawlessness. Only a few hours in La Cruz, and here he was, bent on a lawless occasion that might easily terminate in bloodshed. The situation was out of harmony with the traditions of a family who had given noted jurists to the nation. His own father had been a learned judge.

Mark heard Buck's low voice. "Watch your step—rattler some place close."

He halted. It was his first encounter with a rattlesnake. The faint whirring sound was unmistakable, a sinister warning of lurking death.

Buck's whispered voice came again. "Cain't risk a shot at the critter. Too close to the gaol. Head up the slope, Mark. Good cover in that mesquite up there for us to lay in and take stock of things."

Mark went cautiously up the slope. The brief incident had somehow steadied him. The unfortunate Bill Benton had stepped on a rattlesnake and would soon be a dead man unless something was done about it. This adventure was not an act of lawlessness, but a mission of mercy and justice. To think otherwise was against all common sense.

He lay prone under the mesquite, shadowed from the moonlight by sprawling, twisted branches. Buck came alongside and drew his attention to the low, flat-roofed building some hundred yards away and slightly below them. As he had surmised, they had circled in from behind, and he could see the few lights of the town lower down the slope. Between them and the gaol were more clumps of mesquite, their upper branches frosted with moonshine.

He wondered what their next move would be, waited for Buck to speak. Breaking a man out of gaol was a grim job he had not included in his long-range study of the cattle business. Things were crowding a little too fast for comfort.

Buck said softly, "We've got to figger out a way to fool Teel Furner. Don't want him nor nobody to savvy it was us that got Benton loose."

"I'm feeling awfully useless right now." Mark gazed miserably at the dimly lit gaol. "I don't see how we can get into that place and not be seen—recognized."

"There's ways," Buck told him enigmatically. He was silent for long minutes, eyes scrutinizing the moonlit chaparral, studying the white streak that was the road twisting down the slope towards the town. He muttered a soft exclamation. "That'll be Teel, down there, headin' back to town."

Mark looked, saw a moving shape that vanished the next instant behind concealing bluffs. He said, doubtfully, "We can't be sure it was the town marshal. It might have been anything—a stray horse."

"We'll take a gamble it was Teel, and that means there's only Jess Kinner for us to handle. He's the gaoler." Buck was on his feet. "Let's get real close, and move careful, Mark. Keep in the shadders."

They made a cautious approach, pausing every few moments to listen for any stir in the gaol. They reached the edge of the concealing chaparral. Buck's hand lifted in a signal to halt. The remaining fifteen yards lacked any shred of cover from the revealing moonlight.

They heard steps in the gaol, a gruff voice. Buck was instantly in motion, quick, noiseless strides that carried him to the front of the building. Mark was close on his heels.

The door was open, the office empty. Buck slipped inside, soft-footed as a great cat. Mark followed, saw Buck snatch a gay-colored Navajo blanket from a saddle pegged to the wall and step behind the open door that led into the corridor. Mark crowded alongside.

Buck whispered in his ear, "Put your gun in his belly the moment I get the blanket over his head."

Mark nodded that he understood. He was tingling with excitement, but there was no tremor in the hand he fastened over gun-butt. The forty-five slid up easily to his pull. He stood in a half-crouch, slightly behind Buck.

The rumble of the gruff voice stopped, and now they again heard the heavy tread of booted feet. The flicker of swelling light told Mark that the approaching man was carrying a lantern. He hoped it would be in the gaoler's gun-hand.

The footsteps were close now, and the man's tuneless whistling indicated a complete unawareness of the danger lurking in his office. He was suddenly inside, his back to them, and the Navajo blanket, lifted like a great hood in Buck's hands, swooped over his head and face. At the same instant Mark's gun was hard against the surprised man's ribs.

His first attempt to jerk free of the arms holding the folds of the blanket over his head subsided. He stood very still, and they heard his muffled voice, enraged, frightened.

"Don't squeeze trigger!"

They kept their silence. Mark, at Buck's nod, reached his free hand for the horsehair lariat that hung on a peg next to the saddle. He gave it to Buck who swiftly got a noose over the blanket and coiled the long rope some half dozen times, securing the blanket tight over their victim's arms. He gave Mark a bleak grin of satisfaction, reached under the gay folds for the holstered gun.

"Who in hell are you, and what's your game?" The gaoler's voice was a strangled, muffled whisper. He stood there, frozen with terror, a monstrous, gay-colored cocoon, the lighted lantern still clutched in paralyzed fingers. Mark jerked it from his grasp.

Their continued silence seemed to increase his terror. He spoke again in the same horrified, muffled whisper. "I'm smotherin' to death under this damn' blanket."

A big key ring dangled from his other hand. Mark pulled it from his clutching fingers and at a signal from Buck led the way into the corridor with his lantern. Buck followed with the prisoner, both hands on the blindfolded man's shoulders, pushing and guiding him.

They passed several empty cells, halted at a signal from Mark when the dancing light of his lantern suddenly showed Bill Benton's amazed face peering at the strange procession.

Incredulity, enormous relief, stared from the big ranchman's eyes as he recognized Buck Salten's shadowed face. His quick look at Mark failed to recognize the tenderfoot dude in Red O'Malley's hat and clothes.

Buck's cautioning gesture warned him to keep

silent. He watched, breathing hard, while Mark experimented with the keys on the ring. He found the right key, unlocked the door, stepped into the cell, saw now with savage indignation that Benton wore handcuffs and leg-irons. He searched the key ring again and in a few moments was helping Benton to his feet and out of the cell.

The continued silence was making the gaoler shaky in the knees, and when Buck roughly pushed him into the cell he stumbled, fell flat on his face. Buck stared at the handcuffs and leg-irons, his eyes deadly. He gave Mark a nod, and the younger man, his own face grim, quickly snapped on the manacles.

A muffled groan came from the prostrate gaoler. “I’m smotherin’ to death.”

They ignored him, went softly away, left him alone in that same deadly silence. Nor did they speak until they were outside in the moonlit night, pausing in the office only long enough for Bill Benton to recognize and recover his gun from several others that hung on the wall behind the gaoler’s desk.

The dense mesquite quickly hid them from view of the road, and not until then did Bill Benton break the silence.

“They was fixin’ to murder me,” he said in a hushed voice.

“That’s what we figgered,” Buck Salten told him laconically.

"Jess Kinner bragged I wasn't leaving that damn' gaol alive." Benton drew a long breath of the clean night air. "I was believing him," he added huskily.

"We wasn't wantin' it known who busted you out," Buck warned him. "You'll keep quiet about it, huh, Bill?"

"I'm leavin' it to them wolves to keep on guessin' till they fry in hell," feelingly promised the ranchman. He added wonderingly, "Didn't know you were ridin' on my side, Buck."

"You know it now," drawled Buck. He holstered his gun. "Ain't wantin' Matoon to guess it. That's why we handled Jess Kinner the way we did. Wasn't giving him a chance to get a look at us, hear our voices."

Benton stared at him curiously. "Don't know your game, but you've sure proved you ain't riding with that wolf pack that's got La Cruz by the throat. I owe you my life, Buck, and I want you to know that I'm riding this damn' trail clean to the end with you." He paused, puzzled look on Mark. "Same goes for you, young feller, only I don't seem to remember meeting you before."

Mark lifted his hands, showed his bruised knuckles. "You'll maybe remember these." He grinned. "I'm hoping we'll both soon forget it."

Startled recognition dawned in the ranchman's eyes. He touched his cut chin ruefully. "Don't seem like it's possible, but I reckon you're that dude feller I tangled with."

It was Buck who answered him, his drawling voice touched with dry humor. "Mark's a dude the same way I am," he assured Benton. "Well, let's get movin'. No tellin' but what Teel Furner will be heading back to the gaol."

Mark was thinking about the man they had left wrapped in the smothering blanket. "I wouldn't want that gaoler to strangle to death," he commented worriedly.

"He'll wrastle himself loose from that blanket," chuckled Buck. "No call to worry about *him,* Mark."

They pushed on through the mesquite, went scrambling down the steep side of the *barranca.* Benton halted again. The rush down the boulder-strewn slope had caught his wind. He said, a grim note in his voice, "This business means I'm on the dodge from now on. I've got to hole up some place, or I won't live long enough to even see the inside of that gaol again. Not if Teel Furner lays eyes on me."

"Where's your bronc?" asked Buck.

"Left him in Jim Ball's feed-barn." He gave Mark a rueful smile. "Was my own fault, letting Ab Matoon get the jump on me."

"He claimed you were looking for him with a gun," reminded Mark.

"He's a liar!" exploded the ranchman. "All I

did was to send him word I had to see him for a showdown."

"Ab took it that you meant no good by him," chuckled Buck. "You gave him his chance to lay for you when you hit town."

"I've got to hole up some place," repeated Benton. "Ain't safe for me to head back for the ranch. They'll be waiting for me."

Mark asked sympathetically, "Anybody at the ranch going to be worried about you, Mr. Benton?"

The big ranchman nodded, his granite-hard face softening. "My wife," he said simply. He shook his head sorrowfully. "She's mighty sick—got something wrong with her back, and ain't able to walk. Been layin' in bed for weeks."

Buck said abruptly, "You cain't go back to the ranch. First place they'll hunt for you will be over to Bar B."

Benton nodded, the distress on his face deepening. Buck went on, his voice thoughtful:

"Only one place I know where you can hole up, Bill, and you'll have to make it before sunup at that. Once you're in the Sinks you can thumb your nose at 'em."

Benton nodded again, the gloom still heavy on him. He knew the Sinks, the savage strip of wasteland on the Mexican border, hideout for men on the dodge from the law. "I'll have to get word to Emma," he said, his voice slow, rough with anxiety.

Mark was thinking fast. He wanted to help this man, whose only chance to keep on living was his ability to reach a mysterious place known as the Sinks. That part of the problem was up to Benton himself and to Buck Salten. All *he* could offer was a promise to look after Benton's bedridden wife.

He said hesitantly, "I'll get word to your wife, Mr. Benton. I—I'll watch out for her until this—this trouble is straightened out."

Benton eyed him, his expression doubtful, and Buck's voice broke in, harsh, almost angry. "Listen, Bill, if Mark says he'll keep an eye on Emma he'll do it if the job takes him to hell and back."

"You know him from a long time back, huh?" Uncertainty lingered in the ranchman's voice.

"Known him only since the time you tangled with him in the Horsehead." Buck's good-natured drawl was back. "That's only a few hours, Bill, but I've sure learned plenty about Mark Destin. He's a man to ride the river with, and don't you fool yourself."

Benton's hand went out, and Mark felt the hard grasp of powerful fingers close on his. "I think I ain't needin' to worry about Emma—too much." Emotion choked his voice. "I reckon Buck can size up a man, Mark, and if I weren't so messed up in my mind I wouldn't be needing for him to tell me."

"Thanks, Mr. Benton." Mark's warm smile gave no hint of his own troublesome doubts regarding his ability to care properly for the invalid wife. It was his gloomy opinion that Buck Salten's defense of an unseasoned tenderfoot was more than a little strong. "I'll do my best," he managed to add.

They were moving again now, picking their way through clutching brush and the great boulders that choked the narrow *barranca.*

Buck broke the brief silence. "You know Plácido Romero, don't you, Bill?"

"Sure do," replied Benton. Quick interest edged his voice. "I reckon there ain't a man in La Cruz knows the Sinks like that Mexican does."

"That's right." Buck came to a standstill. "I reckon Plácido's our best bet."

"How come you figger it that way?" queried Benton. "I know the Sinks too. Right now all I'm needing is my bronc."

Buck shook his head. "You're still some messed up in your head." His tone was patient, kind. "Your bronc has got to stay in Jim Ball's barn. They'll be takin' a look there and when they find your bronc is gone it'll be plain hell for Jim. Savvy?"

Benton nodded agreement. "Ain't wanting to get Jim into trouble."

"Sure we don't," agreed Buck. "That makes Plácido Romero the answer we're lookin' for.

He'll fix you up with a bronc, slip you out the back way."

Benton thought it over. "Sounds like good sense," he finally admitted. He shook his head doubtfully. "Won't be easy to get into the *cantina* and nobody see me."

"You'll go in the back way," chuckled Buck. "Won't be nobody to see you. Ain't more'n two or three fellers in La Cruz know the way into Plácido's back yard, and I'm one of 'em."

Mark thought of the closely guarded gate, of the vigilant Rafael, the soft-footed Felipe, the flat-nosed Chato. Only Plácido's trusted friends knew the password that could win the confidence of those three alert Mexicans. The thought gave him a fleeting wonder at Janet Dunbar's reluctance to let Buck Salten personally ask for the loan of the accordion. It was evident that she was unaware of his close friendship with a man whom she regarded as her own trusted friend.

Bill Benton was speaking, a hint of resignation in his voice. "It's up to you to get me in for a talk with Plácido, I reckon, Buck. Only one way I know into that place is the front door."

"I'll get you in," Buck curtly assured him. He looked at Mark. "Won't need you along for the rest of this business."

"I'll get back to the hotel," Mark said. His hand went out. "Good luck, Bill."

Benton's hard fingers closed tight over his.

"*Gracias*, Mark. I won't be forgetting what you and Buck have done tonight." His voice was suddenly husky. "You—you—" He faltered, the question agonizingly plain in his eyes.

Mark said gently, "I'll watch out for her, Bill."

"I'm believing you," the big ranchman said simply. His hand lifted in a weary gesture. "All right, Buck. Let's get on to Plácido's place."

Mark watched them until the chaparral hid their quick-moving shapes from view. Now that he was alone he was conscious of a great weariness. He had never felt so tired, and as he stumbled on down the *barranca* he wondered vaguely at his dreams that had brought him to this remote and violent border town. La Cruz was certainly a rough education for a tenderfoot dude.

He climbed the steps of the hotel porch, stiffened the sag out of his legs. The night man behind the desk had betrayed a pronounced curiosity when he had hurried through the lobby with Buck Salten an hour or so ago. It seemed impossible that hardly more than two hours had passed since he had heard Doc. Bralen telling Janet Dunbar about her stepbrother's accident. The doctor's words were in his ears again.

A fool accident cleaning his gun. Sent a bullet smashing through his hand.

Mark halted on the last step. He felt sick. Could it be possible that Janet knew that Ray Wellerton had tried to hold up the stage—steal his money?

He shook his head, angry at himself, his mind picturing the girl, kneeling by Red O'Malley's side in the dingy little bedroom. No deceit there, no evil complicity in attempted crime. He would stake his soul on her innocence.

Filled with a warming glow he strode into the lobby, flung Cooner a friendly smile as he asked for his key.

The man examined the key-rack, selected a key, and tossed it on the desk. "Things lively at the Horsehead tonight?" he asked.

Mark sensed a trap in the question. "Been down at the stage barn," he answered. He managed an amused laugh. "That old stage-driver certainly has a lot of good stories."

"Sure has," agreed Cooner.

Mark turned to the stair, hesitated. He longed to hurry down the lower hall to the room where Janet Dunbar was nursing a badly wounded man. He had a feeling that Janet would not be pleased to see him, and it was possible that Red O'Malley might be awake and in a mood to ask troublesome questions about Buck Salten.

His look met Cooner's smirking, inquisitive eyes. He asked brusquely, "How's Red O'Malley making out?"

"Doc. Bralen says he's gettin' along fine," Cooner told him. "Mrs. Dorn got in from Silver City unexpected and the doctor put her on the job. The Dunbar gal went off with him." The man leered. "Ain't sayin' she's stayin' the night with him."

Mark held back an impulse to hit the man in the nose. He went upstairs with a briskness he did not feel, found his way down the dark hall to his room, and lit the lamp he saw on the bureau.

His gaze went to the trunk at the foot of the bed. The lock had been forced, was sprung open. He stared for a brief moment, a mirthless grin on his tired face. Somebody had been curious about his trunk. He was too tired to make conjectures, stripped off his clothes and flung himself on the bed. He was not caring about the sag in the springs, was almost instantly asleep.

Chapter 8

The several signs on the front of Ab Matoon's office indicated varied interests. He was a lawyer and general investment agent, bought and sold cattle and ranchlands, made loans large or small. All of which conveniently made a respectable cloak for less savory activities. Like the deceptive, ornate signs on his office door, Ab Matoon's chubby, beaming face was a false front, masked the dark and wily mind of a dangerous crook.

He sat behind his desk, no hint of joviality in him now as he listened to Teel Furner's wrathful and profane account of Bill Benton's mysterious escape from the gaol.

"It's the queerest business I ever heard of," grumbled the worried town marshal. "Jess says there wasn't a word spoke no time. He was so scared when I got him loose from the cell he wasn't able to do any talkin' himself." Furner swore softly, reached for the bottle on the desk, and filled his glass. "He claims it was spooks that come and got Benton away from gaol, says he's quittin' his job, and that no money can make him stay another night in a place where spooks can walk in on him like they did last night."

"Where's Jess now?" asked Matoon. His too-prominent eyes were glassy with anger.

"Got himself drunk, and right now he's sleepin' it off." The town marshal drained his glass, gazed thoughtfully at the bottle. "What do you make of it, Ab?"

Matoon reached for the bottle and slid it into a drawer.

"There's only one answer to that question, Teel, and you don't need me to tell you." The sneer in his voice made the burly town marshal wince. "The answer is that Benton has friends in this town."

"They don't talk out loud they're his friends." Furner glowered at his empty glass. "What the hell are you so stingy with your whisky for all of a sudden?"

"It's a time to keep our heads clear," reminded Matoon. "You've got work to do. Find out who got Benton loose from gaol, and—what's more important—find Benton." He drummed knuckles on the desk, added viciously, "You won't need to throw him in gaol again—when you catch him."

There was understanding in the grin Furner gave him. He said laconically, "I savvy."

Matoon went on, his tone thoughtful, "He won't head for his ranch. Too risky. He'll realize we'll look there for him." He thought for a moment. "Be a good idea to keep an eye on the place, though."

"That's right." Furner looked crestfallen. "I should have sent a man out there on the jump."

"You can send Jess Kinner if you can sober him up before night."

"I reckon we might as well use him that way," agreed the town marshal sourly. "Jess claims he don't want the gaoler job no more." He scowled. "I sure crave to find out who pulled off that spook trick on him. Took plenty nerve."

"Jim Ball," suggested Matoon. "Jim has nerve enough, and he's known Bill Benton a lot of years."

"Jim's too old," demurred Furner. "He couldn't have moved around so fast and quiet, got Jess to swearin' they was ghosts." He paused. "Was over to Jim's barn, lookin' for Benton's bronc. Jim says he ain't seen Benton since he stabled the bronc."

"His horse is still there?" inquired Matoon.

Furner nodded. "Sure is, and ain't nobody in town missin' a horse. Looks like Benton lit out on foot."

The two men were silent for a long moment, worried frowns on their faces as they sought for some solution of the mystery.

"There's Buck Salten," finally suggested Furner. "Him and Benton used to be awful good friends."

"You're wrong there." Matoon shook his head. "You saw how Buck sided with the tenderfoot in the Horsehead. He's no more a friend of Benton than the tenderfoot is."

"That dude kid sure give Benton a beatin'," chuckled the town marshal. "I reckon we can count him *and* Buck out of this business."

A shadow darkened the office window, and Matoon said hurriedly, "Get moving, Teel. Here's young Destin now."

The door opened, and Mark stepped inside. The town marshal got out of his chair, gave him an amiable grin. "Howdy, young feller. I'm thinkin' you're some lucky to be around this mornin'."

"I see you have figured it out," smiled Mark.

"Sure have." Furner pushed out leathery lips, looked wise. "Red O'Malley was wearing your dude clothes, and the killer thought he was you."

"Why would anybody want to kill a stranger just come to town?" asked Mark, with a shrug.

"It was maybe some drunk hombre that just couldn't stand for that dude hat." Furner guffawed, slouched towards the door. "As good an answer as any, I reckon."

"He got away too fast for a man who was drunk," Mark pointed out. "I don't think your answer makes sense."

The town marshal paused at the door, stared back at him, his expression thoughtful. "If we hadn't just throwed Bill Benton in gaol I'd have said it was him done the shootin', only we know he didn't—him bein' in gaol. You sure treated him rough, and he would have wanted to get back at you."

"Mr. Benton has a tight alibi," agreed Mark. "It's a good thing for him that you have him in gaol."

"He ain't in gaol no more," Furner told him. "He busted loose last night."

"Escaped?" Mark showed proper astonishment, gave the two men startled looks.

"Left Jess Kinner locked up in his own cell," grumbled the town marshal. He shook his head, added grimly, "Too bad for you if you run into Benton, young feller. He won't be forgettin' how you beat him up last night."

Matoon broke in, his voice impatient, "It's up to you to get him back in gaol, Teel. I don't want him taking pot shots at me."

"No call to worry, Ab. I'll have him back in no time." Furner's sly wink did not escape Mark. "Benton's awful sure to show up at his ranch on account of that sick wife of his. I'll get Jess on the job pronto." The door slammed behind him.

"Have a chair, Mr. Destin," cordially invited Matoon. "I'm mighty sorry about this shocking attempt to kill you last night. Wouldn't blame you if you decided to take the first stage out of La Cruz."

Mark dropped into a chair, conscious of the other man's probing eyes. "Young O'Malley is the one to feel sorry for." He shook his head at the cigar box Matoon pushed at him. "I have no intention of leaving town, even if my hotel room *was* entered last night and my trunk broken open."

Matoon stared at him open-mouthed, his consternation too genuine to doubt. "You mean—you've been robbed?"

"I think the intention was robbery." Mark concealed his own growing bewilderment. He had been sure that Matoon was responsible for the surreptitious visit to the hotel room. He forced a wry smile. "Luckily I changed my plans about my twenty thousand dollars gold when I heard you have no bank in this town."

The alarm faded from Matoon's chubby face. He nodded gravely. "Most fortunate it was not in your trunk, Mr. Destin."

"You should have warned me." Mark frowned at him. "Naturally I had planned to bank the money upon arrival here."

"The matter never occurred to me." Matoon waved a plump hand at a big iron safe. "Your money would have been quite all right with me." He smiled benevolently. "A lot of people here make use of my safe." He chuckled. "In fact, I'm what you could call a banker myself in a non-profit way. Always glad to accommodate my friends." He paused, and his genial smile found no reflection in sharp, probing eyes. "So you heard in Deming that we have no bank here?"

Mark parried the question. "I heard just in time to make other arrangements."

"You needn't have worried," Matoon again assured his client. "Your money would have been quite safe with me." He gestured. "It's of no real importance whether the money is here or in Deming. Means a little more trouble for us—a tiresome trip to Deming when we close our deal." His fingers drummed on the desk. "Of course, you banked the money in gold?"

"In gold," Mark assured him, and after a moment, his tone hard, "You are the only man who could possibly know that I was bringing twenty thousand dollars gold in my trunk, Mr. Matoon."

The lawyer shook his head, his expression contrite. "I may have thoughtlessly let it drop to somebody."

"Don't you remember?" Mark was thinking of Ray Wellerton, wondering if there was a connection there.

"Can't say that I do." Matoon's tone was rueful. "Careless of me if I *did* make a slip." His voice crispened. "Well, no real harm done, and your money is safe." He fumbled in a drawer, drew out some papers. "I suppose you'll want to have a look at the ranch. In the meantime, here is the deed. You may like to look it over."

Mark took the papers from him, his face showing no hint of his seething thoughts. He had a hunch that Matoon would have heard of his brief encounter with Janet Dunbar on the steps of the hotel porch. Louie Renn could not have failed to hear her words, would have reported them to his boss. His own silence about the affair would arouse Matoon's suspicions.

"A bargain, young man." Matoon's moon face was wreathed in smiles. "Fully equipped and plenty of water, only you'll need some cattle." He gestured. "I can help you there, lend what you'll need to pick up a bunch of good cows and take a mortgage back for the amount." He chuckled. "Perhaps you don't need borrowed money."

Mark replaced the papers on the desk, said slowly, "I'm afraid Miss Dunbar won't sign this deed, Mr. Matoon."

"Nonsense!" The lawyer smiled. "She has very little to say about it, Mr. Destin."

"I ran into her last night," Mark continued. "She was waiting for me on the hotel porch and seemed very disturbed—told me that Diamond D is not for sale."

Matoon nodded good-naturedly. "Yes, I heard that she had—well—been rather rude to you." His eyes took on a glassy hardness. "As a matter of fact, Miss Dunbar is under a grave misapprehension about who is the actual owner of the ranch."

"I'm afraid I don't understand you," Mark said.

"I mean that the ranch is my property," smiled Matoon. "Her father was heavily in debt to me when he—er—died. I have tried to explain the situation to her, but she persists in behaving like a silly child, declares that her father would never have mortgaged the ranch, and that he was not in debt." Matoon shook his head sadly. "It's been most embarrassing to find myself in the role of a hard-hearted moneylender who finds it necessary to protect his own interests."

Mark could almost have believed him. Only he knew that such belief would be folly, after what he had learned since his arrival in La Cruz. This man was a dangerous hypocrite, had turned his hired killers loose on Benton, who would have exposed him for a thieving cheat. He knew, too, that he must continue the role of an unsuspecting tenderfoot, play for time, and help Buck Salten save Janet Dunbar from ruin, thwart the cold-blooded plot to dispossess her of the ranch that had always been her home.

He said, assuming just the right caution for a tenderfoot, "It sounds like a bargain all right, Mr. Matoon, but you know I can't jump into this blind. I'll have to have good proof that you are authorized to make the deal." He managed an uneasy smile. "I'll admit that Miss Dunbar more than upset me. I was awfully disappointed to think I was not going to get the ranch."

"No need to worry," beamed the lawyer. "I was hoping that Miss Dunbar would come to her senses and so avoid the publicity that won't do her father's name any good. Rick Dunbar was a fine, proud man, and he'll turn in his grave to know how his daughter's folly betrayed the poverty of his last years. I'd have given her enough to get away free of personal debts, make a fresh start somewhere." Matoon's hand lifted in an unhappy gesture. "As it stands, she forces me to this role of hard-hearted moneylender, and at that I'll still be in the red, Mr. Destin—very much a loser, letting you have the ranch for twenty thousand."

"I hate to be mixed up in it," worried Mark. He put on a scowl. "After all, business is business. She can't blame me for snapping up a bargain."

"Now you're talking good common sense," approved the lawyer. "Business *is* business, and a man's a fool not to snap up a good thing when it comes his way."

Mark got out of his chair. "Well, I suppose you'll want to talk it over with her, persuade her to see the light."

"I'll do that," Matoon promised, his voice bland. "Not that it really matters, Mr. Destin, only I understand your feelings where a young girl is concerned."

Nobody looking at Mark's poker face would have guessed the rage in him. "I'm not worrying about *her,*" he lied. "I only want to make sure that I'm not buying a pig in a poke, Mr. Matoon." He wondered vaguely what a pig in a poke meant, anyway. It sounded like some silly utterance a young tenderfoot from Boston might be expected to make. "In the meantime I'd like to ride out to the ranch and have a look at the place." He frowned. "Of course, I'd rather Miss Dunbar didn't know."

"Certainly," smiled the lawyer. "A good idea. And don't worry, Mr. Destin. The ranch is as good as yours right now. You have the money, and I *know* that I can deliver a deed conveying honest title."

Mark studied him for a moment. "I met a man in the Horsehead last night—Buck Salten. He said he used to work out at Diamond D ranch. He told me that Miss Dunbar fired him, to use his word for it."

Matoon's grin was wolfish. "Another proof of the girl's childishness," he chuckled. "Buck is a good man, knows the cow-business, was her dad's foreman for years—and she kicks him off the place." He was suddenly looking at Mark, hard. "You mean you want Buck to show you over the ranch, and the girl not know it?"

"That's the idea." Mark looked wise. "I'm thinking he knows Diamond D better than most men, working there so long."

"You're a smart young man," chuckled Matoon. "He'll show you around, and the girl won't know about it. Buck has no use for that young lady."

Mark gave him a knowing smile, turned to the door, halted. "I wasn't aware that no cattle were included in the deal. You said in your letter than the ranch was well stocked."

"So I did," admitted the lawyer smoothly. "However, you may recall that nothing was actually agreed upon about the cattle. I mentioned that the ranch was well stocked but did not say they were included in the deal—not at twenty thousand dollars." Mr. Matoon's voice took on a reproachful note. "That would be too much of a good thing."

"Doesn't Miss Dunbar own the cattle?" Mark asked.

"Miss Dunbar owns nothing—no ranch, no cattle," smiled the lawyer. "She is worse than bankrupt, and doesn't know it, or is stupidly refusing to face the truth."

Mark opened the door. "Well, I'll get on Buck Salten's trail, tell him you want him to show me over the ranch on the quiet."

"Fine!" exclaimed Matoon. "You'll be camping out overnight, but Buck knows the country. He'll look after you."

He sat there for a moment, speculative gaze on Mark's disappearing back, then suddenly he was on his feet, turning the key in the door and drawing the window shades. He returned to the desk, thrust the papers he had offered for Mark's inspection in a drawer, and hurried out of the office through a rear door. A high board-fence enclosed a large back yard. There was a corral, and a watering trough shaded by a cottonwood-tree, and a man, standing near the barn door, leaning indolently on a pitchfork and watching the two sleek bay horses in the corral.

Matoon called to him softly, "Seen Cooner around this morning, Curly?"

"He was loafin' 'round here a while back," answered the stableman. "I reckon he's over to the Horsehead right now. Said he was headin' over there."

"Go get him for me," instructed Matoon. "Tell him it's important and to come in the back way."

Curly nodded, leaned his pitchfork against the barn door. Matoon watched until he disappeared through a narrow, tight-boarded gate. His gaze shifted to the horses in the corral. They were clean-limbed Morgans, trotters, and his eyes took on a momentary gleam of pride as he stared at them.

He turned, went with slow-moving steps into his office, like a man wrestling with a vexing problem. He dropped into his high-backed chair, sat there in the darkened room, rigid, motionless, his face ugly with deepening suspicion.

Footsteps approached up the back hall from the yard. His head turned in a look, and he said gruffly, "Hello, Cooner. I've got a job for you."

Cooner grinned at him, wiped a wet, ragged mustache with his shirt sleeve. "Ridin' night-herd over to the hotel suits me," he said. "I ain't wantin' no new job."

"You'll like *this* job," Matoon told him, with a thin smile.

The man shrugged. "You're the boss."

"I want you to keep an eye on that young tenderfoot who's staying at the hotel."

"The Destin hombre, huh?" Cooner's eyes brightened. "I've a notion he's some slick for a tenderfoot."

"He's no fool, if he *is* fresh out of Boston," grumbled Matoon. "I want you to stick close on his trail day and night."

"Followin' a trail is one thing I'm good at," grinned Cooner. "I can track a crawlin' woodtick in the dark of the moon."

"That is why I'm putting you on the job." Matoon spoke softly, emphasizing each word. "Tell me of every move he makes, who he sees, talks to, where he goes. It's important, Cooner."

A hint of doubt grew in Cooner's eyes. "He's a slick hombre for all that smooth kid's face he wears. I heard about what he done to Bill Benton in the Horsehead last night."

"He mustn't suspect you're watching him," warned Matoon, his voice impatient. "No gun-play, Cooner. He's too valuable until I've finished with this business that hooked him." The lawyer was suddenly silent, his bulging agate eyes fixed intently on the other man. "You were on the desk last night, weren't you?"

Cooner's face showed astonishment. "You know damn' well I was. You come in, asked how Red O'Malley was makin' out, stood there in the lobby talkin' to Doc. Bralen about the shootin'."

"Well, who else did you see in the lobby later—after I was there?"

Cooner's brow furrowed. "Wasn't many fellers in last night. Couple of Flyin' Y boys, Ed Wells in from his Walkin' W ranch." He shook his head. "Only feller Jim Ball brung in on the stage was the dude hombre. I reckon that about totes up the register, boss."

"I'm not asking about the register," fumed Matoon. "I want to know if anybody was in after I left, or if anything happened to attract your attention."

"The Destin feller come in kind of late," said Cooner.

"I'm not wanting to know about Destin," grumbled Matoon. He paused, added softly, "All right, what about him?"

"He seemed some excited." Cooner's eyes narrowed thoughtfully. "He said he'd been having a powwow with Jim Ball over to the livery barn and that Jim sure could tell plenty stories. Got his room key and went on upstairs."

"Seemed excited, you say?" Matoon's voice was sharp.

"Well—" Cooner's grin was sly. "It didn't seem like a feller would lose his wind comin' from Jim's barn to the hotel here. He was sure breathin' kind of hard, and so I figgered he was some excited."

Matoon nodded, asked curtly, "You didn't see him again?"

Cooner shook his head. "Wasn't downstairs while I was at the desk, and I was there until Louie showed up."

Matoon stared at him accusingly. "Destin claims somebody entered his room, broke into his trunk."

"I ain't knowin' nothin' about it," protested Cooner. "I wasn't upstairs the whole doggone night."

"Somebody went up there," snarled Matoon. "Who else was in the lobby last night, not on the register?"

"You're sure wringin' me dry," complained Cooner. "There was several fellers in, and the Dunbar gal. She wanted to know if I'd seen Ray Wellerton."

"Well?" Matoon gave a questioning look.

"Sure Ray was in, only he wasn't stayin' only long enough to take a look at the register. I told the same to the Dunbar gal." Cooner's lips twisted in a sour grin. "That gal sure acts like she'd spit in your eye, give her a reason."

Matoon said musingly, "So Ray took a look

through at the register and then went upstairs."

"Hell, no!" exclaimed Cooner. "He slammed right out the door."

"You can get upstairs the back way from the yard," reminded Matoon, his voice grim.

"That's right," agreed Cooner. His eyes took on a glitter. "I reckon I savvy, boss. You figger it was Ray that went and broke into the dude's trunk, huh?" He broke off, added cautiously, "Ray was wearing a bandage on his hand. Had a piece stuck across his cheek too. Told me to go to hell when I asked him how come."

Matoon's widened eyes showed surprise, then, curtly: "All right, Cooner, get on the job, and keep me posted about Destin's movements."

"Sure." Cooner grinned, got out of his chair. "Don't you worry none, boss. I'll stick to that dude like his own shadder."

"Too bad for you if you don't," Matoon said to his disappearing back. He relaxed in his chair, hand jerking open the drawer that held the whisky bottle.

Chapter 9

A ranch buckboard halted in front of the hotel as Mark approached from Matoon's office. He saw with some surprise that the man in the driver's seat was Buck Salten. A saddled horse trailed in the buckboard on a lead rope.

Curious, half suspecting the reason that was taking Buck out of town, he hastened his step. Buck gave him a brief, unsmiling nod.

"I'm driving Red out to Diamond D," he said, answering the question in Mark's eyes. "Doc. Bralen says he can make the trip, and Janet is bent on having him out there so she can nurse him." Gloom shadowed his face. "Janet ain't liking for me to go along. I told her she wasn't taking Red unless I went with him."

"You should get things straightened out with her," urged Mark.

"No chance." Buck shook his head. "She just won't listen. I sure ain't going on my knees to her."

"Are you going to stay at the ranch long?" Mark's voice was troubled. He had been counting on Buck's help at this time.

"Only long enough to make certain Red is fixed all comfortable. Will likely be back come midnight, or maybe tomorrow noon." His thumb lifted in a gesture at the buckboard-team. "This is Janet's outfit. That's why I'm trailin' my bronc to ride me back to town."

"Fine!" exclaimed Mark, relief in his voice. "I have a lot to tell you, Buck."

"Seen you come out of Ab's place," Buck said.

"I ran into Teel Furner there." Mark lowered his voice. "He was talking to Matoon about Benton's escape from gaol, said he was sending Kinner out to Benton's ranch to watch for him if he tries to see his wife."

"I reckon Bill has made it to the Sinks by now," reassured Buck. "Kinner won't find him out at the ranch."

"I'm thinking about Benton's sick wife," worried Mark. "I promised I'd get word to her that he's safe."

"I can maybe head over to Bar B tomorrow," suggested Buck, a bit reluctantly. "I wouldn't want Matoon to know I was out there. Kinner will sure tell him if he runs into me."

"It's *my* job," asserted Mark. "I gave Benton my word." He smiled. "If I run into Kinner, and he tells Matoon, I can say that I wanted a look at Diamond D and got lost, found myself at Benton's ranch."

A grin flitted over Buck's sober face. "Benton's Bar B don't come within ten miles of Diamond D. At that I reckon Matoon won't think nothing of it—a tenderfoot gettin' off the trail and landin' some place ten miles from where he headed for."

"He said you'd be a good man to show me Diamond D on the quiet." Mark's smile was grim. "He still thinks I'm buying the ranch."

"Yeah?" Buck gave him a sharp look, wrapped the reins over whip-socket, and climbed from the buckboard.

"I'm not saying anything to make him think different," Mark said. "I'm taking cards in this game, Buck; playing along with you."

"I figgered you would." Buck turned to the porch steps. "I'll be gettin' Red loaded into the rig now."

They mounted the steps and Mark said hurriedly, "Listen, Buck—I'll need a horse—directions to the Benton place."

"Jim Ball can fix you up." Buck paused, muttered softly, "Looks like Cooner is some interested in us. Take a look at him, sort of casual. I mean that feller that's loafin' along behind them two Mexicans."

Mark managed a cautious glance, recognized the night clerk. "Do you think he is watching us?" he asked.

"No tellin'. He's awful nosy, and I reckon Matoon finds him useful."

"He doesn't look formidable," Mark said contemptuously.

"Don't fool yourself," Buck warned. "He's a

killer and fast with a gun—likes to use it when you ain't lookin'."

They went into the lobby. Louie Renn looked across at them from his desk. "Doc. Bralen and the Dunbar girl are waiting for you," he informed Buck.

Cooner pushed into the lobby. He hurried toward them. "Say, Mr. Destin"—his voice oozed fawning concern—"was sure too bad about your trunk bein' broke into."

"Nothing taken," Mark said. He followed Buck into the narrow hall, his expression thoughtful. He had told no one except Matoon about the trunk incident. Cooner's remark indicated he must have just come from Matoon's office. Mark was conscious of a quickened pulse. Matoon was not trusting him too much, had put a spy on his trail. His face hardened. He was on his guard now, thanks to Buck's timely warning.

Red O'Malley was sitting on the edge of the bed, looking pale but cheerful. "Hello, fellers." His smile broadened, and he pointed to an accordion that Janet Dunbar was slipping into a leather case. "See what Plácido Romero sent me when he heard mine was busted. She's a beaut—all silver mounted."

"You doggone kid!" Affection made Buck's voice husky. His eyes questioned the doctor.

"He can make it," assured Doc. Bralen. "Take the chuckholes easy, and the trip won't harm him."

"He can use me for a cushion," Janet gave the patient a smile that faded when she became aware of Mark's eyes on her. She said coldly, "Good morning, Mr. Destin." Her chin lifted in a nod at Buck. "We might as well start—if you're ready."

She looked tired, worried, and Mark longed to be able to ease the strain so evident in her. There was nothing he could say, no reassurance he dared voice. Like Buck Salten, he must keep his silence lest some betraying word get back to Ab Matoon, add to her peril. He wished fervently he could have had more time for talk with Buck, tell him about Matoon's asserted claim to the ranch. It was too late now. Jim Ball had said that Doc. Bralen was Matoon's friend. There could be no talk in front of the doctor.

Between them Buck and Mark helped Red into the back seat of the buckboard. Janet climbed in beside him with the cased accordion. Buck got in, gathered up the reins. He looked unhappy, stared ahead, silent, grim, while Doc. Bralen talked in a low voice to Janet, giving her instructions.

"I'll be out in a day or two for a look at him," the doctor promised. He hesitated. "Are you sure you don't want Mrs. Dorn?"

"I can manage," Janet assured him. "Juana will help." She smiled faintly. "Juana's known Red just about all his life—used to make cookies for him."

"She sure did," grinned the cowboy. His head

shifted in a look at Buck's horse on the tie-rope. "Say, where's my Baldy horse, Buck?"

"You won't be settin' no saddle for a week or two," Buck said, not turning his head.

"He won't do no good standin' round in Jim Ball's barn," fretted Red. His eyes went to Mark in a speculative look. His face brightened. "I'm loanin' him to you, Mark. Baldy's a right smart bronc. You tell Jim I said for you to use him."

"Thanks," smiled Mark. "I'll take good care of him."

"He won't know you from me," chuckled Red, "You wearin' them clothes you traded off of me."

The buckboard rolled away, the horses moving at an easy trot. Doc. Bralen picked up his worn brown bag from the porch steps, gave Mark a weary smile. "I've been on the go most of the night," he grumbled. "A cutting scrape and a baby—Ben Stock's wife. She was needing Mrs. Dorn, and I had to ask Janet to stay on the job with Red. The girl's about done up. Looks bad."

Mark felt sorry for him. His eyes were sunk deep in his haggard face. It was obvious that Doc. Bralen was a very tired man, and it was no time to question him about Ray Wellerton. Also a glance at the hotel porch told him that Cooner was lounging there, pretending to be absorbed with shaping a cigarette.

Mark hesitated, gaze following the tall, gaunt physician. He wanted to be on his way to the

Benton ranch, but first he must contrive to get rid of Cooner. The man had suddenly become an annoying problem. It might prove disastrous if Matoon heard about his visit to Benton's wife.

Doc. Bralen was abreast of the Horsehead Bar now. He hesitated, hand on the swing door, then suddenly he was moving across the street, his back erect, his stride the firm step of a man who has made a hard decision.

Cooner came down the porch steps, and Mark heard his sly, amused voice. "I should think the doc would get himself a couple of bottles. He's about due for a bender."

Mark stared at him, dislike and contempt in his eyes. He said coldly, choosing his words with deliberate intent, "You're a low-down liar."

He feared for a moment that the man was too cowardly to resent the insult with violence and thus ruin his hastily conceived plan. Cooner hesitated, sized him up. He was quite as big as Mark, heavier and tough, and bystanders had overheard the remark, were crowding up, faces expectant. He clenched his fists, charged, head down.

Mark's hard right in the belly straightened him up in time to catch a smashing left flush on the jaw. Cooner's knees buckled and he went down.

One of the bystanders swore softly. "Knocked him cold!"

Mark recognized the speaker—the bearded ranchman, one of the riders who had overhauled him in the brush the night before and mistaken him for the man who had shot Red O'Malley.

He said quietly, "You men saw him attack me. I only defended myself."

The bearded man nodded. "We seen Cooner go for you. Good thing he wasn't wearin' his gun. Cooner's awful fast with a gun." He gave Mark a friendly, admiring grin. "No call for you to worry, young feller. If he lets out a holler for the marshal I'll fix it with Teel, tell him how Cooner went for you like a loco bull."

"Thanks," smiled Mark. His keen look at the senseless man told him that the spy problem was settled for the moment. Cooner was going to be out of the picture for half an hour at least, and half an hour was all that he needed.

He went on his way, content with the stratagem that had given him a first victory over Ab Matoon. His immediate objective now was Jim Ball, a horse, and directions to guide him to the Benton ranch.

Despite his haste to reach the livery barn he found himself noticing his surroundings. Seen by daylight, La Cruz proved more attractive than the darkness had led him to believe. He caught glimpses of picturesque adobe walls weathered by more than a century of years and bowered by huge trees—cottonwoods, figs, gnarled peppers. He saw smiling swarthy faces under tall, steeple hats, and gossiping women in gay-colored full skirts, and noisy, shrieking children competing with gaunt, razor-backed pigs for the fallen fruit that littered the ground under the fig trees. These simple homes had been there long years before the coming of the *americanos* with their cheap frame buildings and tawdry false fronts. They belonged in that rugged landscape against the background of circling desert hills.

Jim Ball was in the yard, watching Pedro grease the wheels of his stage. He gave Mark a sharp look, turned on his heel, and led the way into the barn.

Mark said hurriedly, "I'm taking Red's horse, Jim. He wants me to use him, and right now I'm on my way to Benton's ranch and no time to lose."

Jim nodded, limped deeper into the long stable, came to a halt at a stall near the rear door and motioned at a pegged saddle.

"Help yourself, son." He felt for his plug of tobacco, gnawed at it. "You look some excited."

Mark dragged at the saddle, stepped alongside the bald-faced horse. "I had to frame a fight with a spy Matoon set on me. Knocked him senseless. I want to get away from here before he comes to and picks up my trail."

"Who is the feller?"

"Buck said his name is Cooner, and he's got the face of a rat."

"A bad hombre," worried the old stageman.

"Too bad you didn't empty your gun into him. He'll sure lay for you in the brush some place."

"Never mind about *him*." Mark tugged at saddle girth. "Buck said you could tell me how to get out to Benton's ranch."

"Ain't hard to find Bar B," Jim told him. "Ride south up the creek below the barn here and you'll hit Borrego Canyon. Keep goin' until you come to where it forks and turn left. Make sure you turn left. The right fork goes into Diamond D country."

"All right." Mark adjusted the bridle, snatched the tie-rope loose.

"Keep on goin'," continued Jim, "maybe an hour or so, and you come to a place where there's falls when the rains is good. There's a trail that climbs up the right bank, and you're on the flats. Keep on that trail till you come to a lone butte. Take the left fork, and you're headed straight for Benton's ranch."

"I've got it." Mark led the horse from the stall. Jim Ball peeped into the saddlebags. He refastened the flaps, gave Mark a satisfied nod. "Plenty cartridges there," he said. "Hope you won't be needin' 'em, son. Wasn't wantin' you to ride off without plenty loads for your gun—not after what you done to that Cooner hombre."

Mark studied him for a moment. The old man had not wasted time with questions, but curiosity was deep in his eyes. Despite his haste, he was unwilling to leave Jim worried with wild speculations. He gave a terse account of his talk with Ab Matoon.

"I don't want him to know about this trip to Benton's ranch," he warned the stageman. "When Cooner comes around, asking questions, I want him to think that I headed for the Dunbar ranch. Matoon knows I planned to look the place over." He slid into the saddle. "Cooner heard Red tell me I could use this horse. He'll be around to see if the horse is gone. It won't be any use telling him you haven't seen me."

"No need to worry, son." The old man's face creased in a grim smile. "All Cooner will get from me is that you rode off some place, made talk of takin' a look at Diamond D."

"How about Pedro?" Mark asked. "He saw me come here."

"Pedro is a Mex that minds his own business," reassured Jim. He chuckled softly. "Seems like Plácido Romero said some words about you to Pedro that makes you stand ace-high with him."

"Thanks to you." Mark gave his friend a warm smile. "All right, Jim, I'm riding."

The stageman opened the rear door. "Good luck, young feller. You're the doggondest tender-foot I ever laid eyes on."

Mark rode outside, halted the horse, looked back at him with eyes that held a hint of hardness mingled with mirth. "You don't need to use that name on me anymore, Jim." His hand lifted in a gay little gesture. "I'm learning fast."

The old stageman leaned against the barn door, watched until the creek willows below hid horse and rider from view. He spat a dark brown stream, shook his head gloomily, and closed the door.

Chapter 10

The bald-faced horse pulled stubbornly to the right when they reached the fork in the upper reaches of Borrego Canyon. Mark swung him into the left fork and halted under a bluff that offered welcome shade from the noonday sun. The big sorrel's resentfully flattened ears drew a grin from him. He was remembering Jim Ball's words. *Make sure you turn left. The right fork goes into Diamond D country.* Baldy was a Diamond D horse, and for him the right fork meant the home ranch where he had been foaled. Mark vaguely recalled stories he had heard about these horses of the cow-country. Turn them loose, and, if nothing prevented, they would always surely find their way back to the home ranch.

The shade was grateful after the sun-scorched trail that had twisted steeply up the canyon. Baldy, now resigned, heaved a deep sigh, stood with drooping head, and Mark got down from the saddle to stretch his legs and ease the horse of his weight while they rested.

He reflected with some astonishment that less than twenty-four hours had passed since the attempted holdup on the mountain slope. A lot of things had happened, most of them unpleasant. There had been compensations—the friendship of men like Buck Salten and Jim Ball. And there was Janet Dunbar. The thought of her distrust made him wince, although he knew there was cause for her to regard him as an enemy in league with Ab Matoon to gain possession of her ranch. There had been no chance for him to tell her that his only thought now was to help Buck Salten thwart Matoon's ruthless schemes.

Mark thoughtfully rolled a cigarette, his mind on Buck Salten. Buck was first rate, honest to the core, a man without fear, and yet he lacked the qualities necessary in a conflict with a wily wolf like Ab Matoon. Sterling worth and sheer courage were no match for the lawyer's cunning. The game Buck was playing to unmask Matoon would sooner or later end in disaster, with Buck dead—his bullet-ridden body in the chaparral, beckoning the buzzards.

The picture conjured by his lively imagination turned Mark's stomach. He sat down on a fallen boulder, stared with narrowed eyes across the canyon. It was up to himself to do something about it. A man-size job that called for more than physical courage, a job that demanded cool, fast thinking—the shrewd mind that could outwit Ab Matoon. A big job for a young tenderfoot, a stranger in a strange and hostile country.

Mark's head lowered and he stared down at his boots, the big-roweled spurs. Red O'Malley's boots and spurs. He was wearing Red's clothes, his hat, his gun, the garb of a man born on the range. He suddenly felt years older, hard, toughened by his less than a day in the little border town of La Cruz. Those brief, danger-ridden hours had already rubbed the tenderfoot softness from him. What was it he had said to Jim Ball? *You don't need to use that name on me anymore.*

He continued to sit there in that brooding stillness, his mind probing, grasping, seizing on scattered fragments, assorting, piecing them together in a picture that might make sense. Janet Dunbar, Buck Salten, Ab Matoon, *Bill Benton*—

The thought of Benton lifted Mark to his feet. He stubbed his half-finished cigarette under boot-heel and swung into his saddle. His first job was to get to the Benton ranch, do what he could to carry comfort to the fugitive ranchman's helpless wife.

He had been gone perhaps less than half an hour when another rider came up the canyon trail. The paint horse under him was in a lather of sweat, and Cooner reluctantly reined to a standstill a few yards up the right fork. He had pushed the chase a little too fast and he was going to find himself on foot unless he gave the horse a rest.

He eased in the saddle and felt in his shirt pocket for tobacco pouch and papers, indifferent to the gasping heaves of the winded horse under him. He felt no pity for the horse, only anger because of the enforced halt that was increasing the miles between him and the young tenderfoot who had so craftily bested him.

He thumb-nailed a sulfur match and lit the hastily rolled cigarette, inhaled deeply. Ab Matoon was going to take his scalp if he failed to pick up young Destin's trail. Ab had no use for a man who fell down on the job.

Cooner's dark, leathery face twisted in an ugly grimace as he recalled certain mysteriously missing men whose failures had incurred the fatal displeasure of the boss. He knew the answers to those unexplained disappearances, answers that he and the buzzards alone shared with Ab Matoon.

Force of habit drew his restless eyes to the trail ahead, and his face took on the sharp look of a fox. He straightened out of his slouch, leaned forward, intent gaze studying the trail that led to Diamond D ranch. His eyes narrowed to speculative slits, and after a few moments he slid from the saddle, bent his head in a closer look. It was what he failed to find that worried him. The trail was bare of fresh hoofprints, and Cooner knew then that something was wrong. Destin was not headed for Diamond D, as Jim Ball had led him to believe.

His eyes like shiny black buttons, Cooner ran back to where the canyon trail forked. His had been no idle boast to Ab Matoon. *Can track a crawlin' woodtick in the dark of the moon.* Once on the alert he was like a hound not to be turned from a hot scent.

He found the fresh hoofprints of Mark's horse in the left fork, followed them to the bluff where Mark had dismounted. He squatted on his heels, studied the half-smoked cigarette, scrutinized the impressions in the dust made by the shod hoofs of the standing horse. The deepened hoofprints told him that the halt had used up some ten minutes. He fingered the cigarette end. It was cold.

Cooner straightened up from his crouch, his expression deeply puzzled. The tracks were plain enough, told him that his quarry was riding up the left fork, which made no sense if his purpose was to take a look at the Dunbar ranch. The left fork would lead him straight to the Benton ranch, a lot of miles away from Diamond D, his supposed destination.

The perplexed spy touched his bruised chin, stared with vicious eyes at the blood that came away on his fingers. He was following the trail, and when he came up with Destin there would be no swinging fists—only gunsmoke and hot lead from the gun that now nestled against his thigh in tied-down holster.

Cooner hurried back to his paint horse. The job was to his liking. An unsuspecting tenderfoot on the trail ahead—a gunshot crackling through the stillness of the desert hills, and again stillness—and some time later, a few days, buzzards circling the blue sky, winging down to another feast.

Chapter II

Mark found the lone butte described by Jim Ball, and now the trail leveled straight across the mesa towards a grove of trees. Benton's ranch, Mark guessed, and he sent the horse into an easy lope.

The trail cut into a dusty road, and soon he was following an avenue that wound through the grove. He saw a white picket fence, and a low house, hardly visible in the green tangle of shrubs and trees. The signs of neglect and decay were everywhere. There were breaks in the picket fence, and it was evident that no attempt was being made to care for the garden.

He came to the yard gate, opened it, and led the horse through. The place depressed him. It was like a ghost ranch, deserted, lifeless, the only sound the harsh creak of a windmill. He wondered why someone did not stop the spinning windmill. Water overflowed the sides of the big wooden tank, flooded across the yard, and the long watering trough was spilling a steady stream.

The horse was thirsty, and after a moment's inspection of the trough Mark found a place where he could reach it without wading through mud. He watered the horse sparingly, tied him to a hitch-rail, and walked across the yard to a small gate that led into the garden. The thing was getting on his nerves. Bill Benton should be here, caring for his ranch, not forced to flee for his life from a scoundrel whose treachery had apparently brought him to ruin. This was Benton's home. He had put his sweat into it, no doubt had even planted the trees that now made so brave a showing of green against the background of desert hills.

His heart heavy, Mark pushed through the little gate. A piece of chain weighted with a broken grindstone pulled it shut behind him, and its sharp creak was evidently a familiar sound; it drew a woman to the kitchen door. She held the screen open with one hand, peered at him anxiously. She was large and heavy, with carroty hair streaked with grey, and a big, sunburned face. Alarm filled her eyes, when she failed to recognize him. Her other hand appeared, a gun in clasped fingers.

"Don't you come any closer," she warned, in a harsh voice.

Mark held his step. He knew that this woman could not be Bill Benton's bed-ridden wife. Whoever she was it was plain that she was ready to use the gun leveled at him.

He removed his hat, smiled. "I came to see Mrs. Benton. I'm a friend of her husband."

The suspicion continued in her eyes. She shook her head. "You sayin' you're his friend don't make you one."

"Do you know Jim Ball?" he asked. "And Buck Salten?"

The woman nodded. "I'd trust *them* two anywheres."

"It was Jim Ball who told me how to get here," Mark said.

"I didn't see you on the road no place." She spoke doubtfully.

"I came up Borrego Canyon—the short cut," he explained. He held on to his patience, and his smile. "It's very important for me to see Mrs. Benton. I have a message from her husband. She'll be worried about him."

"She sure is . . ." The woman paused, added defensively, "Mr. Benton told me I wasn't to take chances. There's a lot of snakes crawlin' around these times."

"I've *got* to see her," persisted Mark. "You can hold your gun on me while I talk to her." His smile widened. "You won't need to use it, I promise you."

She considered him, her expression dubious. The windmill creaked and clanked, and her eyes lifted in a troubled look. "That plagued old thing," she muttered.

"What's the matter with it?" Mark asked.

"The rope that pulls it out of the wind is broke, and I'm too heavy to climb the ladder to fix it." The gun was dangling against her apron now. "The boss turned it on when he went to La Cruz yesterday, and the thing's been goin' like mad ever since, the wind bein' high all day. The tank is floodin' all over the place and me not able to stop it."

"I'll climb up and fix it for you," Mark offered.

"That will be grand of you." Relief wiped the lingering suspicion from her face. "I'm that bothered, the boss not back from town, and no man about the place to do anything at all."

"I must see Mrs. Benton first," bargained Mark.

"And what might be your name, young man?"

He told her, and after a brief hesitation she held the screen door open. "You can come in this way and wait here in the kitchen while I tell my poor lamb."

He stood there in the kitchen, aware of a growing respect for the big woman as he gazed about. The place was in sharp contrast to the run-down condition of the yard—the fences—the ranch buildings. Everything was spotless, the stove bright with polish, the pots and pans gleaming, the floor well-scrubbed, a red-checked cloth on the table. It was plain that here at least was no submission to defeat.

She returned in a few moments, said briefly, "I'll take you in to her now, Mr. Destin."

He followed through a hall and into a large bedroom with windows that overlooked the jungle of garden.

"Here he is," the big woman said. She made no

move to leave the room, stood there, concealed gun bulging her apron.

The woman under the bedcovers looked intently at Mark. The inspection seemed to satisfy her. She smiled faintly. "Tildy says you have a message from my husband, Mr. Destin."

Despite the smile, there was stark apprehension in her eyes, and Mark said quickly, "He's all right, Mrs. Benton. He wanted you to know he won't be home for a few days. I promised I would come and tell you."

"He—he's hurt?" The question came in a little gasp.

"Not hurt," Mark assured her. "There's been some trouble, and it seemed best for him to stay away from the ranch."

She lay very still on the pillow, eyes closed for a moment. Her face showed remnants of a beauty that suffering and anxiety had wasted away, and there was a hint of grey in the dark hair. She looked very frail. Mark's heart went out to her, and to the husband kept from her side by men who sought his life.

Her eyes opened on him. "I suppose the trouble was with Ab Matoon?"

"Yes," Mark said.

"Tell me about it." Then, seeing the hesitation in his eyes, "I'd rather know than lie here thinking the worst."

"You're very brave," Mark said.

"A woman has to be brave—in this country." Her eyes were beseeching him. "Please tell me."

He told her about the arrest, the gaol-break, the decision for Benton to seek safety in the Sinks. "He doesn't want you to worry. I promised to see you and explain why he couldn't come home."

"Matoon will have the ranch watched," she whispered.

Her words jolted Mark's memory. He heard the town marshal's confident voice. *I'll get Jess on the job pronto.* Perhaps the man was already snooping around, watching for Benton, waiting for a chance to send a bullet into his back. There had been no signs on the trail, but he *could* come by the longer road.

He said gravely, "I think they're almost sure to watch for him here, but they won't harm you, Mrs. Benton."

Tildy's voice broke the brief silence. "Just let 'em try." Her voice was grim. "I'm good at shooting wolves." The gun under her apron stirred in the grip of her hand. "I've got a Winchester in the kitchen, and a shotgun, both of 'em loaded."

"They won't harm women." Mark did not feel the confidence he put into his voice. He was not so sure what men like Kinner might do. He continued, warning in his voice now. "If anybody does come around it's important they don't know that I've been here."

"I won't tell 'em nothin'," Tildy said harshly. "All I'll tell 'em is to get away from here if they don't want a dose of buckshot. I'll be gettin' Mr. Destin a cup of coffee," she added hospitably. She left the room, her step surprisingly light, and for a moment there was a silence, Mrs. Benton motionless under her covers, her eyes closed. She said presently, "Tildy Hogan is as good as two men around the place." A hint of color touched her white cheeks; her voice grew faint. "We had to let all our men go. . . . No money to pay them. Ab Matoon has dreadfully cheated my husband, and it does seem as if the end is close."

"Don't say that, Mrs. Benton." Mark spoke softly, but his voice had the edge of steel. "Your husband has friends fighting on his side."

"I'm so useless," she half wailed. "I'm only a burden on him, ever since my back was injured when my horse fell with me."

"Don't say that either, Mrs. Benton." Compassion took the steel from Mark's voice. "You'll be up and about again."

"I could be, perhaps—" Her thin hand lifted in a hopeless gesture. "My husband has been wanting to take me to a doctor in Santa Fe—a delicate operation that might cure me." Her hand lifted again. "It means money—and we have none—now that Ab Matoon has robbed us."

"There's a doctor in La Cruz," began Mark.

"Not *that* man." She shook her head. "Anyway,

he's a friend of Matoon and he's just no good—a drunkard, we've heard."

Mark held his peace, but the thought of Doc. Bralen stayed with him. He had seen the doctor at work, sensed in him an amazing ability. He made a mental note to speak to Doc. Bralen about Mrs. Benton. He liked the man, despite the talk against him.

Tildy came in with a cold beef sandwich and a cup of coffee on the tray. "You've a starved look to you," she said. "I won't be wrong guessin' you've not had a bite since early mornin'."

"You've guessed right," grinned Mark.

He ate and drank quickly, anxious now to be on his way. The thought of Jess Kinner showing up worried him. It would complicate matters if Matoon heard of his visit to Benton's ranch. Matoon was already suspicious, had put Cooner on his trail. He had given Cooner the slip, but Kinner was something different.

"You won't be forgettin' that plaguey windmill," reminded Tildy. "Looks like the wind's goin' to blow all night."

Mark replaced the empty cup on the tray. "I'll tackle the job now." He went to the bed, leaned down, and took Mrs. Benton's hand gently in his. "Don't forget what I said. Your husband has friends fighting on his side now, and you're going to pull through—both of you."

She gazed up at him, wonder in her eyes. "You

seem so young," she whispered. "Hardly more than a boy—but you are very comforting, Mr. Destin. I can almost believe you, and I thank you for coming."

He followed Tildy Hogan back to her kitchen and out to the busy windmill. They stared up at the whirling vanes. The woman shook her head worriedly.

"It's a new rope we're needin'," she said. "And where to lay me hands on one I can't tell you."

"We can look in the barn," Mark suggested.

"There's no rope in the barn," she told him. "Only some of those rawhide lariats and all of 'em too short."

"That braided rawhide is strong," Mark pointed out. "I can tie a couple of them together."

"It's a bright mind you've got under your hat," beamed Tildy. "Come on, lad. They're hangin' there on pegs in the saddle-room."

She scurried up the dusty yard, hair and skirt blowing in the wind. Mark kept pace with her. He was curious about her, ventured a question.

"Have you known Mrs. Benton long?"

"Sure and I've known her a lot of years, ever since her pa got killed leadin' a cavalry charge against a bunch of raidin' Apaches." She added, in a soft voice, "My man, Pat, was the Captain's corporal and got himself killed in that same skirmish, bless his soul."

"She's lucky to have you with her these days," commented Mark.

"She's my lamb," Tildy told him, with a toss of her head. "The very day she married Bill Benton I said to her, 'Whither thou goes, I will go; and where thou lodges, I will lodge!' They was words I'd read in the Bible some place and they sounded *just* the way I felt about the lamb. I've been with her ever since."

They were in the barn now. The stillness there depressed Mark. Anger against the evil man who was the cause of this sinister quiet hardened his resolution to destroy him, use every weapon he could muster, match cunning with cunning, ruthlessness with ruthlessness. There could be no compromise.

Mrs. Hogan's brisk voice dragged him from his somber thoughts. "You'll find 'em in the saddle-room, yonder, young man, and I hope you can make use of 'em before that plaguey windmill bangs itself to pieces." She looked at him curiously. She had never seen a face so granite hard with implacable purpose. The face of a fighter. The thought cheered her. There was need here for a fighter.

Mark stepped into a dark little room that smelled of leather and harness oil. He found the coils of rawhide, slung them over an arm.

"They'll do the job," he said briefly.

"It's a job that should have been done long

ago," Mrs. Hogan grumbled. "The boss has been so crazy-like these days he just hasn't been good for much, fumin' and frettin' and swearin' he'd kill Ab Matoon." She shook her head sadly. "Bill's a good man, only he's been goin' round in a kind of daze and not able to think straight."

Climbing a windmill tower was another new experience for Mark. He crawled up the ladder cautiously, an end of the tightly knotted rawhide ropes looped over an arm. He reached a little platform, knelt there, his head a scant foot under the racketing wooden planes of the windmill. The rope had broken off short. He got a grasp on it, pulled steadily until the big vanes shifted out of the wind. The revolutions slowed, and in a few moments he had the great wheel at a standstill.

He worked fast now, made his improvised rope secure, looked down, saw that the other end was within reach of anyone standing below.

"That's fine," Tildy Hogan called up to him. "You're a smart lad, Mr. Destin."

Mark was not finished yet. The platform offered a good view of the country, and there was a chance that a look might discover Jess Kinner lurking in the vicinity.

His gaze went first to the road that twisted endlessly through the chaparral, circled gullies, and finally dropped from view behind low hills. No sign of dust lifted in the distance. He could detect no stir of life there.

"Whatever be you starin' at?" Mrs. Hogan called up, her tone uneasy.

"Just looking," replied Mark. He shifted his gaze finally to the lone butte across the mesa, the landmark that had guided him from Borrego Canyon. He was suddenly tense, eyes narrowed, concentrating on something that moved there, a crawling black dot that disappeared behind a clump of sagebrush, came in sight for a moment, and again vanished in the chaparral.

Mark continued to gaze. The sun was low behind him, and as the slow-moving dot reappeared he caught the glint of sunlight on metal. A gun—a rifle in saddle-boot. The moving dot was a lone rider, and the chances were good that he wore the name of Jess Kinner.

Mark's heart sank. He did not want Kinner to find him at the ranch, nor did he now relish the thought of riding away, leaving the women alone. He longed desperately for a pair of binoculars that might help him to establish the identity of the approaching horseman.

His searching mind suddenly recalled something he had noticed on the kitchen table. An ancient brass telescope, evidently much used by Tildy Hogan, ever watchful of the road. In an instant he went scrambling down the precarious ladder.

Mrs. Hogan gave him a keen look. The expression on his face put alarm in her eyes. "What is it, lad?"

Her quick fright steadied him, and he forced a reassuring smile. "Almost tangled my feet in those rungs coming down." He glanced up at the dangling rope. "You won't have any more trouble with the windmill, I think."

"You looked a bit upset," she said. "Got me to wonderin' what it was that scared you."

"I *was* scared." He managed a rueful grin. "I wouldn't like a tumble from that ladder."

Suspicion still lingered in her eyes. "Well, a mighty lot of thanks to you for fixin' the rope."

"It's a grand view from the platform," Mark continued. "Was wishing I had my binoculars . . . a good telescope."

"Sure now and I've got one of them things," exclaimed Mrs. Hogan. "Use it myself a lot these days, keepin' watch on the road and all. I'll get it for you, Mr. Destin."

He waited with an impatience he was careful to conceal when she hurriedly returned from the house, the telescope in her hand.

"Take your time with it," she said indulgently. "I'll be in the kitchen when you fetch it back. Got a pan of bread to slip into the oven."

The garden gate shut her from view before Mark regained the tower platform. He leveled the long telescope, felt an extraordinary relief as the lone rider sprang into view. The approaching horseman was Cooner. He could hardly believe his eyes. Jim Ball must have made a slip. The idea was to let Cooner think that the tenderfoot was headed for the Dunbar ranch.

One thing was certain. Cooner's business here was not Bill Benton. *His* job was to stick close to the tenderfoot. It was all too apparent that the man had managed to pick up the trail.

Mark wasted no time for a second look, scrambled hastily down the ladder, and ran for the garden gate. It was up to him to fox the trail, lead Cooner a long way from the lonely ranch house.

The tell-tale screech of the gate drew Mrs. Hogan to the screen door. "You wasn't takin' much of a look." She gazed at him hard, her eyes sharp, again suspicious.

"I just realized the sun is getting low." Mark kept his voice casual. "I want to get down into the canyon before dark." He put the telescope into her hand. "Thanks, Mrs. Hogan. I'll try the glass again some other day when I have more time."

"You're welcome," Mrs. Hogan said graciously. A softness crept into her voice. "I want you to know that your talk hasn't got me fooled. You've spotted somethin' you don't like, but I'm trustin' you, young man, and I'm not worryin' too much. I've seen the same look in my long dead-and-gone Pat's eyes, God rest his soul. I'm prayin' that God will ride with you and keep your wits bright and your gun hand ready for whatever comes this day." She gave him a warm smile. "I'm talkin' too much—and you with work to do."

Mark was already moving fast. He slammed through the gate to his horse, snatched at the tie-rope, paused briefly to examine the carbine in the scabbard of Red O'Malley's saddle. A .44 Winchester. It was fully loaded. He thrust the gun back into its leather sheath and stepped into the saddle.

His immediate purpose was to draw Cooner into a running chase away from the ranch house. It meant risking a shot from the rifle he suspected the man carried. What happened afterwards depended on his own wits. Once he gained the dry wash of the creek, the screening willows, he would have an even break with the man Jim Ball had said was a ruthless killer. He was putting himself now into the same deadly mood that had kept Cooner clinging to his trail. He would kill too, be as merciless, as cold-blooded as the man who sought to kill him. He was under no delusions about Cooner. The man's venom would be in full flow because of the beating that had left him senseless, an object of derision. He would not be content now with merely spying on the tenderfoot, carrying tales to Ab Matoon. Only one thing remained to satisfy the thirst for revenge in him. A *dead* tenderfoot, lying somewhere in the chaparral.

The fast-moving horse under him drew the fringing willows close. A shot crackled above the thud of Baldy's hoofs, and Mark heard the screeching whine of a bullet. He glanced back, saw Cooner's horse swing from the trail.

Baldy was on the dead run now, and in another moment Mark was reining the horse deep into the screening willows. He halted, slid from his saddle, jerked the carbine from its scabbard. The pounding hoofs of the paint horse drew closer, died away, and a hush came—a stillness that sent a chill through Mark, and at the same time steadied him. He crouched there in the bushes, Red O'Malley's carbine in lifted hands, every sense in him on the alert for the killer who stalked him. He had never felt quite so cool, so filled with ruthless determination.

Chapter 12

The willow brakes drew longing looks from Jess Kinner as he jogged his horse along the road. He was not feeling any too good after his night's debauch. He felt that he would rather be anywhere than sitting in a saddle. His head ached horribly, and there were moments when the landscape blurred in front of his bloodshot eyes. Teel Furner should have known better than to send him out on this job to the Benton ranch. Teel should have let him sleep it off a few more hours, get himself in better shape. He had told Teel that he was as sick as a poisoned pup, but the town marshal had practically booted him into the saddle, with ominous threats of worse things to come from Ab Matoon if he delayed in getting out to the ranch in a hurry.

"Benton will likely show up there on account of his sick wife," Furner had told him. "You're forkin' saddle right now, or I'm putting you back to tendin' gaol ag'in."

The ultimatum had drawn lurid protests from Jess Kinner. His weird experience of the previous night had given him a horror of the town's gaol. His decision to resign his custodianship was final. He used very positive language in making the town marshal understand that no inducement could change his mind, and if he had to do *something* to appease Ab Matoon he chose the lookout job at Benton's ranch.

"Ab ain't askin' for you to bring Benton back to gaol if you run into him," Teel Furner had said significantly. "You'll want to look out he don't see you first—get his gun on you."

The town marshal's words were loud in Kinner's ears now as he neared the ranch. He had an uneasy feeling that an encounter with Bill Benton at this time would be highly unpleasant, in fact disastrous, with himself on the receiving end. His head felt like a balloon about to burst, his nerves were jumpy—his hands shaky. He was in no shape for this business. He would be a sitting duck for Benton's gun.

The next rise would bring him in full view of the ranch house. Kinner reined his horse to a standstill, bleary gaze again on the willow brakes, his still befuddled mind wrestling for a solution of the problem that vexed him. What he was needing was sleep, a couple of hours more sleep to clear his aching head, take the twitch out of his nerves. The willows would be a first-rate place for a man to bed down in for some sleep. Come sundown he could be on the job again, on the lookout for Benton, ready for a chance to empty hot lead into him. Teel Furner had been plain enough about it. Ab Matoon had sent him out here to kill Benton, and right now he was in no shape for the job—not until he had some sleep, got his mind clear, the shake out of his hand.

He swung the horse from the wheel-rutted road and made for the willow brakes less than a mile away. The ridge hid him from possible view of watchers at the ranch house. His presence in the willows would not be suspected, and when darkness came he could do some prowling with practically no risk of running into gunfire. Kinner was a firm believer in the ambush, a safe chance to fix the gunsight on his unsuspecting victim's back.

He reached the thick-growing willows and after a brief search found the retreat he was looking for—a soft bed of dry bunch grass, a round little hillock for his aching head, the wind in the willows making lullaby music.

He cached the horse behind a concealing clump of bushes, where the animal could browse on the bunch grass, extracted a pint flask of whisky from the rolled slicker tied to the saddle, and returned to the spot he had chosen for his rest. He pulled the cork, tipped the flask to his lips, and gulped thirstily. The whisky sent a comfortable glow through him. He sighed, eyed the flask reflectively, shook his head, and pushed in the cork. He would be needing a good drink or two later, when he had finished the job he had come to do.

He stretched out on the bed of bunch grass, closed his eyes, his black Stetson within hand's reach, the whisky flask under it.

He came awake with a start, lay still for a moment, not immediately comprehending where he was. The noise that had dragged him from his sleep had seemed like a shot. He wondered vaguely if he had been dreaming, fancied with a cold prickle of horror that something stirred in the thicket behind him.

Kinner sat up, careful to make no sound. He was still confused, moved his head in stupid looks from side to side. The stealthy movement in the willow brakes had hushed. He could hear nothing, see nothing. The stillness recalled the gaol visitation of the spooks, and a rush of superstitious dread turned his blood to ice, held him rigid in a paralysis of terror. The spooks had picked up his trail!

He strained his ears; he heard a faint swish of sound that might have been the wind in the willows, or the stir of bunch grass under a man's boot. Whatever it was, he felt a quick relief. Spooks had invisible hands that could squeeze a man's throat and tie him up with ropes, but spooks did not make sounds.

He thought it over for a moment. What he had heard was some animal—a coyote, a jackrabbit. He grinned, reached for his hat and pulled it on. The movement uncovered the whisky flask.

His grin widened. Time for another drink. He picked up the flask, was appalled to hear a blast of gunfire startlingly close. The flask shattered in his hand.

Kinner gazed stupidly at the fragment of glass still clutched in his fingers. A second shot crackled. He felt a sharp sting across his scalp. His hat lifted, settled back.

The pain sobered him, galvanized him to action. He jerked at the gun in his holster, rolled behind a thick bush, furious gaze seeking the source of the gunfire. He knew the answer now. Bill Benton had somehow discovered his presence, was stalking him—meant to kill him.

Stillness settled down again, and Cooner, crouched a few yards away, was careful not to disturb that stillness. He was uncertain that his bullets had found the target. He was taking no chances with the tenderfoot. He had glimpsed the black Stetson, the green-and-yellow shirt sleeve, and sent in two quick shots. His mistake was natural enough. Matoon had not told him of the plan to send Jess Kinner to watch out for Bill Benton, nor had he seen Teel Furner after leaving Matoon's office, or the town marshal might have told him that Kinner was already on his way to the Benton ranch. He had gathered from Jim Ball's vague talk that the tenderfoot had said something about riding out to the Dunbar ranch for a look at the place, a plan suggested by Ab

Matoon. He had picked up the tenderfoot's trail, discovered in time at the fork that his quarry had taken the wrong turn and was heading for the Benton ranch instead of Diamond D. And now he had him cornered in the willow brakes below the ranch house. There was no mistaking the black Stetson—the green-and-yellow checked shirt the tenderfoot had got in a trade from Red O'Malley.

Cooner licked a fleck of blood from his swollen and cut lower lip. No kid tenderfoot was going to slam him round and get away with it. He grinned contentedly, waited for some betraying sound in the bushes beyond. Sooner or later the tenderfoot would make the rash move that would mean his finish.

Mark Destin too was careful to make no sound that would draw attention to himself. Like Cooner he was unaware of Kinner's presence in the willows. The two quick shots, the curl of gun-smoke in the bushes a good hundred yards away only meant one thing to him. Cooner apparently thought he had sighted the man he was trailing and the long silence indicated that he was waiting for some reaction from the tenderfoot.

Again smoke curled like blue mist from the bushes, and as Cooner's gun roared Mark was amazed to hear the sharp crack of another gun, see smoke lifting from a second clump of bushes. He could hardly believe his senses. A third character had mysteriously appeared on the grim scene. Who the third man might be was a puzzling question, but it was obvious that Cooner believed him to be the tenderfoot. The thought appalled Mark. He was reluctant to allow the thing to continue, let Cooner kill an innocent and probably very bewildered man.

The rattle of gunfire hushed, and the mystery man lurched from behind a clump of sagebrush. Mark realized that the strange duel was finished, and apparently Cooner was not the victor. No need now to interfere.

The man, gun in dangling hand, moved unsteadily towards a dark shape that lay sprawled in the brush. Amazement widened Mark's eyes. The stranger was Jess Kinner.

Something of the truth came to him as he watched. Kinner's black hat and gaudy checked shirt were similar to his own. Cooner's blunder was natural. He had glimpsed the tell-tale shirt and hat and mistaken Kinner for the tenderfoot he was stalking.

Unaware that he was under Mark's interested observation, Jess Kinner gazed with bewildered eyes at Cooner's sprawled body. He had expected to find Bill Benton lying dead here, and for a few moments his liquor-sodden brain refused to comprehend the truth. He wondered if he were going crazy, or if the spooks were again at work with their ghostly tricks.

He rolled bloodshot eyes in a nervous look

round. The stillness revived the superstitious dread he had striven to banish from his mind with drink. He thought longingly of the flask smashed by Cooner's first bullet.

Kinner glowered at the dead man, wondered dully why Cooner had tried to kill him; and slowly his confused mind seized upon the only answer that seemed possible. Ab Matoon had sent Cooner to kill him. Cooner had picked up his trail, followed him into the willow brakes bent on murder.

It was an answer that put Kinner in a cold sweat. Ab Matoon had no use for a man who fell down on the job. He was not liking Bill Benton's mysterious escape from the gaol. It was possible that his story about the spooks had made Matoon suspicious of his part in the affair.

Kinner wiped his hot face, felt something sticky on his fingers. He stared at the red stains. His scalp was bleeding—his cheek a smear of blood. Cooner's second bullet had nearly done for him. Only luck had saved him. His lifeless body could have lain there in the brush for days on end, and the buzzards alone would have known.

Kinner's face creased in a mirthless smile. The buzzards would soon be winging to the scene, but it was Cooner's body that would draw them, not his—not the body of the man Ab Matoon wanted dead.

Smoldering rage mingled with the fright in

him. He was not giving Matoon another chance at him. He would fork saddle—keep on going, head for the Sinks—maybe hide out in Mexico. To return to La Cruz now would be signing his own death warrant.

Kinner turned abruptly on his heel, started for his concealed horse. He came to a standstill, gazed back at the dead man. He was craving a drink, and Cooner was almost certain to have a flask on him.

Engrossed with his search, he failed to notice Mark's stealthy approach. His fingers closed over the bottle, and, sitting on his heels by the side of the dead man, he pulled the cork, tilted the flask to his lips.

The search had dragged a soiled envelope from one of Cooner's pockets. Kinner stared at it as he pushed in the cork and pocketed the flask. Some thought seemed to amuse him, put a savage grin on his face, and still sitting there on his heels he fumbled a stubby pencil from a pocket and picked up the envelope.

He smoothed it out on his knee, laboriously scrawled on the back, mouthing the words as he wrote. His grin widened. He leaned over the dead man, pushed the folded envelope into his shirt pocket, and got unsteadily to his feet.

Mark watched as he stumbled away. The man was a killer, and Matoon had sent him here to shoot Bill Benton on sight. It seemed a mistake to let him continue to live when a slight squeeze of the rifle's trigger could so promptly send him to join the slain Cooner.

Squeezing the trigger was something Mark found impossible to do. Also he had an idea of the purpose in Kinner's mind. The man was running away, convinced that Matoon had sent Cooner to ambush him. Terror would be riding Kinner hard, and he would want to get a long way from La Cruz.

Unaware that he was under observation, Kinner found his horse and rode away. Mark stalked him through the willows, watched until he vanished into the chaparral, and, satisfied now that the man had abandoned his job as lookout on the Benton house, he hastily returned to the scene of the shooting, curious to read the note Kinner had tucked inside the slain spy's pocket.

As he had suspected, the scrawl was addressed to Matoon, and Kinner had left no shred of doubt as to his immediate intention to put distance between himself and the sinister little lawyer. The blunt-penciled message was brief.

> You pizen snake I shore fixt Cooner for the buzerds to find and you wont nevver see me agin no time, you low-down skunk.

Mark tucked the envelope back in the dead man's shirt pocket, conscious of a curious gratitude to the fleeing Kinner. He had not thought it possible ever to feel grateful to the ex-gaoler. The man's boastful admission of the killing would convince Matoon that Cooner's death could not be blamed on the tenderfoot. It would have been Matoon's first thought that Mark had killed the spy who had trailed him to the Benton ranch. Kinner's scrawled words made an alibi not to be disputed, although he would have been amazed to know that, in his wish to hurl defiance at the man he believed had planned his murder, he had unwittingly earned Mark's grateful thanks.

Mark gazed thoughtfully at the dead man. He was not satisfied to leave the body lying there. Sooner or later the buzzards would draw attention to the place, and, although Kinner's note alibied the tenderfoot, the fact that the killing had occurred so near the Benton ranch house would give Matoon cause for dangerous speculations. He had put Cooner on the tenderfoot's trail, so would guess that the trail had led to the Benton ranch.

The shadows were lengthening. Mark realized he must make a decision and be on his way before darkness caught him in the willow brakes. He wondered if Tildy Hogan might have heard the shots. She would be alarmed, perhaps think he had run into a man sent to keep a lookout for Bill Benton. It was hardly probable she could have heard the gunfire. The thick-growing willows would have muffled the shots, and the ranch house was a good mile away.

There was only one thing he could do to keep Matoon from guessing the truth, and, his decision made, Mark soon found where Cooner had cached his horse. He led the animal back to where the dead man lay and untied the coil of rope from the saddle. The paint horse smelled death, was nervous, and Mark was forced to tie him short to a willow stump before he could get the body roped to the saddle.

The sun was close to the western hills by the time he rode down the Borrego Canyon trail, the paint horse following on a lead-rope and now reconciled to its burden.

He reached the fork that led to the Dunbar ranch and halted to consider just what to do with the dead man. It seemed the place to stage the locale of the ambush that had resulted in the death of the man Kinner had thought was bent on murder.

Mark got down from his saddle, and after a brief search found a clump of sagebrush close to the trail. He led the paint horse over, and in a few moments had the lifeless body sprawled face down behind the bushes, his gun under stiffening fingers.

He was still not quite satisfied. He wanted the place to show all the signs of a man waiting in ambush for his intended victim, and after a brief hesitation he extracted three cigarettes from the pack in the dead Cooner's shirt pocket. He had no time to smoke them down to the stubs a man would discard, grind under bootheel. He reached for his knife, cut off the ends, lit and smoked the improvised stubs. They looked natural enough after he heeled them into the dust—good evidence of a man who had been lying there, waiting to use his gun.

The pinto needed no urging to head downtrail for town. Matoon was due for an unpleasant surprise when news of the riderless horse reached him. He would soon have men searching for his missing spy.

Mark swung into his saddle and rode up the trail that led to the Dunbar ranch. He was tired—physically and mentally. Events were moving too fast, and as he rode through the yellowing light he wondered gloomily what still lay ahead. Sheer luck had saved him from a killer's gun—a freak circumstance, resulting in one man dead and another in frantic flight from an imagined peril.

He smiled grimly. Tenderfoot's luck, perhaps, and already stretched to the limit. He should have listened to Jim Ball—taken his advice, and the next stage out of La Cruz.

He halted the horse, turned the idea over in his mind. There was still time enough to get back to La Cruz, redeem his gold from Plácido Romero, and take the morning stage for Deming.

Baldy stamped a restive forefoot, tossed his

head, impatient for the home-ranch barn. Mark grinned, sent him up the trail. There could be no turning back now, not while dark danger so ominously threatened Janet Dunbar.

He had a job to do. Not the job that had brought him to La Cruz, full of hope of dreams to be realized. He knew now that for a time those hopes must remain dreams, make way for sterner things—the grim realities of life and death.

He thought of Bill Benton's crippled wife, so brave and so helpless. She had given him her trust, was depending on him. He felt a responsibility there not to be ignored. He had more to think about now than Janet Dunbar. He was in a fight to the finish. It might be an unpleasant finish, with himself lying like Cooner, somewhere in the chaparral. No one would know. Only the buzzards, ever on the alert when death struck.

His gloomy thoughts annoyed him. It was no time to let dark forebodings soften him. The business that now bound him to La Cruz demanded unfaltering courage—a cool mind.

The sunset glow faded; stars began to wink overhead as darkness crept over the landscape. Janet Dunbar would be surprised to see him so soon again, and no doubt more than displeased. It was necessary to have a talk with her, break down the barriers of her distrust. She needed his help, and Buck Salten's help. Her continued enmity could only make her situation more perilous—

result in ruin, perhaps death. Ab Matoon would not hesitate at any infamy that furthered his purpose.

Baldy's head lifted high, ears pricked forward. Mark instantly reined the horse from the trail and found cover in the thick juniper scrub. He was not taking any more chances. Vigilance was the price of safety now. Failure to keep on the alert might easily result in disaster.

He could hear no sound as he waited there. Only the soft sigh of the night wind in the chaparral. He was confident, though, that something had attracted Baldy's attention. It might have been anything—a coyote, a stray horse—or it might have been Buck Salten, approaching from the Dunbar ranch, on his way back to town.

The continued deep stillness began to fret him. Thick-growing junipers shut out the starlight, and he could see nothing in that blanketing darkness.

He remained rigid in the saddle, strained his ears for some betraying whisper of sound. The horse seemed quiet enough now, and Mark decided that his first guess was right. Baldy's momentary excitement had been caused by some vagrant scent of coyote on the night wind that came so gently from uptrail.

It was a reasonable explanation, and he was surprised to find himself rejecting it. He could not take a chance, allow any easy answer to draw him into a fatal ambush. He was remembering that Ray Wellerton also lived on the Dunbar ranch. It was not impossible that Matoon had managed to get word to him to be on the watch for the tenderfoot. The fact that Matoon had set Cooner to spy on him was sure proof of the lawyer's suspicions. There was an ugly connection between the two men. Ray Wellerton could have known only from Matoon about the twenty thousand dollars in gold, although his attempted holdup of the stage might have been his own idea, a scheme to double-cross Matoon.

Mark continued to hesitate, low voice quieting the restive horse. If his hunch was right Ray Wellerton might be lying in wait for him somewhere up the trail. The man would have learned by now that his attempt to kill the tenderfoot had failed. He would be in an ugly mood, quick to make use of the dark night, the lonely trail.

Mark thought it over, wondering what to do. Once he left the trail it would be a hopeless task to find the Dunbar ranch house in that darkness. He could leave his horse tied in the brush, try and locate the suspected ambush. He played with the idea, abandoned it. He was new to this business, lacked the experience that would have made it a simple matter for a man like Buck Salten.

A low voice suddenly broke through the stillness. Mark froze in his saddle, wondered wildly if thinking of Buck could have done things to him. He heard the voice again, amusement in the familiar drawl.

"It's me, Mark. Don't you get jumpy . . . or go for your gun."

The cold prickles left Mark's spine. He relaxed, turned his head in a look at the vague shape a scant five yards from him and hardly distinguishable from the surrounding junipers.

The stumpy shape moved, came close, showed Buck Salten's face, grim, unsmiling, gun in lowered hand. "You wasn't watchin' very sharp." His tone was reproving. "Good thing I wasn't after your scalp, Mark."

Mark said softly, fervently. "I'm thinking the same, Buck." He slid from his saddle, gazed with relieved eyes at the taller man. "When it comes to this kind of business I'm afraid I'm still a fool tenderfoot—a babe in the woods."

"It takes time to learn scoutin'," Buck said. "You're doin' right smart." He began shaping a cigarette. "Looks like you heard me up the trail, or you wouldn't be cached back here in the scrub."

"It was Baldy." Mark's tone was rueful. "He's smarter than any tenderfoot."

Buck chuckled. "You figgered there was somethin' up on the trail from the way he acted, huh?"

"That's right."

"Well . . ." Buck lit his cigarette, and the flame showed a hint of laughter in his shrewd eyes. "You acted quick, hunted cover, and that ain't what a *real* tenderfoot would have done. A real tenderfoot wouldn't have took no notice—just kept going and maybe run smack into an ambush." He nodded his head. "I reckon you've sure graduated, Mark."

"*Gracias*." Mark grinned. "I'm still mighty green at it, letting you get so close. I didn't hear a sound, Buck. How did you manage to sneak up on me?"

"I been scoutin' a lot of years," drawled Buck. "You'll pick up the trick, give you time."

"You heard me coming up the trail?"

"My bronc did," chuckled Diamond D's ex-foreman. "It seemed like a smart notion for me to scout round some. I sure ain't takin' chances right now, not with all this hell goin' on."

"Same with me," agreed Mark. "I thought it might be Ray Wellerton watching for me. He would, if he happened to know I was up this way."

"Ray is at the ranch now." Buck's voice hardened. "He's got Janet believin' his story of an accident with his gun, the doggone liar." He shook his head, added harshly, "I'd sure like to know for a fact that it was him that shot Red, thinkin' Red was you."

Mark felt no doubts about the would-be assassin's identity. The mantle fitted Ray Wellerton too well to leave room for doubts. He had no wish to draw Buck into the matter at this time and abruptly changed the subject, gave his friend a brief account of the strange duel in the willow brakes that had left Cooner dead, and the man he had mistaken for the tenderfoot seeking safety in panic-stricken flight.

"Cooner was a killin' snake," Buck said. He shook his head, and alarm crispened his voice. "Makes two times since you got in on the stage last night, Mark. Why—you ain't been here much more than twenty-four hours and two different fellers tryin' to kill you. I sure don't like it."

"I'm not liking it either," Mark said dryly.

"A feller's luck cain't hold that good *all* the time," worried Buck. He gazed at Mark thoughtfully. "There ain't no good reason for you to stick round just to get yourself filled with lead."

"You know better than that," Mark said. He thought of Janet, thought of Mrs. Benton.

"No sense for you to stay," fumed Buck. "You wasn't knowing none of us until you hit La Cruz. Ain't good sense for you to get mixed up in the hell that's bustin' loose. You should catch the first stage and get out while the going is good."

"Is that what you would do—in my place?" Mark asked softly.

Buck grinned, dropped his cigarette, and ground it under his bootheel. "I reckon good sense and me never did keep close company," he drawled. "Well, I done my best, and it ain't *my* fault if you ain't got sense enough to catch Jim Ball's stage."

"I'm sticking," Mark told him. "I'm riding with you all the way—to the end of the trail. Isn't that the way you want it?"

"Sure is," Buck said, his voice low, husky with emotion. "Well, I'll get my bronc and head back to the ranch with you."

"I thought you were returning to town," Mark said, surprised.

"I'm sticking close to you this trip," Buck told him. "Ray Wellerton is at the ranch, and I've a notion he won't like it, you showin' your face there. Ray is one mean hombre, if Janet *does* think different about him. That girl ain't got a lick of good sense in her." He paused, added with a grim chuckle, "I reckon she's got even less sense than you and me, Mark."

He found his horse, and they followed the trail that twisted interminably across the starlit mesa.

A light began to wink at them from the far distance, and Buck Salten said laconically, "That's Diamond D yonder."

Mark pushed his horse alongside. There was a question he wanted answered.

"Listen, Buck. I'm wondering why Rick Dunbar got you to homestead that Borrego Creek strip."

"Wasn't nobody else he could trust to deed it over to him after the homesteadin' was finished."

Buck's head turned in a surprised look. "What for you ask about it, Mark?"

"Well—" Mark hesitated. "Couldn't Janet have used *her* homestead rights on it?"

"She ain't old enough," explained Buck. "Rick couldn't wait for Janet to be twenty-one. I reckon she's got to go more'n a year yet before she's twenty-one." His voice stiffened. "No call for *you* to worry about that Borrego strip. I'm not going back on my promise to Janet's dad, even if he *is* layin' in his grave."

"I'm not worrying about what *you'll* do," Mark said. "It's only that I want to get the thing straightened out in my mind."

A silence fell between them, and Mark set his mind on the job that was taking him to see Janet Dunbar. He had to convince her of Buck Salten's loyal if secret devotion, win for himself her friendship and trust. It would not be easy, with Ray Wellerton there to harden her resistance, fan the flames of suspicion against him.

Chapter 13

Janet had never felt so tired. There had been no sleep for her during the long night at the hotel, playing nurse to Red O'Malley. Her eyes were heavy, her spirits low—the door wide open to crowding fears.

"You look *muy malo*," worried Juana; "so pale, *señorita*, and the beeg black circles under your eyes."

"I feel terrible," Janet admitted.

"You go upstairs and take a bath and then have long, nize sleep," advised the Mexican woman. "I will give Red the soup w'en eet ees ready."

Janet offered no protest, went up to her room and took a bath, and, after a longing look at the bed, slipped into a fresh dress. She had too much on her mind to think of sleep yet. There were questions she wanted to ask her stepbrother. They were not pleasant questions, but she was determined to ask them. The past hours had raised an uneasiness in her about Ray.

She stood at the open window and gazed speculatively into the darkness beyond, her thoughts busy, shaping and reshaping the things she wanted to say to Ray. She would need to be careful, not let him suspect her disturbing suspicions. She had never liked him much, but he was her stepbrother, the son of the woman who for a few years had been her father's wife.

The marriage that had made Ray and his mother members of the Dunbar household had always been a shock she had carefully concealed from her father. She had not grieved when death had again made him a widower. Also it was her secret thought that Rick Dunbar had felt more relief than sorrow for his loss. The marriage had been a total failure so far as his happiness was concerned.

Janet's heart constricted, as it always did now when she thought of her father. She longed passionately to learn the identity of the assassin who had killed him from ambush. Ray had thrown out hints that Buck Salten knew more than he should about the dreadful business.

Doubts were again crowding in fast. She leaned out of the window, looked up at the stars, let the soft night wind cool her hot cheeks. Certain odd happenings had drawn her attention to Ray Wellerton, made her wonder if she was all wrong about Buck Salten. Her father had thought a lot of Buck, and she had never known him to be mistaken in his estimate of a man. She knew, too, that he had long ago taken Ray Wellerton's measure and found him lacking the qualities he demanded.

Janet was conscious of a dull surprise at her own stupidity in not sooner recognizing so important a truth. She had chosen to go against her father's unerring judgment. It was Ray's talk that had set her against Buck Salten, the man her father had trusted.

She thought miserably of Red O'Malley—his indignation over her treatment of Buck. It must have been hard for Red to leave Diamond D and throw in his lot with Buck. An Indian raid had left Red an orphan, and her father had practically adopted him, treated him almost as a son. Diamond D had been his home since he was a small boy. She and Red had been playmates, and she loved him like a brother.

She realized now, with some amazement, that Red was wiser than Rick Dunbar's daughter. Like her father, Red could see the rotten spots in a man. She might have known from his studied politeness to Ray that he disliked him. He had never said so in words, but his blue eyes would frost when Ray was around.

Janet's hand lifted in an impatient gesture. She had been a little fool, refusing to listen to Buck. He had tried in his stumbling, awkward way to warn her. She had turned on him like a wildcat. There was nothing else he could do but ask for his time and say goodbye to Diamond D.

She thought uneasily of the young Easterner who seemed to be mixed up in the scheme to steal the ranch. She could not make up her mind about him. Red O'Malley liked him, and she respected Red's judgment. She only knew that he was a friend of Ab Matoon. The lawyer had written an amazing letter, informing her that he had sold Diamond D to Mark Destin. She had puzzled over it for hours, could remember every word.

> . . . and you must realize that I cannot carry this loan indefinitely and so am forced to call in the mortgage. The deal I propose to make with Destin will clear the debt, and I trust you will cooperate and sign the quit-claim deed I have prepared. I would much dislike being forced to take more drastic steps. . . .

A frightening letter, and to think of it sent shivers through her. The talk about a mortgage was absurd. Her father would never have borrowed a cent from Ab Matoon, let alone put a mortgage on his beloved ranch.

She wished now that she had shown the letter to Buck Salten. But Buck himself had come under suspicion. The fact that he had filed homestead rights on the Borrego Creek strip had a bad smell. The strip controlled most of the water on the Pioche range. Losing the Pioche would hit Diamond D hard.

Buck had resented Ray's sneering comments about it. The memory of the unpleasant scene made Janet wince. They had just returned from the new grave under the tall trees in the garden, and she had flung herself down on the big sofa in the living room, closed her eyes, tried to keep back the tears, shut her ears to the sound she fancied she heard—the earth falling from the spades of the men they had left to fill the grave.

It was Ray Wellerton's sneering voice that had brought her upright from the cushions. Her step-brother stood in the doorway as if to block Buck from leaving the room, and there was a wicked rage in his shiny black eyes.

"Got the jump on me, huh, Buck?" His voice was a low tight rasp. "You couldn't wait for Rick Dunbar to get cold before you filed on the Borrego Creek strip."

"How come you know I filed?" asked Buck in his mild voice. "Looks like you was over to the land office in Silver City."

"Sure I was over there!" shouted Ray. "Now that Rick Dunbar is dead it's my duty to protect Diamond D, and that's something *he* wasn't doing."

"You're awful wrong, Ray." The soft drawl had gone from Buck's voice. "It was Rick's own idea for me to homestead the Borrego Creek strip. He'd never got title to that land, and the way folks was headin' into the La Cruz country scared him plenty. He figgered it was time to act quick and told me to file in my name."

"Your talk doesn't make sense," sneered Ray. "Why should he ask *you* to file?"

Buck hesitated, gave Janet an embarrassed look. "Rick wasn't tellin' me, and I wasn't needin' to ask him. I reckon he figgered I'd play square with him, deed the land over when I got title from the Government."

"Your talk don't make hay with *me,*" sneered Ray. He was a tall, wide-shouldered man and darkly handsome. "Why should he pick on *you* to homestead the strip?"

"There wasn't nobody else." Buck kept his voice quiet. "Rick knowed I hadn't used my homestead rights."

Ray glared at him, his expression ugly. "I could have filed!" he exploded. "Rick knew I hadn't used *my* homestead rights. If he was so anxious to save the strip from land grabbers he'd have asked *me* to file."

Buck said coolly, "I reckon he had his reasons for not wantin' you to file."

"You're a liar!"

Buck moved with lightning speed, big fist lashing out. The blow caught Ray on the jaw, and he staggered, stumbled over a chair, and crashed to the floor.

Janet had screamed, rushed between them. "Stop it!" She was thankful that neither of the men were wearing their guns.

"Are you believin' his talk that your dad didn't

tell me to homestead the strip?" asked Buck.

She had hesitated a fraction too long, the doubt in her eyes plain, and Buck said grimly, "I reckon you ain't needin' me here on Diamond D no more."

He was gone before her confused mind could quite grasp his meaning. Her stepbrother got slowly to his feet, hand caressing his bruised jaw. He seemed in no hurry to follow the foreman into the yard.

"I'm getting my gun," he said hoarsely. "I'll kill him."

Janet clutched him with both hands. "No—no! Let him go."

"He's a low-down thief, stealing our land." Ray pushed her hands off. "I'm betting he's the skunk who shot the old man in the back."

She had given him a horrified look and fled into the yard to the barn. Buck was already throwing a saddle on his horse. He faced round at her call, his eyes bleak.

"Buck!" She flung the question hysterically. "Do you know who killed Dad?"

His face went blank, and after a moment he said softly, "I aim to find out for sure before I do any talkin'."

"Ray says that—that—" She faltered, unable to repeat the accusation, saw by his expression that he understood what she wanted to tell him.

"If you're smart you won't be listening to Ray

too much," he said, with a bitter smile. He turned back to the horse, jerked the tie-rope loose.

Perhaps if he had been more gentle, less contemptuous, things might have been different. She was too wrought up, her grief for her father more than she could bear. She felt that Buck was running away, leaving her in the lurch. She had become hysterical, told him that his flight was a sign of guilt and that she hoped the day would come when she would see him hanged.

Buck had only looked at her once, his eyes anguished, full of pity, and he had ridden away, grim, wordless. Red O'Malley had witnessed the wretched scene and, outraged, had quickly followed his friend.

"Your dad would turn in his grave if he could be hearin' your fool talk to Buck," the young cowboy had told her sorrowfully. "I'm sayin' *adiós*, Janet."

The memory of it all held her rigid with horror as she stood there at the bedroom window. She must have been out of her mind, a driveling little fool unable to use the common sense that was her birthright as Rick Dunbar's daughter. Her sanity was back now, her mind able to reason and for the first time able to grasp the significance of various incidents that she had blindly ignored.

Voices reached her from the ranch yard, and her quick look recognized her tall stepbrother revealed in the lamplight that glowed from the open door of the men's bunkhouse. Another man appeared in the doorway and handed Ray a lighted lantern. Ray said something that drew a guffaw from the man, and then he was moving through the darkness towards the barn.

Janet turned hastily from the window and hurried from the room and down the stairs. There was nobody in the kitchen, and she guessed that Juana was giving Red O'Malley his soup.

The big chinaberry trees that shaded the adobe walls of the dairy house shut out the starlight, and it was very dark in the back garden. She managed to stay on the path that led to the yard gate, from where she could again see the barn. A light glimmered from the stable.

She pushed through the gate and went swiftly up the yard, thankful that the bunkhouse door was closed. She did not want to attract the attention of the men there. They were new hands Ray had recently put on the payroll without a word of explanation to her. She only knew that the old timers had disappeared and guessed that Ray must have discharged them. She did not like the new riders. Border scum, her father would have called them. He would have kicked them off the ranch.

Ray heard her quick step and peered at her from the stall where he was saddling his bay horse. "What do you want?" He stepped into the runway, and even in that dim lantern light she could see that he had been drinking.

Janet studied him for a moment, lowered her gaze pointedly to his bandaged hand. “It wasn’t an accident,” she said. “Why have you lied about it, Ray?”

“Who’s saying it wasn’t an accident?” His tone was sullen.

“The doctor says the wound wasn’t made by a bullet from a .45 gun, and your gun is a .45 Colt.”

“A lot Doc. Bralen knows about guns,” sneered her stepbrother. “He was so drunk he could hardly get a bandage on me.”

Janet shook her head. She was remembering the doctor’s skillful removal of the bullet from Red O’Malley’s shoulder. “He wasn’t drunk last night, and it was last night he treated your wound.”

Ray scowled, teetered on his high heels. “Well—what about it? I don’t care a damn what you and the doc think.”

“I’m thinking a lot of things,” Janet retorted. “I’m thinking it is very queer about Red. *That* shooting was no accident.”

He was silent, his expression uneasy, and, looking at him, Janet felt her vague suspicion had become a sickening conviction.

“You were trying to kill Buck Salten,” she accused. “You took a shot at him through the screen and nearly killed Red instead.”

"You're crazy," he muttered.

"You don't deny it," she persisted. "You hate Buck and you tried to kill him."

An angry smile twisted his lips. "I hate Buck, and that's no lie, but I sure wasn't gunning for him last night."

She changed the subject. "I don't like these new men you've put on the payroll. Father wouldn't have allowed such trash to set foot on the ranch."

"Rick doesn't have anything more to say about it," Ray told her with another hard smile. "He's dead."

"*I* have something to say about it," flared the girl. "Father's will left Diamond D to me. I'm the boss now."

"Like hell you are," sneered her stepbrother. "Ab Matoon is the *real* owner of this ranch—or will be, quick as he calls in the mortgage. Ab has put me in charge, and I'm doing the hiring and the firing."

She looked at him steadily. "You know the mortgage is a forgery—a fraud. I don't trust you any more, Ray."

He said roughly, "Get out of here. I'm not wasting time with talk." He swung away, snatched the tie-rope, and backed the horse from the stall.

Janet held her ground, refused to let him pass. "You and Matoon are in this wicked business together." Her voice broke. "I've been a fool, trying to think the best of you."

His face was ugly now. "Get out of here," he repeated.

She stood there, rigid, defiant. "Father knew you were no good, and so does Buck Salten. I should have listened to Buck."

"It was Buck who killed your dad," gibed Ray. "I'll prove it on him."

The hint of malicious mirth in his drink-inflamed eyes sent a shiver through her. She said in a low, horrified voice, "You know the murderer's name, Ray, and you know it isn't Buck Salten." Her hand lifted in a tragic gesture. "It makes me sick even to guess, but I know now that you hated my father. I'm asking Buck to come back on the job. *He'll* know what to do."

He took a step towards her, and, frightened by the ugly look on his face, she dodged his outstretched hand and turned to run into the yard. Her foot slipped on the straw, and she felt herself falling, felt a dizzying pain as her head hit hard against a stall post. She knew nothing more.

Her stepbrother bent over her, saw that she was unconscious. He straightened up, continued to gaze at her, eyes narrowed thoughtfully. Something like a grin touched the harsh set of his lips. He stooped again and gathered the senseless girl into his arms.

Chapter 14

Moonlight was flooding over the mountains when Mark and Buck rode into the ranch yard. The big barn loomed dark and silent in the ghostly mist. A lone horse nickered softly from the corral.

They reined to a standstill and gazed across the yard at the sprawling bulk of the ranch house under the shadowing trees. Lights still burned there, and in the long bunkhouse to the left of them, near a windmill silhouetted against a starlit sky.

"It's too quiet," Mark said, his tone uneasy. He had always been sensitive to his surroundings, and the stillness seemed ominous, aroused vague fears in him.

Buck nodded, his face grim. "Things is going to hell fast," he muttered. His look shifted to the bunkhouse, and his frown deepened. "Like as not Ray is over there playing poker with them renegades he's put on the payroll. Hope he'll stay there until we get done with your business here."

"I'd just as soon meet him," Mark said.

"He'd like to see you and me layin' stiff and cold in the brush some place," Buck told him. "I had a look at those fellers he hired, and they're killin' gents. Ray'll jump at the chance to start their guns smokin' at us."

Mark gazed thoughtfully at the bunkhouse

lights. He was thinking that this remote ranch was indeed a dangerous place for a lone young girl. He was glad he had come, and more than ever resolved to destroy the sinister forces that had flung so black a shadow over Diamond D and even threatened the life of Janet Dunbar herself. The girl was in very real peril, and it was up to him to do something about it.

Buck broke into his somber reflections. "I reckon the broncs could do with a feed before we head back to town." He slid from his saddle and led his horse into the stable.

Mark followed, and they stalled the horses, removed bridles, loosened saddle girths, and shook hay down into the mangers. The horses had already been watered when crossing the creek below the barn, and there was no need to go to the trough near the bunkhouse, risk letting their presence be known to the men there.

There were other horses in some of the stalls. Buck moved cautiously along the dark runway behind them to the rear door. He slid the draw-bar back and returned to Mark.

"We might want to get away from here fast," he explained. "We could head across the horse pasture and take these broncs standin' here along with us."

"If it comes to that Janet is going too," Mark said. "We're not leaving her here alone again."

"That's the shoutin' truth." A hint of self-reproach touched Buck's voice. "I shouldn't have left her the way I done. It made me see red this evenin' when I seen them border wolves that Ray has got loafin' around here. I'm sure glad I met you on the trail, Mark. It ain't right to leave Janet alone on this ranch."

He led the way down the yard, careful to hug the shadows of the fence. Buck said softly, "There's a hole here." He ducked under a rail, crawled through a tall, ragged tamarisk hedge. Mark followed close on his heels, saw they were in the back garden, with the kitchen porch only a few yards away.

They went up the porch steps quietly. The door was open, and Buck peered for a moment through the screen into the lighted kitchen. Mark looked over his shoulder, glimpsed an elderly Mexican woman seated in a chair, her face bent absorbedly over something she was carefully mending with needle and thread.

Buck spoke softly. "Hello, Juana."

Her head lifted, and she fastened startled eyes on them. "Señor Buck! You come back queek!" She broke off, continued to gaze at him, a hint of alarm shadowing her face. "W'at ees wr-rong to breeng you back?" Her look went briefly to Mark. "Who ees thees man?"

Buck said abruptly, "Where's Janet? I'm wanting to see her." And then, remembering, "Mark Destin is a friend of mine."

Juana got slowly out of her chair, and Mark recognized the shirt in her hands—the one that he had traded to Red O'Malley. She had been mending the ragged tear made by the bullet. The sight of it made him wince.

"You look like you much worry, Señor Buck." Her voice was sharp with apprehension. "W'at ees wr-rong that you come for see the *señorita*?"

"We've got to see her in a hurry, Juana. Where is she?"

"She upstairs in her room." Juana shook her head. "She very tired w'en she come 'ome weeth poor Red. I make her lie down for good sleep."

"You tell her that Mark and I want to see her." Impatience touched Buck's voice. "Hurry, Juana! It's important!"

Juana hesitated, her face troubled. She said worriedly, "Too bad to wake her, but I weel tell her you 'ave come back for see her." She folded the shirt over a chairback and reluctantly left the room.

They stood there, listening to her slow ascent of the stairs. No other sound broke the stillness, and Mark was again conscious of an unpleasant stirring in him. Something was wrong here.

The footfalls upstairs hushed, and after a moment the silence was broken by a frightened exclamation, and now they heard the quick pad of Juana's sandaled feet hurriedly descending the stairs.

She halted in the doorway, breathless, gazed at them wildly. "She—she ees not in her room!" Her voice was frantic. "The bed no 'ave been slept on. *Ay de mí*! Somet'ing terrible 'ave 'appen' to my *señorita*!"

Buck looked like a man turned to stone. He could only stare at her helplessly.

"Perhaps she is with Red," suggested Mark.

Juana gestured despairingly. "No, no—she not weeth Red. She went upstairs. She no come down again. I would 'ave 'eard. *Madre de Dios*! I am much frightened for her."

Buck came out of his trance, pushed past her, and ran down the hall. Mark and Juana followed, overtook him in Red's room. They heard Red's startled voice from the darkness.

"It's me," reassured Buck. It was plain that he was making an effort to keep calm. He looked back at Juana. "Give us a light."

She felt her way to the table and lit a lamp. Red gazed at them from his pillow. "What's the excitement—bustin' in on me so sudden?" He broke off, his look fastened hard on Juana. "What's got you so scared, Juana? You're shakin' somethin' awful."

"You talk like you got a fever," interrupted Buck. He forced a sickly grin. "Has Janet been in here recent?"

Red shook his head, eyed him suspiciously. "She ain't been in since before Juana fetched me my soup." His voice sharpened. "What for you askin' if she was *here?*"

Buck hesitated, refused to meet the young cowboy's look. "I reckon she's out in the yard some place." He turned on his heel, went swiftly into the hall. Juana fled after him, wiping at her eyes with her apron.

Mark stood for a moment, his warm smile on the disturbed cowboy. "Take it easy with that shoulder," he said. "Doc. Bralen won't want you working up a fever."

"You ain't foolin' me, Mark," grumbled Red. He frowned. "Somethin' has got all of you awful scared." He paused, the worry deepening in his eyes. "Buck left for town two-three hours ago, and now he's back, and from the look on his face I sure smell plenty trouble."

"Listen—" Mark spoke firmly. "If there's trouble here I'm riding with Buck. Don't you worry, Red. You stay put and get that shoulder in good shape again." He threw the cowboy a reassuring grin and went swiftly into the hall.

He found Buck and Juana in the kitchen. The Mexican woman had collapsed in a chair, was weeping softly into her apron. Buck turned in a grim look at Mark.

"She's gone to pieces," he muttered. "I cain't make any sense of her talk."

Mark went to the woman, put a hand gently on her shoulder. "Listen, Juana—" There was kindliness, yet a quality of hardness, in his voice that seemed to steady her. Her face lifted.

"*Sí, señor.*"

"Tell us all that you know about your *señorita*, since she came home. Did she mention going any place?"

Juana dabbed at her eyes, shook her head. "I know *not'ing,*" she wailed. "She go upstairs for 'ave sleep. I no see her anymore."

The two men exchanged dismayed looks, and after a moment Mark spoke again. "Where is Ray Wellerton?"

"Señor Ray not here. He say he go to La Cruz." Juana lifted an expressive shoulder. "I not know if he tell the truth about where he go." Her tone indicated distaste for Janet's stepbrother.

The cigarette Buck was shaping dropped from his fingers. He asked harshly, "How long has Ray been gone?"

"He gone long time now. Hour—maybe more."

"Did he talk to the *señorita* before he left?" asked Mark.

Juana shook her head. "Señor Ray come in and ask for *señorita*. I tell him she upstairs for 'ave sleep. He go upstairs and soon he come back to kitchen. He say *señorita* still sound asleep and he no like to wake her."

"Looks like she was in her room an hour or so ago," Buck said in a puzzled voice. "Sure is mighty queer she'd go off and not leave word."

"Is there anything else you can remember about Ray?" queried Mark. "Did he say why he was going to La Cruz?"

"He no say—" Juana paused, eyes widening with sudden recollection. "He 'ave his saddle-bag weeth him w'en he come downstairs," she added.

Buck said grimly, "We're wastin' time. I reckon our next move is a talk with them fellers over to the bunkhouse."

Mark nodded, his expression thoughtful. "It might be a good idea to have a look in the barn first, find out if her horse is gone—or the buckboard." He paused. "Juana, you go up to her room and have a look around, see if any of her clothes are missing. She may have gone off in a hurry without telling you—thinking she would be back soon."

The woman left the room, and their impatience made the few minutes of waiting seem interminable. Buck fidgeted, fingered the butt of his holstered gun.

"We're wastin' time," he repeated.

"I don't think so." Mark spoke quietly. He was the cooler of the two in this moment of crisis. "She was last known to be in her bedroom. We must start from there."

"She wouldn't have gone off and leave no word," argued Buck. "Something's awful wrong—" His voice cracked. "I'm half crazy!"

"There's a chance she was worried about Mrs. Benton and went to see her," Mark suggested.

"She'd have left word," insisted Buck.

Juana hurried into the kitchen, a look of bewilderment on her face. "Her ranch clothes, her hat, her boots, not in room—"

"I reckon she was wearin' 'em when she went off," interrupted Buck.

"*Sí.*" Juana nodded, added in a puzzled tone, "Her pink muslin dress gone too. I no un'erstan' why she take her pink dress!"

The two men gazed at her stupidly, and after a moment Mark broke the silence. "Her pink dress you say?"

"*Sí, señor.* I no un'erstan' why she take it."

Mark said in a tight voice to Buck, "All right—let's go."

He took a quick step towards the door, halted, gazed back at the Mexican woman. "Stay close to Red, Juana."

"*Sí, señor.*"

"Have you a gun?" he asked.

She nodded. "I can use a gun good."

Her matter-of-factness pleased Mark. He smiled at her. "If anything seems wrong lock yourself up in Red's room. Use the gun on any man who tries to get in."

"*Sí, señor.*" Juana followed them to the door, closed it behind them, and locked it. She stood for a moment, listening to the quick tread of their feet fading into the night, then, with a hasty dab at her eyes, she hurried into the hall.

Instinctively the two friends slowed their pace as they reached the yard gate. The moon was well up now, and they had no wish to draw the attention of the occupants of the bunkhouse. Lamplight still glowed from the windows there, and they could hear the low murmur of voices as they drifted past, soundless as ghosts.

They reached the barn, and darkness hid them again. Mark heard Buck's low whisper, "The buckboard ain't in the yard."

"Can you tell what horses are gone?" Mark asked. "It's awfully dark in here."

"Ain't needing a light to make out what horses are in the stalls." Buck's feet made soft rustles in the straw as he went from stall to stall. Mark waited, and his hand touched something soft that clung to the end-post of the empty stall near the door. Unconsciously his fingers closed over it, and it came free in his hand. It felt like a piece of cloth.

Buck returned from his inspection of the stalls. "Ray's bronc is gone," he reported, "and the bay team. Not the team Janet was using today."

Mark absorbed the information. It did not offer much to explain the girl's disappearance, except that, either willingly or unwillingly, she had gone off in the buckboard. He said as much to Buck.

"I reckon that's the answer," agreed Buck.

"She wouldn't be riding Ray's bronc. She would have used her own mare. Anyway, her saddle is hangin' back there on the peg."

Mark became conscious of the bit of flimsy cloth in his fingers, and suddenly a cold prickle ran through him. He held the cloth close to his eyes. It was too dark to see what it was. Not a piece of sack or canvas, but something light and dainty that did not belong in this stable.

He said softly, "I wish we had a light."

"What for you want a light?" asked Buck.

"I found something sticking to the post here," Mark told him. "It feels like a piece torn from a dress."

"Let's crowd back in the stall," suggested Buck. "I'll strike a match so we can take a quick look."

They pressed close to the manger, and Mark held the piece of cloth ready. A sulfur match in Buck's fingers hissed, flickered into a tiny flame, enough to show that Mark's find was a torn strip of pink muslin.

They stood there in the darkness, rigid, something of the truth taking vague shape in their minds. Buck said, huskily, "It looks like she run into trouble here—got knocked against the post."

"It's our first clue, all right," agreed Mark. He felt sick, forced himself to keep his mind cool. "It doesn't make good sense," he went on thoughtfully. "Juana said the pink dress was missing, but so are her riding clothes, and boots and hat. This bit of muslin indicates that she was wearing her pink dress when she was here in the barn. I'd like to know what became of her other clothes."

"I'm cravin' a talk with them fellers in the bunkhouse." Buck was breathing hard. "I'm gettin' my hands on 'em—make 'em tell what's been going on here."

Mark's voice held him back. "Just a moment, Buck. Let me think this out."

"There ain't nothin' more we *can* think out," fumed the older man.

"I'm not so sure." Excitement touched Mark's voice. "Here's the story as I begin to see it. Janet was wearing her pink dress when she came to the barn, perhaps to have a talk with her stepbrother. Something happened—and she did not get back to the house. Juana told us that Ray was in the house asking for her, went upstairs, and came down with his filled saddlebag."

A stifled groan from Buck interrupted him. "I'll kill him if he has harmed her!"

"We've got to hope that he has not," Mark said, his voice unsteady. "Let me finish, Buck. As I see it, Ray pretended to Juana that Janet was still asleep in her room. He went in, packed up her ranch clothes, carried them off in his bag, telling Juana that he was going to La Cruz."

There was a momentary silence, broken by Buck. "You figger he has taken her off some place, huh?"

"Yes," Mark said grimly. "It's the only answer to this bit of torn dress." He slid his gun from its holster. "Come on, Buck. It's time now for us to have a talk with those men in the bunkhouse."

They moved cautiously, careful to give no warning of their approach, and in a few moments were peering through one of the windows. Mark saw two men seated at a table, cards in their hands, a whisky bottle between them. A third man lay on a bunk, listlessly turning the pages of a dog-eared mail-order catalogue.

Guns ready, they edged stealthily to the door. Buck noiselessly turned the knob, kicked the door open.

"Keep awful still, fellers." His gun menaced the cardplayers at the table. The third man, on the bunk, muttered a startled oath, made a frantic grab at the gun in the belt that dangled across a stool within arm's reach.

"Don't try it," warned Mark. He slid past Buck, his .45 leveled at the man. "Get out of that bunk, and keep your hands up."

The man sullenly obeyed, joined his companions now on their feet. Mark snatched the gun belt from the stool and tossed it into a corner. He saw the gun-laden belts of the cardplayers, lying on a bench near the table. He added them to the one in the corner.

Buck studied the trio of scowling faces. "Where's the other feller?" he asked.

"Pima went off with the boss some place," answered the man Mark had routed out of the bunk. His legs were too short for his bull-shouldered body, and he had sandy hair and pale unwinking eyes set in a flat face badly in need of a shave. "Who the hell are you?"

"I'm asking the questions," Buck told him. "You fellers do the answerin'—and no back talk."

"Go ahaid," invited the dwarfish man, with an insolent grin. "I've got you pegged now. You're Buck Salten."

"That's right." Buck waggled the gun at him. "I'm wanting to know where they took the girl."

"Don't know nothin' about the girl," answered the man.

"I'm repeatin' the question." Buck's voice was brittle. "I'm killin' you now if you don't tell me about what's happened to the girl." His gun lifted. "One of you talk, and talk fast."

"He sure means business, Stumpy," muttered one of the other men. He was as long and lean as Stumpy was short and heavy. He fixed frightened eyes on the menacing gun. "Ray went off with her in the buckboard."

"How do you know she went with him in the buckboard?" asked Mark.

"Seen her settin' there in the seat when they drove out of the yard," answered the lean man.

"Was Pima with them—in the buckboard?" Mark watched their faces intently as he asked the question. The sly look that Stumpy flickered at his companions did not escape him.

The lean man hesitated the merest instant, shook his head. "No. Pima didn't go with 'em."

"Where did Pima go?" persisted Mark. He stared hard at the bull-shouldered Stumpy. "You said that Pima went off some place. Where did he go?"

"I heard the boss tell him to head for the Borrego Creek camp. Cain't swear that he did, me not trailin' him." Again the insolent grin flickered across Stumpy's sunburned face. "You can ask questions till hell freezes, and there ain't no more answers."

Buck said curtly, "Turn around and rub your noses against the wall."

The three men reluctantly obeyed, pressed close to the wall, and Buck said to Mark, "Get a rope over their hands." He gestured at a coiled lariat hanging on a Peg.

Mark reached for the rope, cut off several lengths, and quickly tied the prisoners' hands behind their backs. Stumpy's arms were abnormally long, and there was something repulsive about the huge, sausage-like fingers. The powerful, dwarfish man was decidedly the most dangerous of the trio, and he drew the knots extra tight over the thick wrists.

"All right, fellers," Buck said. "You can turn around again."

Stumpy's eyes were pits of hate. "The boss will sure take your skelp for this business," he croaked. "He'll feed you to the buzzards."

"I'm the boss now," Buck told him with a hard smile. "I'm running Diamond D again, and my first job is to fire you off the payroll."

The prisoners gazed at him stupidly, and the lean man shook his head in disbelief. "You cain't do this to us. Ray Wellerton's the boss here."

"You're awful wrong," Buck said frostily.

"All right." Stumpy's mouth twisted in a crafty grin. "If we're fired give us our time and we'll fork saddle away from here."

"You're not forking saddle for any place," Buck told him. "I'm keeping you hombres in a safe place, and if any harm has come to Janet Dunbar I'm swinging the bunch of you from the nearest tree." He motioned them out to the yard.

"What are you going to do with them?" Mark asked as Buck prodded the prisoners across the moonlit yard.

Buck gestured at a low adobe building, a dark shape under clustering chinaberry trees. "The old granary will make a good calaboose," he said. "Walls three foot thick, and no windows—only six-inch ventilators. No chance for 'em to bust out of *that* place."

The heavy, iron-strapped door was unlocked. Mark swung it open, and Buck pushed the prisoners into the darkness. Stumpy swore, tried to resist. He was as powerful as a bull and only ceased his struggle when Buck tapped him on the head with the barrel of his gun.

Mark closed the door, snapped the heavy padlock, and handed Buck the key. "We haven't learned much," he said gloomily.

"We've got to get help," Buck muttered. "It's going to be a tough job, pickin' up Janet's trail."

Mark nodded, his expression thoughtful. "Stumpy lied when he said Pima had ridden for the Borrego Creek camp."

Buck pocketed the key. "How come you think he's lying?" he asked worriedly.

"Pima wouldn't be riding Ray Wellerton's horse," Mark pointed out. "It's my guess that it was Pima who drove off with the buckboard and Janet. Ray's horse is missing, and that means that Ray has likely headed for La Cruz for a talk with Matoon."

"Sounds like you guessed it," Buck admitted. His tone was dejected, hopeless. "This thing sure has me buffaloed."

"It's not much use for us to start a search blind . . ." Mark was thinking aloud. "I don't know this country," he added. "One trail looks like another to me."

"We got to get help," Buck repeated.

They gazed at each other, their minds desperately searching for some solution of the problem. Mark broke the silence.

"Plácido Romero," he exclaimed. "Plácido is the answer, Buck."

"He sure is!" Relief briskened Buck's voice. "Plácido will come on the jump if we can get word to him. Bring a bunch of his Mex riders with him, too. I reckon one of us must fork saddle for town."

Mark nodded, said simply, "I'll need a fresh horse if you can pick one out for me."

Buck turned on his heel, silently led the way back to the barn.

Chapter 15

The mountains made a black wall under the moon. Janet was puzzled. They were not the same mountains she could see from her bedroom window. She wondered vaguely if she had somehow managed to go to sleep in her father's room that overlooked the western hills. She had often sat with him there at the window and watched the moon lift above the horizon. She closed her eyes. It hurt her head to think, and her arms and legs felt oddly numb.

Awareness of her surroundings became more acute, and suddenly she realized she was in the back seat of a buckboard. She heard the clatter of shod hoofs, the grind of wheels—felt the jolt and sway of a fast-moving vehicle. She tried to straighten up, found that her wrists were tied to the seat rail. Terror surged through her.

Her frightened exclamation drew the attention of the driver. His head turned in a brief look. She failed to recognize the sharp profile distinct against the moonlight. No word came from him, and she found herself again staring at the back of his head. She wondered hysterically if it were all just an ugly nightmare. The jolting buckboard, the cords numbing her wrists and ankles, were painful proof positive that she was wide awake;

and now she was remembering the scene in the stable . . . her stepbrother's murderous expression when she had turned to run from his reaching hands.

Janet lay very still, tried to fill in the gap between that last conscious moment in the barn and her awakening in the buckboard. She could remember nothing, could only use her imagination as to what must have happened. She had been too rash, letting Ray know that she suspected him. She had as good as accused him of shooting Red O'Malley, believing him to be Mark Destin. An attempt at cold-blooded murder. She had also charged him with conspiring with Ab Matoon to steal her ranch, warned him that his day at Diamond D was done and that she was putting Buck Salten back on the job as foreman.

Another and more dreadful thought drew a shiver from Janet. Ray Wellerton had very good cause to fear her—decide that while she lived his own life was in deadly peril. She had let him know that she suspected him of the murder of her father. If her suspicion was true Ray would not hesitate at a second murder to conceal his terrible secret.

Horror seeped through her as she gazed at the dark shape of the driver. It was all too plain that her suspicion was true. Ray Wellerton was a murderer—this thing that was happening to her was proof she could not doubt. She was being hurried away to some remote spot far from the ranch. Nobody would know where to look for her. Ray would concoct a plausible story to satisfy the curious—arrange to make her death appear an accident if the trail was ever picked up.

She wanted to scream, realized she must save her strength, hold on to her sanity. At least she was still alive, and while life was in her there was always a fighting chance.

She found courage for speech. "Who are you, and where are you taking me?" Her voice sounded thin above the rattling of the wheels.

The driver's head turned in another look; and after a moment he reined the team to a standstill, wrapped the lines over the brake, and climbed from his seat.

He came around to the side of the buckboard, peered at her over the wheels. "My name is Pima, ma'am." His voice was toneless, devoid of expression. "Are you feelin' bad?"

"What do you think?" She flung the words at him. "Untie these ropes!"

The man tipped his hat back, slowly drew tobacco pouch and papers from a pocket. "Sorry, ma'am. I ain't takin' them ropes off—not yet. The boss was feared you might hurt yourself unless you was tied safe in the seat."

Janet recognized him now. One of the new men Ray had put on the payroll. He had the look of a half-breed, Mexican or Indian—perhaps a little of both. She gazed at him wildly, tried to find something in him that might give her a shred of hope, could see only callous indifference and cruelty in the heavy-featured face.

She asked desperately, "You know who I am, don't you?"

"Sure do." Pima lit the cigarette, gave her a faint grin. "The boss says you're loco."

"*I'm* your boss—the owner of Diamond D. How dare you do this to me?"

"Well, ma'am, you claimin' to be boss don't make it so." The man's tone was touched with malicious amusement. "Ray figgered you was out of your haid, which is why I'm takin' you to a place where you can rest up and folks not know you're havin' a crazy spell."

Janet looked at him, appalled. "You mean that my stepbrother plans to have me killed." It was a statement rather than a question, and for the first time she detected a hint of uneasiness in his manner.

"Ray said you'd make crazy talk." He turned away with an impatient gesture.

Janet wanted to do all she possibly could to delay the journey to her unknown destination. She called out frantically, "I'm shivering with cold! This dress is so thin!"

Pima hesitated, came back reluctantly, reached an arm over the wheels, and picked up a blanket from the buckboard floor. He threw it over her, uncovering a saddlebag she recognized as Ray's.

She asked, curious, "What is the bag for? Is my stepbrother joining us?"

Pima glanced at the bag. "It's got some clothes the boss sent along for you." He left her, climbed into his seat, and in another moment they were again following the rough road through the mesquite.

Janet stared at the shapeless bag at her feet, conscious of a sudden if faint hope. Ray would not have sent extra clothes along if murder were in his mind. She tried to find comfort in the thought.

The buckboard struck a series of deep chuck-holes that bounced and swayed her in the seat. The bag bounced and slid too, toppled across her feet. One of the straps had worked loose from its buckle, and she saw the heel of a boot squeeze through the opening. Another series of violent bumps spilled more things that she recognized even in that tricky moonlight—the workaday clothes she usually wore on ranch business, linen blouse and short skirt. Her Stetson hat was there, too. She could see its white brim, mashed under the boot. She had left the things lying around in the bedroom, when changing into the fresh muslin dress. Ray must have hastily stuffed them into the bag.

Fear again laid cold fingers on her. Only some evil purpose could have made Ray pack her things in his own bag. There were better bags for her clothes in the closet. He had used his own bag to keep Juana from suspecting anything wrong. Juana would have been curious if she had seen him carrying off one of the *señorita*'s bags. She might have gone up to the bedroom to investigate.

It was not the chill of the night wind that made Janet shiver. She was divining the significance of that hurriedly crammed bag. Sooner or later Juana would discover that she was not in the house. It was Ray's scheme to have her believe that some emergency ranch business had called Janet away. The missing buckboard and team would confirm such an impression. She wondered dully if Juana would notice the absence of the pink muslin dress. Juana would be puzzled, perhaps realize that something was wrong.

The road dipped into a wide, sandy wash. The wheels sank deep, slowed the horses to a walk. Janet looked despairingly from right to left. If it were not for the cords that held her prisoner she could jump out, quickly lose herself in the thick-growing willows.

She tugged futilely at the binding cords. It was no use. She lay limp in the seat. It seemed that she was indeed doomed.

They pulled out of the dry wash, and the road began to wind between low hills—bleak, barren upthrusts of rock. Janet straightened in the seat. There was something familiar about these desolate hills. She had seen them before. She racked her memory. The occasion had been years earlier—a trip with her father to the notorious Sinks country. Her heart skipped a beat. She knew now that Pima was taking her to the land of lawless men.

For long moments she sat rigid, resolutely forced her mind to steadiness. All hope would be gone, once she reached her journey's end. She must think coolly and fast, use her wits, and the courage that was her heritage. She could not afford to let the dark face of danger weaken her resistance. Her one remaining chance for life was *escape.*

She tugged again at the cords that tied her wrists to the seat rails on either side of her, felt her fingers close over the smooth, cold iron, and she suddenly remembered something. The screw-nut that bolted one of them to the back of the seat had fallen off. She had forgotten to have it replaced.

She considered the possibilities carefully. It would not be easy to loosen the rail without attracting Pima's attention. She studied the slouching, dark shape. He seemed almost half asleep, apparently confident of her inability to escape. He never even troubled himself to give her an occasional glance.

Reassured, she pressed an elbow firmly against

the rail, felt it give. She waited a moment, tried again, and suddenly the socket slipped off the bolt. She kept very still for another long moment, her gaze on the man in front of her, wondering if he had heard the slight screech of metal. Apparently the sound had been covered by the rattle and creak of the swaying buckboard.

She pushed gently on the loosened rail until it swung away from the seat, then cautiously, inch by inch, she slid her bound wrist along the smooth iron, felt wrist and rope slip off the end.

She was watching Pima intently, saw that he remained unsuspecting. The cord was still knotted round her wrist, but the hand was free now, and swiftly, noiselessly, she replaced the rail socket over the bolt.

Again she paused. Her next move would be more easily noticed if Pima chanced to look round. Her heart pounding, she reached her free right hand across to the opposite rail, set to work on the knots that bound her left wrist. They were tight knots, and it took several moments to loosen them and slip the cord off. The effort and suspense left her weak. She relaxed against the cushioned back, kept both hands outstretched on either rail. A chance look now from Pima would not discover anything amiss. In fact, it would need more than a casual glance to notice that anything was wrong with his prisoner. Clouds had massed above the mountains, closed over the moon. She was grateful for the welcome darkness.

Steadiness returned, the tremble left her fingers. Using her left hand, she swiftly loosened the knotted cord from her right wrist and slipped it off. Both hands were free now, but untying her ankles offered a far more difficult problem. She would have to bend over to reach the knots, and the risk daunted her for a moment. She steeled herself to make the attempt. She had gone too far to hesitate now.

It was fortunate she had waited those few seconds. Pima's head turned in a look at her. To all appearances her wrists were still bound to the side rails.

Janet dared a bold move. She said pleadingly, "Won't you please untie me? These cords hurt." She knew he would refuse the request. She was right.

"Ain't takin' them cords off till we get to where we're goin'." His voice was unexpectedly surly, and she sensed an impatience in him to reach their destination and be finished with the job. "Ain't wantin' no more yelps from you, savvy?" He returned his attention to the road ahead.

His threatening manner spurred her to swift action. She bent over, fingers of both hands working on the cord round her ankles. She slipped them off and leaned back in the seat, hands again on the side rails. For the moment she had done all that seemed possible. She could only wait—and pray.

The moon was completely lost behind the spreading clouds, and the darkness seemed to worry Pima. He held the team down to a walk, leaned forward in his seat, gaze intent on the road. The buckboard lurched and swayed over deep, storm-washed ruts. Janet held herself steady against the jolts, every nerve tense for the chance she prayed would come.

She sat very still, ears alert for sounds that might tell her of the nature of the country. It was impossible to see a thing in that darkness. A jump from the slow-moving buckboard could send her hurtling over a cliff. The thought held her impatience in check. She wanted a fighting chance when the right moment came.

She saw Pima's crouched frame relax, heard the faster beat of the horses' hoofs, and knew they were through the pass and that the road was leveling down to open country again. The sharp tang of sagebrush came to her—pungent, exciting. Given a chance, she could quickly lose herself in that vast expanse of chaparral. She prayed for a few moments of moonlight. When she made the leap she must be sure that her flight would carry her deep into the concealing bushes.

The wheels slowed—she heard the grind of sand and guessed they had reached another dry wash. She continued to wait, gaze frantically probing the darkness on either side, and to her relief the moon suddenly broke through the clouds, gave her a brief glimpse of thick growing desert shrubs. A willow thicket, she guessed, and huge, sprawling mesquite trees. Darkness came blanketing down again, but she had had the moment for which she prayed.

The sand dragged at the buckboard wheels—they seemed hardly to move. Jane tried to nerve herself for the leap, could not force her legs to obey her will. The thought of failure terrified her. She would not have a second chance.

She gazed despairingly at the hulking shape of the man in the front seat, caught the pale glimmer of his face peering back at her. Evidently satisfied that his prisoner was still secure, Pima drew a flask from his pocket, pulled the cork, and tilted the bottle to his lips. The cork slipped from his fingers and dropped to the floor. He muttered angrily and bent over to search for it.

Janet realized that her chance had come. She turned in the seat and swung lithely over the back, felt her feet dig into sand. In another moment she was alone, stumbling through the darkness.

Sharp thorns clawed at her thin dress. She gave them no heed, pushed frantically through the cruel tangle. Too late she realized that her blind flight had carried her into a dense growth of cat's-claw.

She reached a little clearing in the bushes,

halted, breathless. No sound touched her ears. The deep stillness frightened her. Pima had discovered her escape and had halted the team.

She cowered there. The least sound would draw his attention. She prayed again that the moon would remain hidden under the clouds.

His voice broke through the fearsome silence, his words distinct, profane, promising shocking things. She heard the harsh crackle of bushes under his running feet. She stood motionless, a rabbit hiding from a furiously questing hound.

The sounds faded off to the right. Relief surged through her. Pima had decided that she would not have dared the horrors of the clawing tangle of cat's-claw. He was pushing the search into the willow brakes.

Her legs and arms were badly scratched, her dress torn to shreds, but she was content. The price was not too high. She had made her escape against insurmountable odds and was humbly thankful for the answer to her prayer that had so strangely recalled the memory of the vulnerable bolt. Escape would have been impossible if she had not remembered that lost screw-nut.

It was suddenly very still there, and new fears sent cold prickles down Janet's spine. Pima had abandoned his noisy search and was making a silent stalk through the chaparral. She had left pieces of her dress clinging to the cat's-claw. Once he picked up the trail he would swiftly overtake her. Any moment might find him leaping at her from the darkness.

She found an opening in the tangled growth, moved stealthily deeper into the scrub, pausing every few moments to listen for some betraying sound from her pursuer. Sharp thorns clawed again at her dress, and the sound of tearing cloth horrified her. She halted, tried to pull the skirt free. It was no use—the barbed thorns clung with fiendish persistence, and she had to cautiously rip off nearly half the remaining tatters of the dress. Alert now for each reaching, treacherous branch she continued her stealthy progress. Dry thorns underfoot pierced the thin soles of her slippers. She longed for the boots in Ray's saddlebag—the serviceable ranch clothes.

A gunshot startled her ears, held her rigid. Pima must have imagined he had seen her, was trying to make a quick finish of the business.

A second shot shattered the night's stillness; a third, a fourth crashing report followed. Janet knew that the last two shots were from a heavier gun. She was familiar with guns, and the third and fourth shots were unmistakably the bark of a Colt .45 revolver.

She was out of the cat's-claw now and crouched low under a concealing gnarled mesquite. She waited for some sound that might explain the mystery of the two guns. She could only surmise that Pima's search through the chaparral had brought him in contact with some third person.

It seemed a good idea to keep going as fast as she safely could while Pima was involved with the mysterious owner of the .45 revolver. He would be a very puzzled man and wondering how the girl who had escaped from him had managed to get possession of a gun.

She stole quietly towards the next mesquite. It was so dark she could hardly see where to place her feet, was in terror of a twig crackling underfoot.

No more shots disturbed the silence of the night. She would have liked some sound that would warn her. The thought of bumping into one of the unseen men kept her frayed nerves on edge.

She found her feet sinking in sand, realized with sickening dismay that she had made a complete circle and was back on the road. She halted, gazed wildly at the dark bulk that she knew was the buckboard.

Any moment might bring Pima, and she forced herself to stumble towards the buckboard, where she could hide from immediate discovery. It would be the last place he would think of looking for her.

The deep silence continued, broken only by an occasional restless movement of the horses. She managed a closer look, saw that Pima had tied the team to a bush. She wondered if she dare loosen the tie-rope, jump into the buckboard, and drive away. She abandoned the idea. The soft sand of the dry wash made a fast getaway impossible. Pima, on foot, could easily overtake her—and he had a gun.

She leaned against the side of the buckboard, sick, bewildered, uncertain what next to do. The soles of her feet were smarting from the thorns that had pierced her slippers, and again she thought of the boots in the saddlebag, now within arm's reach. She wasted no time, aware of stealthily approaching footsteps.

The bag clutched in her arms, she backed away, careful to make no sound, sank to her knees behind a bush close to the roadside. After all, she could find no safer place for the moment. Pima supposed she was a long way from there by now.

The half-breed slunk up silent as a shadow, untied the horses, and climbed hastily into his seat. He was a bewildered and frightened man. The turn of events had unnerved him, and his one thought now was to put distance between himself and the unknown prowler in the chaparral. He had not expected any trouble recapturing his prisoner, had decided to use his gun on her at the first opportunity. The stealthy movement in the willow brakes had drawn his immediate fire. The answering gunshots, the vicious whine of bullets, shocked and terrified him. He could only guess that friends of the girl had picked up the trail.

They were welcome to her. He was not going to linger on the scene, try to argue the matter.

He kicked off the brake, and in another moment the buckboard vanished into the darkness. Relief surged through Janet, crouched behind the bush. She could hardly believe her senses. Something must have dreadfully frightened the half-breed to have sent him off in such panic-stricken haste.

She put her mind on her own immediate problem. Pima might recover from his fright and decide to return, continue the search. He was going to be surprised to find the saddlebag missing. She must lose no time getting away, and which direction to take had her guessing. She only knew that she must be somewhere in the Sinks. She could follow the road back, or else find shelter under a mesquite and wait for daylight. There were no stars, no moon, to give her an idea of the time—past midnight, she guessed. Pima had traveled fast, despite the rough road, and the several hours must have carried her some twenty miles from the ranch.

The thought appalled her. She ached all over from the jolting ride, and she became acutely aware of her smarting scratches. She gazed down at the bulging saddlebag. Now was as good a time as any to change from her tattered dress and torn slippers to the stout boots and ranch clothes. She put on the boots first, slipped out of the ruined muslin, and was soon clothed in the denim skirt and flannel blouse. She smoothed out the white Stetson and put it on. The change made her feel better, restored confidence in her ability to cope with anything that might come. She wished she had a gun.

From a long way off she could hear the rattle of wheels fading into the distance. The sound reassured her. Pima was still going, would probably not stop until he reached his destination.

A glow warmed Janet. Pima would arrive without his prisoner. Her courage and wits had defeated Ray Wellerton's purpose. She had made her escape against frightening odds.

The night was very still again, and very dark. She would have liked some moonlight now, dreaded again stumbling into more of the vicious cat's-claw. A coyote called from a nearby sandhill. She was familiar with coyotes, and the eerie yipping caused her no alarm. It was another sound that held her frozen with sudden terror behind the roadside bush.

She had almost forgotten the mysterious gunshots that had sent Pima scurrying away. Someone still lurked nearby in the chaparral—an armed man who might be fully as dangerous as Pima. Only men who lived beyond the law frequented the remote and savage wilderness of the Sinks.

Janet waited, hardly daring to draw a breath.

The faint crackle of brush came again—closer now, and again silence, broken only by the wild call of the coyote.

Janet's heart stood still. She was being stalked. Sooner or later the stalker would pick up the trail.

She resisted the impulse to run. It was too dark, and it was quite likely that the prowler would shoot. Quietly, careful to avoid crackling branches, she crept away, pausing every few steps to listen. No more sounds came to her. She surmised that the man was listening too. His caution indicated that he was wary of exposing himself to a possible shot.

The willow brakes closed round her, and, miraculously it seemed, the moon again appeared. The clouds were breaking, and now she could see her surroundings quite distinctly. Her cautious walk became almost a run.

The road was soon far behind. Janet had no idea of direction, only knew that the road was dangerous and that she must keep to the concealment of the willows—follow the wash deeper into the hills.

She halted frequently to listen and look. Once she thought she glimpsed a vague shape in the moonlit clearing behind her.

Janet did not wait for a second look, hurried on, tried to keep to the shadows as much as possible. It seemed to her that she had been stumbling and running for hours. Her legs ached, and she felt that there must soon be an end. Sheer physical exhaustion would defeat her, make her an easy victim to the unknown pursuer.

The wash began to climb, and the sand gave way to tumbled boulders and slippery shale that told her she had reached the mouth of a narrow canyon. She forced her lagging feet to the ascent, rounded a sharp bend, and came to an amazed standstill, gazed joyfully at the cabin less than a hundred yards away. A faint light showed there.

The crunch of bootheels down in the wash below aroused her, sent her into a stumbling run towards that beckoning light. Anything was better than the unknown terror behind. Her heart pounding, she almost fell against the door, beat on it with clenched fists. She dared one quick look over her shoulder, glimpsed a man's tall shape silhouetted against the moonlit wash below.

She heard a movement inside the cabin, and suddenly the door opened, framed a big-shouldered man, gun in hand. His grim expression changed to stark amazement. He said in a shocked, startled voice, "My God! *Janet!*"

She pushed past him, breathless. "Quick!" She motioned frantically at the door. "Close it! A man out there. He's been following me for miles!"

He closed the door, slid a heavy bar, stood gazing at her. The bewilderment and incredulity in his eyes were reflected in Janet's as she recognized him.

"Mr. *Benton!*" Her voice trembled. "Oh, I'm so thankful it is *you!*" Her knees gave way, and she sank on the floor at his feet, began to cry. "I—I can't help it," she sobbed. "It—it's a miracle!" She broke off, stared apprehensively at the door.

Benton too had heard the stealthy movement outside. He turned, blew out the single candle on the table. Janet got unsteadily to her feet, felt for him in the dark, stood close to him, heard his low whisper.

"Who is this man you say has been following you?" he asked.

"I don't know." Janet was frightened, horrified. She knew that he was a fugitive from men who sought his life. She had perhaps all unwittingly brought death to his doorstep. It was too much. Her heart sank.

Benton stood rigid, close to the door. The stealthy movements outside had hushed. He was completely bewildered by Janet Dunbar's mysterious arrival at his remote hideout cabin in the Sinks, and there was no time for questions.

A voice broke the stillness—hoarse, plaintive. "I seen you, Benton, when you opened the door for the girl."

It was a familiar voice, and Benton's fingers tightened over the gun in his hand. He called out harshly, "What do you want, Kinner?"

"I'm bleedin' to death," answered his former gaoler. "Let me in, Benton. I need help bad."

"You're lying," Benton accused. "It's a trick to get me back in your gaol."

"I ain't lyin'—" Kinner spoke huskily. "I'm awful sick."

"It's a trick," repeated Benton.

"I've quit workin' for Matoon," Kinner said. "The damn' skunk sent Cooner to dry-gulch me. I was faster—left him layin' in the brush for the buzzards and lit out for the Sinks like you done."

Benton thought it over. If Kinner were lying he could not afford to let him get away with the news of the hideout cabin. If he were not lying it would be safe to open the door and easy to overpower him.

He asked another question. "Why were you following Miss Dunbar?"

"Wasn't knowin' it was the Dunbar girl," answered Kinner. "I was down in the willows when a feller jumped me, shot me in my leg. I smoked my gun back at him and he went away fast—climbed into his buckboard and drove like hell up the road." Kinner was silent for a moment. "I ain't got it figgered how come Miss Dunbar was mixed up in it." His voice was feeble, hardly audible through the door. "I reckon she got away from the feller, and he was lookin' for her when he jumped me."

Benton heard Janet's low whisper. "He's telling the truth." She gave the ranchman a brief account of her horrifying experience—the escape from Pima.

She raised her voice for Kinner to hear outside the door. "Why did you follow me?" she asked.

"I figgered you was headed for some place where I could get help," Kinner replied. "You went so fast I couldn't catch up with you, my leg so lame."

"You could have called to me," Janet told him furiously. "You frightened me dreadfully."

"I was feared you'd take a shot at me if you got me located," Kinner explained. He groaned. "My gawd, I'm bleedin' awful . . ."

Benton opened the door suddenly, and the moonlight revealed Kinner's long, gaunt frame slumped on a nearby boulder.

Benton said, "Lift your hands, Kinner. I'm taking a chance on your story."

The man lifted his hands, got up slowly from the boulder. Benton stepped outside, gun leveled.

"Get that gun from his holster," he said to Janet. She came quickly from the dark cabin and in a moment had Kinner's gun in her hand. Benton handed her a block of sulfur matches.

"Now go and light the candle."

Janet ran into the cabin, lit a match, found the candle, and touched the flame to the wick. Kinner limped through the doorway, Benton's gun at his back. He lowered himself to a bench. They saw that his right boot was wet with blood.

Benton got the boot off and examined the wound. "The bullet went clean through the calf," he told Kinner. "You'll be all right when we stop the bleeding."

He improvised a tourniquet and got the wounded man stretched out on the cot. "You'll be all right," he repeated. "Nothing more we can do for you now. It's up to you to lie here if you don't want to bleed to death."

"I ain't movin' a step," Kinner said fervently.

Benton studied him, his expression speculative. "Where's your horse?" he asked. "You didn't come to the Sinks on foot."

"I sure didn't." Kinner repressed an oath. "My fool bronc broke his leg in a pothole. I had to shoot the critter." He choked down another oath. "Would have been across the border by now," he grumbled.

Benton seemed to forget him. He went to the door, stood there, gazing into the night. The moon was low in the west. Dawn would soon be breaking over the eastern hills.

His head turned and he looked at Janet. "I've got to get you away from here," he said. "Wellerton and his ruffians will be looking for you."

She nodded, waited for him to continue. She was too weary to think. It was up to him to devise some plan.

Benton sensed her hopelessness, wanted to comfort her. There was no time to waste, and he went on quickly to explain what was in his mind. "My horse is cached in a gully back of the cabin. We'll have to ride double."

Janet found her voice. "Where can we go . . . hide?" she asked.

"I'm taking you to my ranch," he said "Wellerton will be looking for you here in the Sinks. He won't think to look for you at Bar B."

"How about yourself?" she asked. "You can't risk being seen at your ranch. It will mean gaol if they catch you."

"We'll forget about *me,*" Benton told her gruffly. He crossed over to the cot, gazed down at Kinner. "I shouldn't leave you alive to do any talking," he said.

"I won't do any talkin'," Kinner muttered sullenly.

"I'm thinking about Miss Dunbar's safety." Benton spoke savagely, lifted his gun.

"No!" exclaimed Janet. "Don't—"

"Thanks, ma'am." Kinner's horrified face turned in a look at her. "I won't ever tell of runnin' into you or Benton."

They left him, and Benton led the way down a slope to the concealed horse. He hurriedly adjusted saddle and bridle, mounted, and gave a hand to the girl. She slid up behind him, and they rode out of the gully and through the pass that opened on the flats below. The moonlight was fading. Dawn touched the hills beyond.

Chapter 16

Ab Matoon glanced at his fat gold watch. Two hours past midnight. He frowned. Teel Furner was taking his time to investigate the mystery of Cooner's riderless horse.

Matoon's frown darkened. It was almost certain that his spy was dead. The bloodstains on the saddle told an ominous story. There seemed only one answer to the strange affair. Young Destin must have discovered that Cooner was trailing him. He would resent the attempt to spy on his movements, and the ensuing argument had developed into a shooting affray. It was entirely possible that the young tenderfoot was also lying somewhere in the chaparral. Cooner was deadly fast with a gun. The fact that Destin's horse had not returned to town was no proof that Destin was still alive. Teel Furner had learned from Jim Ball that Red O'Malley had given the tenderfoot the use of his bald-face, and if Destin had been knocked from his saddle, killed, the horse was almost sure to wander back to Diamond D, where he had been raised from a colt.

The lawyer looked at his watch again. He would give Furner another ten minutes and then get to bed. It was obvious that the town marshal was having difficulty in locating the scene of the shooting.

He became aware of low voices in the back yard. Somebody tapped on the rear hall door. Matoon got out of his chair, hurried down the hall, and reached for the bolt.

"Is that you, Curly?" he asked.

"Yeah," answered his stableman. "Ray Wellerton just got in and wants to see you."

Matoon slid the bolt and opened the door. Ray Wellerton pushed into the hall. He looked both tired and excited, and after a quick, searching glance at him, Matoon closed the door and led the way into his office. Ray found a chair, and, with another keen look at the younger man's dust-grimed, haggard face, Matoon opened his desk drawer and set out whisky bottle and glasses.

Ray muttered, "Thanks—" and filled one of the glasses. He emptied it at a gulp, set the glass down, said harshly, "Janet went loco tonight. I had to get rid of her."

"Are you telling me she is—*dead?*" Matoon's voice indicated annoyance rather than grief. His bulging eyes grew agate hard. "I trust that she is *not* dead, Ray. I have some unfinished business with her."

Janet's stepbrother shook his head. "I've sent her to the Sinks." He paused, added sullenly, "If you're thinking about that quit-claim deed—she'll *never* sign it."

"She may change her mind." Matoon's smile was not pleasant.

"You don't need that deed," argued Wellerton. "The fake mortgage you fixed up does the business." He grinned. "Rick's closest friends would swear he wrote that signature."

Matoon's pudgy hand lifted in a dissenting gesture. "A deed is more simple—saves a lot of trouble."

"You can fake hers just as good as you faked her dad's." Ray scowled. "I'm telling you now that Janet ain't leaving the Sinks alive. She's figured out the truth and give her half a chance she'll raise plenty hell for both of us."

"You can leave *me* out of it," Matoon said softly. "I had nothing to do with the murder of Rick Dunbar." His look went slyly to the hall door. Curly stood there, a vague, still shape, and, as if reassured, Matoon's voice hardened with vicious anger. "You're a damn' fool, Ray. Thinking you could double-cross me—get your hands on Destin's twenty thousand dollars. It was careless of me to let it drop he was bringing the gold in his trunk." The lawyer smiled contemptuously. "You must have been disappointed when you broke into his trunk over at the hotel the other night."

"You're crazy," muttered Wellerton. His eyes lowered in a quick look at his bandaged hand.

Matoon noticed the brief glance. "Doc. Bralen doesn't believe you shot yourself accidentally," he went on, his voice a purr. "You might as well tell me the truth, Ray. It will explain why you nearly killed Red O'Malley, thinking he was Destin. You didn't know they had just traded clothes."

"I sure didn't," growled Wellerton.

"Ah, so you admit you tried to kill Destin, eh?"

"I ain't admittin' anything."

"I'm not fooled," Matoon said. "You expected to find the gold in Destin's trunk, and, not finding it, you went over to the Horsehead and tried to kill him." Matoon paused, waggled a finger at the younger man. "You had some other reason for trying to kill him, something to do with that bullet wound in your hand."

"All right." Wellerton eased back in his chair, his uninjured hand on the gun in his holster. "I stopped the stage up on the divide. Destin tricked me, started his lead flyin'."

"Served you right for trying to double-cross me," smiled Matoon.

Wellerton eyed him suspiciously. "I'm damn' sure the gold was in that trunk. I could tell it was heavy when he heaved it up against the side of the rig. It's mighty queer where that gold got to."

Matoon was suddenly thoughtful, drummed fingers speculatively on his desk. "You're quite sure, eh?" A frown darkened his face.

"You bet I'm sure." Wellerton glanced briefly at the big iron safe against the wall. "Your talk don't fool me, Ab. Destin's twenty thousand is locked away in your safe. He would have left it with you."

Matoon's limp gesture neither confirmed nor denied the accusation. He asked abruptly, "Who took the girl to the Sinks?"

"I sent Pima with her," Wellerton answered. "You needn't worry about Janet. No chance for her to get away from Pima." He flicked a sly look at the big safe.

Matoon asked another question. "Where was Buck Salten when Janet got ugly with you? Buck helped her take Red out to the ranch."

"He'd left for town," explained Wellerton. He gave Matoon a puzzled look. "Ain't Buck showed up yet?"

The lawyer shook his head, looked worried. "I'd like to know what's become of him—and Destin too, for that matter." He told Wellerton about Cooner's riderless horse, the blood-stained saddle. "Teel Furner went on a scout. I've been waiting for him to get back."

"I'm hoping Cooner filled that damn' tenderfoot with lead," Wellerton said viciously. He paused, added, "I'd like to know why Buck ain't showed up in town."

"I'm wondering . . ." Matoon stared hard at him. "It might be that you know the answer."

Wellerton grinned. "I ain't ambushed him, if that's what you mean. I figure Buck is going to be some useful to you and me when it comes to a showdown about who killed Rick Dunbar." His eyes narrowed in a wary look at the lawyer. "The day Buck swings for murder I'm filin' homestead rights on the Borrego Creek strip. That's the deal we made, Ab, and don't you forget it."

"You'll mess things up yet," fretted Matoon. "I made no deal with you."

Wellerton glared at him. "You said if I'd let you swindle Janet out of the home ranch you'd keep quiet about who killed her dad. I don't trust you, and that's why I figured to get hold of Destin's cash money and hit the trail for some place a long way from here. Not gettin' the money, I sure aim to get title to that Borrego Creek strip. I can clean up plenty on those water rights."

Matoon's hand lifted in a derisive gesture. "You're a fool, Wellerton. I'm the one who cracks the whip in this town. If I choose to speak it won't be Buck Salten who will hang for the murder of Rick Dunbar." He slid another look at the vague, still shape of the man in the dark hall. "I have a way of dealing with fools like you."

Wellerton reached for the bottle, splashed whisky into his glass. He drank, set the empty glass back on the desk, studied his hand curiously as if surprised by the trembling fingers.

"So that's the way you figure it, huh?" His gaze lifted, and there was fear and smoldering rage in his eyes. "Listen, Ab! Janet only suspects, but *you* know, and so don't fool yourself." His voice tightened, was hardly more than a whisper. "You're taking a ride tonight, Ab, clear out to the Sinks."

Matoon sat motionless in his chair, his smile venomous. "Keep your hand off that gun, young man, and take a look behind you."

"Take a look your own self," retorted Wellerton. His gun slid over the desk. "You're all wrong about that whip-cracking stuff."

Matoon turned his head in a look at the hall door. His smile froze, became a horrified grimace. The gun in Curly's hand was leveled at himself.

The stableman grinned. "Some surprise, huh, boss?" Malicious amusement was in his voice.

Matoon was speechless. His look shifted back to Wellerton, now on his feet. He licked dry lips, gazed stupidly at the younger man.

Wellerton pushed the gun back in his holster, gave him a dangerous smile. "Curly feels the same way about you," he said significantly. His look went to the old-fashioned safe. "I want that gold Destin left with you, Ab."

Matoon found his voice. "Destin didn't leave his money with me," he croaked.

"Open that damn' safe," rasped Wellerton. "I'm findin' out how big a liar you are."

Matoon felt in a pocket, drew out a key. Wellerton snatched it from his shaking hand, went quickly to the safe, and got the door open.

He swore, said disgustedly to Curly, “Ain’t more than a few hundred bucks in the damn’ box.”

“I told you Destin didn’t leave his money with me,” mumbled the lawyer. “I’ve never seen his money.”

“I’m asking Pegleg,” snarled Wellerton. “Keep your gun on him, Curly, while I go ask Pegleg.” He pushed into the hall.

The stableman eased his back against the wall, his grin wide, his gun steady. “You look some pale, boss,” he taunted.

Matoon remained silent. His hold on these men had managed to slip a knot. It seemed that Pegleg was mixed up in the business, too. Pegleg was another whose fear of the hangman’s noose had kept him obedient to the crack of the whip. There were others who had done his bidding for the same reason—fear of him, because of certain grim secrets in his possession. Cooner, Jess Kinner, Teel Furner, and Louie Renn. All of them men on the dodge from the law’s hangman. He had protected them—for a price.

Ab Matoon now knew fear himself. He felt physically ill, but his mind still functioned, cool—crafty. The outlook was grim, yet when it came to brains he was the master of them all.

He considered their possibilities. Cooner was undoubtedly dead, but he could hope for loyalty from Teel Furner and Jess Kinner and Louie

Renn. He had always been more than generous with them, allowed them more than a jackal's share of the lion's kill. Buck Salten too offered a ray of hope. He had instinctively distrusted the lanky ex-foreman's show of friendship, sensed some dangerous purpose.

The lawyer's agile brain raced. Buck Salten had no use for Janet's stepbrother. If he could somehow manage to get word to Buck, tell him the name of the man who had shot Janet Dunbar's father in the back, there might be a chance that Buck would take swift action.

Matoon's momentary hope faded as he considered Buck Salten. It was quite possible that Ray Wellerton had already killed the former Diamond D man. If Buck had reached town he would have shown himself at the Horsehead as usual. His failure to appear indicated that he had run into serious trouble.

Hurried footsteps approaching up the hall interrupted his gloomy speculations. Wellerton stamped into the office, his face dark with disappointment.

"Pegleg says he don't know a thing about Destin's money," he told Curly. "Beats hell where Destin cached the stuff."

Matoon came out of his lethargy, reached for the bottle, and poured himself a drink. "You're both acting like fools." He drained the glass. "If it's money you want I can fix you up with a couple of thousand apiece—give me time to get it from Deming."

"Like hell you will!" sneered Wellerton. He stared at the lawyer thoughtfully. "At that it's not a bad idea, huh, Curly?"

"I'll believe him when I see the *dinero* in my hand," chuckled Curly.

Wellerton fixed an unpleasant smile on the lawyer. "It's a good idea at that, Matoon," he repeated. "We'll talk it over when we get to the Sinks." He looked at Curly. "All right, let's get started." He corked the whisky bottle, put it in his pocket, and flapped his bandaged hand at Matoon. "Outside, mister!"

Matoon got stiffly out of his chair. Wellerton said, "Don't forget your hat." Matoon took his hat from a wall-peg and put it on. He was a very frightened man.

"Get him into the buggy," Wellerton told Curly. "I'll be right out, quick as I've cleaned up the cash in the safe."

Curly prodded his former boss down the hall and out to the moonlit yard. Matoon's dismay increased when he saw his team of Morgans already hitched to the buggy.

Urged by the gun against his spine, he climbed into the seat. "You and Ray had it all fixed up," he said bitterly.

"Sure we did," grinned the man.

"You'll be sorry," Matoon prophesied.

"I'll be settin' pretty—with Ray boss of Diamond D," boasted Curly.

His words deepened the lawyer's grim forebodings. With himself and Janet Dunbar dead, nobody else could prove that Wellerton was the murderer of Janet's father. He would become sole owner of the ranch and, no doubt, would soon dispose of Buck Salten and gain possession of the valuable Borrego Creek strip.

"You'll be sorry," he again warned Curly. "Now that Ray has started, he'll make a clean job of it. You'll end up feeding the buzzards."

Curly gave him a startled look, then grinned disbelievingly. "It's worth a gamble," he said laconically.

The light in the office winked out. Ray appeared. He closed and locked the door and approached the buggy.

"You drive," he said to Curly. "I'll trail you." He looked at Matoon, limp in the seat. "No monkey business, Ab. I'll be watching you close."

He waited for Curly to drive out of the yard, closed the gate, and swung into his saddle. Cloud-drift darkened the night as they headed quietly away from the sleeping town.

Chapter 17

The ride to La Cruz seemed intolerably long to Mark. The intervals of darkness while the moon played hide-and-seek with drifting clouds confused his sense of direction, and he began to suspect that he had lost the trail.

The clouds broke, drifted behind the mountains. He could see stars again and the moon, now low in the west. His fears evaporated with the clouds, and he halted the tired horse and gazed with relieved eyes at the dark huddle of buildings in the valley below.

Dawn lay pale on the eastern peaks when he reached the livery barn. Pedro met him in the dark entrance, a lighted lantern in hand, and back in the office, which was Jim Ball's bedroom, he could hear the stage-driver moving around.

Mark slid from his saddle, gestured to the Mexican to take the horse, and hurried to the office door. Jim must have heard him. The door jerked open, revealed the old stageman's astonished face.

Mark said, "Janet has disappeared! We can't find her anywhere around the ranch!"

Jim gave him a thunderstruck look. Mark allowed him no time for words. "Buck wants Plácido Romero to send out a bunch of his riders."

Jim motioned him into the office, closed the door. "Keep talkin', son, while I finish dressing." He reached for his flannel shirt. "Gettin' ready to take the stage out on the Deming haul."

Mark gave him a brief account of the situation at Diamond D. "We don't know where to start looking, Jim. We can only guess that something happened to her in the barn." He showed Jim the torn fragment of muslin.

The stageman shook his head gravely. "It sure looks like Ray has made off with the girl." He tucked in his shirt and threw open the door. "Pedro!" he called.

The Mexican emerged from a stall. "*Sí, señor.*"

"Get Destin over to Plácido, pronto!"

Mark said gratefully, "Thanks, Jim. I'll be back here as soon as I've seen Plácido." He followed the swift-moving Mexican outside.

A few minutes' walk brought them to the front entrance of the *cantina*, set back in a grove of large cottonwoods. A *mozo* peered cautiously from the door at Pedro's knock. "*Quién es*?" His sharp scrutiny changed to a recognizing smile. He opened the door, gestured for them to enter.

A light burned low in the room. Mark saw tables and chairs piled against the wall, a short bar—an array of bottles and glassware. The *mozo* had evidently been cleaning. He leaned on his broom, inquiring gaze on Pedro.

Mark spoke quickly in Spanish. "I desire word with Señor Romero. It is important."

The *mozo* hesitated, looked at Pedro, who nodded confirmation. "Make haste, slow one," he urged.

The *mozo* rested his broom against the bar, disappeared through a doorway. Mark waited, impatience at fever-heat. Too much time had passed since leaving Buck Salten at Diamond D. The possibilities frightened him. Janet might already be dead.

The *mozo* was suddenly back, soft-footed as a cat. He looked at Mark, eyes bright with curiosity. His hand lifted in a summoning gesture, and, wordless, he turned back into the dark hall. Mark and Pedro pressed close on his heels, and Mark was aware of familiar ground—the wide patio, the murmuring fountain—Plácido Romero framed in a doorway that opened on the long *galería.*

Plácido said, "Ah, my good frien'! Thees beeg 'appiness to see you so early!"

"Let us speak in Spanish, *señor,*" Mark interrupted. "You remember that I know your language."

Romero gave him a penetrating look, asked quietly, "There is trouble, my friend?"

"It is life or death," Mark told him, his voice not quite steady. "Janet Dunbar is missing from her home. We need help, Plácido. Buck Salten sent me to tell you that we need your help." The words grew husky in his throat. "Every moment is precious."

Perhaps for a space of five seconds Romero stood rigid, his eyes without expression as he looked at the young *americano*. His hand lifted, and he spoke sharply to the *mozo*, his voice deep, resonant. "Rafael, Felipe—Chato! Tell them to come!"

The *mozo* vanished down the *galería*, still dark, not yet touched by the lifting dawn. Plácido motioned Mark into the room, and Pedro, sensing his own work was done, slipped away.

Romero looked keenly at his visitor. "You are very tired, my friend, a man almost drained of strength." He opened a cupboard, took down a cut-glass decanter. "A little brandy will be good for you."

Mark offered no protest, swallowed the drink. "Thank you, Plácido." He spoke wearily. He had never felt so completely done, mentally or physically. He had hardly rested a moment since leaving for the Benton ranch the morning before, and his only food had been the sandwich from the hands of Tildy Hogan.

Romero was watching him, his eyes like gimlets. "I would know more about this affair," he said. "Tell me everything."

Mark related the little he knew, showed him the bit of muslin found in the barn. "It's the only clue we have, and we don't know where to start looking for her." His voice broke. "We're frightened, Plácido."

Plácido nodded gravely. "It is bad business, but do not lose heart, my friend. I command many sharp eyes, and we will find our little *señorita*, no matter how hidden the trail." His voice hardened, and he held up both hands with thumb crossed over forefinger. "*Por esta cruz*! It will be too bad for Ray Wellerton if one hair of her head is harmed!"

Mark told him about the three men Buck had imprisoned in the granary. "They're a tough bunch, Plácido," he worried.

Romero was already buckling on his gun belt. "I am on the way, my friend," he reassured him. "Twenty good men will ride at my back."

Mark hesitated. "I would like to ride with you, but there are things I must do in town first. It is possible that I can force Matoon to talk, to tell me what he knows, or give me some idea about where Wellerton might have taken the girl."

Romero nodded. "You go ahead, my friend. Do what is in your mind. In the meantime, you have my promise to ride like the wind out to Diamond D and start the search."

Mark left him, and the *mozo*, back from delivering his message, conducted him to a gate and let him out of the patio. Romero watched from his door, beckoned to the group of approaching

Mexicans. He gestured at Mark, who was disappearing through the gate.

"Rafael—" He spoke gravely. "Follow wherever he goes. Never let him out of your sight. Guard him as you would guard me. I am fond of the young man, and no harm must come to him."

"To hear is to obey," Rafael said. "I will be his shadow."

Mark found Jim Ball in conversation with a stranger, whom he introduced as Matt Dawson.

"Matt's been haulin' freight for a mining outfit back in the hills," Jim said. "He got laid off because of a shut-down, and I've fixed it up with him to take out the stage for me. I aim to stick 'round and help find Janet." Jim paused, eyes questioning. "Did you see Plácido?"

Mark nodded. "He's on his way to the ranch as soon as he can round up his riders."

"Ain't you ridin' with 'em?" Jim asked.

"I want to see Matoon," Mark explained. "There's a chance he knows something—if he can be made to talk."

Jim studied him. "You look awful tired, son. You should grab yourself some sleep."

"I'll be all right when I get some food in me," Mark told him. "I'm too worried to think of sleep."

"We'll head over to Ah Gee's and get some breakfast," Jim said. "We can do some more talkin' while we eat." He gave his relief driver a parting nod. "All right, Matt. I'll tell Ben Stock you'll carry the mail today."

Matt Dawson rubbed a bristly chin. "I'll go get cleaned up some," he drawled. "So long, Jim, if I ain't seein' you ag'in." He drifted into the street.

Mark waited for the old stageman to cram on his hat. "I wish we had a sheriff handy," he fretted. "I'd like to have Matoon thrown into gaol, and that is something Teel Furner won't do for us. He's nothing more than Matoon's hired gunman."

Jim eyed him thoughtfully, muttered an ejaculation, and slid open his desk drawer. He rummaged in the tumbled contents for a moment and drew out a tarnished silver badge. He dusted it against flannel sleeve and pinned it on his shirt.

"It's been a lot of years since Sheriff Bolger gave it to me," he said with a reminiscent grin. "Bolger's dead, but the new sheriff ain't never called this badge in, so I reckon I'm still a deputy sheriff."

They went down the street to the Chop House. Ah Gee greeted them with an affable smile and hastened to set out cups of hot coffee.

"Ham and eggs velly good," he told them.

"Make it a double portion," smiled Mark. "I'm starving."

Concern was in the sharp look the Chinese gave him. "You velly tired. I bling ham and eggs heap quick." He sped away to his kitchen.

"You should get over to the hotel and grab some sleep," grumbled Jim. "You're in bad shape, Mark."

"I've got to see Matoon first, just as quick as I get some food into me." Mark took a drink of coffee. It tasted good, and he drained the cup.

"How come you think Matoon knows anything about the girl?" Jim asked.

"I've been finding out things about Matoon." Mark's tone was grim. "I had a talk with him yesterday morning, just before I left for the Benton ranch. He said enough to make me very suspicious, tried to make me believe he held a mortgage on Diamond D and that he can force Janet to sign a quit-claim deed. Of course, Matoon would get the twenty thousand. Ray Wellerton is mixed up in the business, and that is why I think Matoon will guess what has happened to the girl."

"I can't arrest him just on suspicion," worried Jim. He broke off, glanced at the street door. "Teel Furner," he muttered. "Looks like hell. Must have been ridin' all night."

The town marshal's roving gaze fastened on them, and surprise widened his eyes as he recognized Mark. He slouched across the room, pulled out a chair, and sat down at their table.

"It's sure been one hell of a night," he grumbled. He gave Mark a sour grin. "We found Cooner's body layin' in the brush up at the

Benton Fork. Some lucky for you that he had this piece of paper on him, Destin."

Mark said curtly, "I don't understand."

Furner tipped his hat back on his head, malicious amusement in his eyes. "It's like this, Destin. You and Cooner had a scrap yesterday morning just before you forked saddle for your trip out to Diamond D. At least, you told Ab Matoon you was heading out that way. It looks like Cooner trailed you, and when his bronc showed up in town last evenin' and him not in the saddle, we figgered that he caught up with you and that you shot him. There was plenty blood on his saddle."

Mark said quietly, "He *didn't* catch up with me, and I *didn't* shoot him."

"That's why I'm repeatin' it's lucky we found this piece of paper on him. Here, take a look at what this writin' says."

Mark picked up the torn scrap of paper Furner tossed at him and read it aloud, and nothing in his voice betrayed the fact that he had seen it before. It was addressed to Ab Matoon from Jess Kinner.

> You pizen snake I shore fixt Cooner for the buzerds to find and you wont nevver see me agin no time, you low-down skunk.

Jim commented soberly, "It sure *is* lucky for you, Mark, that Kinner writ that note. The killin' would have been pinned on you for certain."

Furner pocketed the piece of paper. "What beats me is how come the pair of 'em got to shootin' it out? It don't make sense, them two smokin' their guns at each other."

Mark offered no comment. He could have explained much to the perplexed town marshal, but to tell what he knew would have betrayed his own presence at the Benton ranch.

"Did you fetch the body back to town?" Jim Ball asked.

The town marshal nodded. "Doc. Bralen will hold the inquest this afternoon, I reckon." Furner grinned. "I stopped by the doc's house on the way in, figgerin' he'd pull off the inquest right now and get done with it. He went on the prod, told me to go to hell. He weren't drunk, nuther—cold sober. Said he'd been up all night with another baby case. Eased up on his drinkin', seems like," added the marshal, almost resentfully.

"I don't blame Doc for bawlin' you out," chuckled Jim. "He was up most of the night before, getting Ben Stock's baby borned."

Worry furrowed Furner's brow. "I'm some puzzled about where Ab Matoon is. He said he'd wait up for news about Cooner. I was over to his office, where he sleeps in that back room he fixed up. I banged on the door plenty hard." The town marshal rubbed his nose thoughtfully with a blunt forefinger. "If he *is* in he sure acts like he's dead. I've a mind to bust the lock and have a look."

Ah Gee appeared from the kitchen with the ham and eggs. Furner eyed the food hungrily and got out of his chair. "Fix me up the same thing," he told the Chinese. "I'll be right back quick as I've had another look at Ab's place." The street door slammed behind him.

Ah Gee placed the dishes on the table, asked Mark blandly, "You buy cow-ranch yet?"

"Not yet," Mark answered. He sensed more than idle curiosity in the question. Ah Gee knew that something was wrong and was frankly worried. "Keep it to yourself, Ah Gee, but Miss Dunbar has disappeared, and we're afraid something bad has happened."

The Chinese sucked in his breath, stared at him, his face an expressionless mask. "Too bad," he said softly. "She nice lady. Too bad."

"Keep your eyes and ears open for anything suspicious," Mark told him. He thought a moment. "Get in touch with me or Jim Ball if you hear anything, but don't talk to Furner about it, or to anybody else."

Ah Gee nodded. "Furner no good," he said. He shook his head. "This La Cluz town no good."

"We've got to do something about it," Mark told him grimly. He drank the last of his coffee and pushed up from his chair. "All right, Jim.

Let's help Furner find Ab Matoon. If he's not in town it means he's left for some place in a hurry. I don't like it, Jim."

They paid Ah Gee and hurried into the street. Sunlight was spreading over the eastern hills, laying crimson and gold on the clouds that draped the higher peaks. Jim caught sight of Ben Stock framed in the doorway of the Great Emporium, superintending a Mexican who was sweeping the porch. He was reminded of his promise to Matt Dawson.

"I've got to tell Ben about Matt taking the stage out for me," he said to Mark.

They crossed over to the store. The lanky postmaster greeted them with a smile that oddly softened his austere bearded face. He handed Mark a cigar.

"If you haven't heard about it, it's a boy," he said sonorously. "My first, Mr. Destin." He beamed. "My seventh child, but the others are all girls."

Mark pocketed the cigar, feigned an interest he did not feel. "Congratulations." He forced a smile. "Seven is a lucky number, I've heard."

Jim sensed his impatience, hastily informed the postmaster about the substitute stage-driver. "Somethin' important come up and I ain't able to leave town." He hesitated. "Seen Ab Matoon any place this mornin'?" he asked.

Ben Stock shook his head. "Teel Furner was

asking me the same question. No, I ain't seen Ab since last evening when I bought him a drink over at the Horsehead." He grinned apologetically. "Celebrating the arrival of Ben Stock junior, you might say."

"Ab don't seem to be in his room," Jim said. "Come on, Mark. Let's go and see what Furner has found out."

Matoon's office door was open—the lock broken, they noticed. They went inside, met Furner and Louie Renn hurrying from the hall that led to the back room.

"Ab ain't here!" the town marshal told them frantically. He gestured at the open safe. "Looks like he's cleaned out all his money in the safe and hightailed it off some place. His buggy and team ain't in the barn, and Curly's gone too."

Mark gazed at the safe. "Was it broken open?" he asked.

"The key's in the lock," Furner pointed out. "Nobody but Ab had a key to that safe, and that means he opened it his own self."

Mark was careful to avoid Jim Ball's eyes, but Jim was less cautious. "Looks like you figgered it right," he muttered.

Teel Furner was suddenly bristling with suspicion. "What do you mean by that remark, Jim?" He stared at Mark, his expression ugly. "Are you a law officer, a Pinkerton man?"

"I'm neither," Mark replied.

“I’ll bet you’re back of this business!” shouted the town marshal. He looked at Louie Renn for support. “We should toss him in gaol, huh, Louie?”

“You’re the law in this town.” The hotel clerk’s death’s-head face had taken on an even more ghastly pallor. He glanced furtively at the door as if longing to be gone from the place. It was obvious to Mark that he was frightened by Furner’s talk of a Pinkerton man.

Furner’s hand was on his gun. “I’m throwing you in gaol,” he blustered to Mark.

Jim said mildly, “Don’t try any funny business, Teel.” An ancient .45 suddenly appeared in his hand. “You can call yourself a town marshal, but I’m deputy sheriff, and I’ll sure use this gun on you if you don’t mind me.” He touched the tarnished silver star on his shirt. “There’s plenty authority in this badge, mister, and I aim to use it.”

The town marshal’s hand dropped from his gun, and he gazed open-mouthed at the old stageman. “You—you’re loco,” he muttered.

A shadow darkened the doorway, was suddenly gone, but not before Mark recognized the swarthy face of the man who had made the shadow. He wondered briefly why Rafael should be watching the scene, made a shrewd guess that Plácido Romero was not passing up any bets. Rafael was obeying orders to watch out for him. He would have killed Furner if Jim Ball had not gained command of the situation. The thought sent a tingle through Mark. He had not dreamed that his life meant so much to Plácido Romero.

Another shadow darkened the doorway, and Pegleg stumped into the office, surprise on his beefy face as he gazed round.

“What’s goin’ on?” asked the barman. His look fastened on Jim Ball. “What’s the idea of that gun, Jim? Pullin’ off a holdup?”

The man’s pretense of amazement was so obvious that Mark reached for his gun, leveled it at him. “You don’t need any answers, Pegleg,” he said. “Put up your hands.”

“Huh?” Pegleg goggled at him, reluctantly lifted his hands. “No savvy your talk.”

“I think you can tell us what has become of Matoon,” Mark said. “Talk fast, Pegleg.”

Fright stared from the bartender’s piggish eyes. “You askin’ about Ab? Why—I ain’t seen Ab since—since—” Pegleg looked around at Ben Stock suddenly framed in the doorway. Relief chased across his moon face. “Sure and it was when Ben was in settin’ up drinks for the house that I seen Ab last. Ben was celebratin’—”

“Shut up, Pegleg!” The storekeeper’s profile was a stern Lincoln-like mask. “I’m not obliged to you for telling tales.” His look went to Jim Ball. “It seems that Matoon is really missing and it occurs to me that I have a clue.”

“We sure crave to hear about it,” Jim said

gruffly. He kept eyes and gun on the town marshal. “What’s on your mind, Ben?”

“You were asking when I’d seen Matoon last.” The storekeeper hesitated, his expression embarrassed. “My—er—my new little son was crying. I—er—was nervous, and I got out of bed and stood at the window for a few minutes.”

“Yes,” urged Mark. “You mean you saw something when you stood at the window?”

“It was moonlight,” Ben Stock continued. “I saw something, Mr. Destin. A team and buggy, followed by a lone rider. Is it possible that Matoon was in that buggy.”

“Was he alone in the buggy?” asked Mark.

The storekeeper gestured regretfully. “I cannot say, Mr. Destin. It is difficult to see things clearly in the moonlight. I only know that I saw a buggy and a lone horseman.”

“I’m bettin’ it was Ab Matoon in that rig,” growled Jim Ball. He glared at Teel Furner. “I reckon you ain’t sayin’ I’m wrong, huh, Teel?”

The town marshal had no words, kept his sullen gaze on the ransacked safe. It was Pegleg who broke the momentary silence.

“I ain’t knowin’ nothin’ about Ab Matoon,” he lied smoothly. “I only know if he’s skipped town I’ll be full owner of the Horsehead Bar and I’m settin’ up drinks right now for the crowd.” His genial smile was back. “No sense holdin’ your gun on me, Destin. I sure crave to get my hands down."

Mark ignored him, spoke to Ben Stock. "Which way would that buggy have been traveling?" he asked.

"South," answered the storekeeper. He added after a moment's thought, "The Sinks country is over that way."

Jim said, softly, "You figgered right, Mark. I reckon Matoon will meet up with Wellerton and the girl over in the Sinks."

Mark stared at him, eyes dark with deepening anxiety. "I don't know, Jim . . ." He spoke slowly. "It is possible that Janet was in that buggy, which means that the lone rider with them was Ray Wellerton." His gun lifted. "We can't waste time with these men. Throw them in gaol, Jim. I'm following the trail of that buggy."

Jim Ball muttered a dismayed ejaculation. "Where's Louie Renn got to. He was standin' there by the wall—and he's sure gone."

"Louie went into the hall," Ben Stock said. "He slipped off when I was telling you about seeing the buggy." The storekeeper's tone was rueful. "I didn't know he was one of your prisoners, or I'd have stopped him."

"He'll likely make for the Sinks and warn Matoon," Jim worried. He looked at Mark. "Maybe you can overhaul him, son."

Mark said thoughtfully, "I think the best is just

to follow him. The trail will lead to the place where they're keeping Janet."

"Go fork your saddle," urged Jim. "He ain't got only a few minutes start on you." He paused, growing doubt on his face. "Don't seem sensible, you goin' lone-handed. Sure wish Romero's outfit hadn't pulled out for the Dunbar ranch so quick."

"It's too late to stop them now." Mark moved towards the street door. "I'm going, Jim. It's our best chance to find Janet, if I can stick to Renn's trail."

"You don't know the Sinks country," argued Jim. "Louie does, and he'll give you the slip. He's a foxy hombre."

"I won't be alone," Mark told him with a grim smile. "Romero has sent Rafael to keep close on *my* trail. He's out in the street now, and I'll take him along."

Jim Ball's worried frown vanished. "You won' lose Renn with Rafael readin' sign for you," he chuckled. "Get movin', son. Ben and me will hustle these fellers over to the gaol."

Mark slammed through the door and beckoned to Rafael, who was leaning indolently against the hitch-rail in front of the Great Emporium.

"I am not deceived," he said in Spanish when the Mexican approached. "You have been ordered to follow me."

"It is true," admitted Rafael. "I hope you are

not angry that I obey orders," he added politely.

"Say no more," smiled Mark. "I am glad Romero sent you. I can use you."

"I am your servant," the Mexican assured him.

"Did Romero tell you about Miss Dunbar?"

Rafael nodded, his dark eyes suddenly fierce. "After he told me to follow you," he said.

Mark explained about Louie Renn's flight. "We think his trail will lead to Miss Dunbar. Climb your saddle and chase after him and keep him in sight, only don't let him know he's followed. I'll overtake you."

"*Sí!*" Rafael snatched the tie-rope loose, slid into his saddle, and was gone in a cloud of dust that made yellow mist in the early sunlight.

Mark broke into a run for the stage barn, a warm feeling in his heart for Plácido Romero. No danger now of losing sight of the man whose trail would lead to Matoon's secret hideout in the Sinks. A dangerous trail to follow, but no risk was too great if it meant the life of Janet Dunbar. He knew now that Janet was the most important thing in the whole world and that he loved her.

Chapter 18

The sunlight slanted in through the window, laid scorching fingers on Jess Kinner's face where he snored on the cot. He stirred, awoke, pulled himself up on one elbow, and gazed about, bewildered, still in a drunken stupor and unable to remember where he was.

A whisky bottle lay on the floor. He reached out a hand and picked it up. It was empty. He muttered an oath, hurled the bottle across the room, and got to his feet. The sharp stab of pain in the calf of his leg somewhat cleared his befuddled mind. After Benton's hurried departure with the girl from the cabin he had investigated the meager stock of supplies and found a nearly full quart bottle of whisky.

Kinner stared ruefully at the shattered bottle. He should have saved himself a couple of good drinks. His head ached viciously, and more whisky was the medicine he craved. He limped painfully to Benton's abandoned saddlebags, with the vague hope of finding another bottle. He swore disappointedly. Only cans of beans and peaches, the half of a loaf of bread.

He gazed round for water, saw some in a tin bucket. He upended the pail, drank thirstily, the water spilling over and drenching his shirt.

Sounds reached him, and he hastily set the bucket down, limped to the door, and opened it, surprise widening his bloodshot eyes as he recognized the approaching horsemen—Ray Wellerton, Curly, Pima, and a half score of other riders, one of them Ab Matoon.

Fear held Kinner rigid for a moment when he saw Matoon, and then the fright was gone and a grin spread over his face. Matoon's hands were tied to his saddle horn, and he had the look of a man who had lost all hope. No need now to be afraid of the sly schemer who had sent Cooner to ambush him.

Ray Wellerton's gun was out, and his voice, harsh and menacing, drove thoughts of Matoon from Kinner's mind. He lifted his hands, fright wiping the grin from his face.

"Where's the girl?" Wellerton asked.

Kinner shook his head, too frightened for words, rolled horrified eyes at the group of riders. Some of them were friends, companions in many a ruthless affair, but now he read only hostility in their hard faces.

"Pima was taking her to the Hidden Valley place," Wellerton continued. "She got away from him down in Dry Creek wash. Pima says some feller helped her, started shooting. He went on to Hidden Valley for help."

Kinner found his voice. "Wasn't knowin' it was Pima stalkin' the brush," he said. He sent a puzzled look at Matoon. "What for you got *him* tied up?"

"Curly and I were taking him to the Hidden Valley place when we met Pima and the bunch on the road below Dry Creek," explained Wellerton. "We ditched the buggy and picked up the girl's trail. Wasn't hard to find with Pima reading sign."

The half-breed was studying Kinner curiously. "I figger them was *your* tracks we picked up with the girl's," he said. "You were limpin' bad, Jess."

"Caught one of your slugs in my laig," admitted Kinner. His fright was leaving him. He felt that he saw the way out of a difficult situation. "I was trailin' Benton after he bust loose from gaol. Lost him down in the willow brakes and was waitin' for daylight when you run into me lookin' for the girl. I figgered you was Benton and started shootin'." Kinner's sly look went to Matoon. The lawyer's expression told him that he was still unaware of Cooner's fate.

"All right." Wellerton showed impatience. "You followed the girl to this cabin. Where is she?"

"I figgered it was Benton I was trailin'," Kinner lied smoothly. "I was too lame to get close enough to make out it was a girl I was followin'. I got here and seen Benton open the door and let her inside. Benton seen me and got the drop on me." Kinner managed a wry grin. "Benton ain't here now. He took my gun and left me hawg-tied and hightailed it away from here with the Dunbar girl."

Wellerton swore, flung from his saddle, and pushed into the cabin, took a brief look and turned savagely on Kinner. "Which way did they go?" he asked angrily.

"He said he was takin' her back to his Bar B ranch," answered the ex-gaoler. "No call to stick your gun in my face," he added complainingly. "Ain't my fault Benton got away with the girl."

Wellerton lowered his gun. "How long have they been gone? Talk fast, Kinner—and no lies."

"I reckon it was close to sunup," Kinner told him. "I was some time gettin' loose and couldn't follow, my laig so bad hurt and no bronc handy."

"So you lay here guzzling redeye," sneered Wellerton.

"Wasn't nothin' else better to do," Kinner candidly admitted. "The bottle was handy and my laig hurtin' bad."

Wellerton strode outside. "Get Matoon into the cabin. We've got to ride like hell for Benton's ranch."

Pima and Curly hustled Matoon down from his horse and into the cabin.

"Want him tied up?" Curly asked.

Wellerton nodded, and they roped the helpless lawyer to the cot.

"I reckon he's safe enough till we get back," guffawed Curly. Sudden doubt creased his hard face. "Ain't so sure we should leave him layin' here alone at that. Worth too much *dinero* for us to risk his bustin' loose."

"I'll watch him for you," eagerly offered Kinner. He fastened an ugly look on the prisoner. "You damn' skunk—sendin' Cooner to lay for me in the brush." He spat contemptuously. "I sure fooled you, Ab. It's Cooner that's layin' out in the brush for the buzzards, not *me*." Kinner broke off, warned by their attentive faces that he was arousing dangerous curiosity. He was reluctant to betray the true reason for his presence in the Sinks, wanted them to believe his story of following the fugitive Benton's trail direct from the gaol.

"What's this talk of Cooner trying to kill you?" Wellerton asked suspiciously.

"Waal . . ." Kinner did some fast thinking. "I figger Matoon wasn't wantin' Benton back in gaol and sent Cooner to stop me for sure."

"The man's lying," Matoon mumbled from the cot.

"I'd sooner believe him than you," sneered Wellerton. He studied Kinner thoughtfully, noted the bandaged leg under the upturned pants. It was plain that the man was in no shape to sit a saddle.

"All right," he agreed. "You stay here with Matoon, and be damned sure he's still here when I get back."

"No chance for him to get loose," grinned

Kinner. "Not with *me* on the job. I'm needin' a gun," he added.

They supplied him with gun and cartridge belt, also a flask of whisky that Curly grudgingly dug out of a pocket. Kinner felt fine again. He stood in the doorway, watched the riders drop from view into the valley below. He heard Matoon's furious whisper from the cot behind him.

"You damn' fool. I never sent Cooner to dry-gulch you."

Kinner closed the door, turned, and looked at his prisoner. "You sure did, Ab. I was layin' there in the brush, watchin' for Benton to show up at his house, when Cooner sneaked up and started smokin' his gun at me."

"He was trailing young Destin," Matoon said bitterly. "Cooner mistook you for Destin because of that shirt you wear. It's like the one he traded from Red O'Malley."

Kinner gave him an appalled look. "Hell!" he muttered. "I reckon that's maybe the answer, boss." His unconscious use of *boss* indicated dawning realization of his mistake, and something like hope touched Matoon's grey face. He pressed his point.

"Of course it's the answer," he said, in a stronger voice. "Get these ropes off me. We must be a long way from here before Wellerton is back."

Kinner was not disposed to be rushed. As he read the signs, it was apparent that his old boss was on the way out and Wellerton's star in the ascendant. Turning Matoon loose might have highly unpleasant consequences. He limped over to the table, lowered himself to a bench, uncorked the flask in his hand, and took a long drink.

"How come you and Ray has locked horns?" he asked.

"I know that he killed Rick Dunbar." Matoon was impatient. "Don't waste time, Jess. Get these ropes off me."

"Seems like he'd fix you the way he fixed Rick Dunbar," commented Kinner. He tilted the flask to his mouth. The whisky was warming him. "Don't make sense—him not shuttin' your mouth with hot lead."

"I've promised him fifty thousand dollars if he'll turn me loose," explained Matoon. "I'm to give him an order on my Deming Bank, and he says he'll turn me loose when he gets the cash." Matoon groaned. "Of course he won't, but I'm pretending to believe him. I'd have been dead hours ago if I hadn't talked money to him. I underestimated that young man. He's a cold-blooded wolf."

"Fifty thousand bucks, huh?" Kinner's eyes took on an avaricious glitter. "Some *dinero*, boss." He tilted the flask again, drank, replaced the cork, and carefully set the flask on the table. "Maybe me and you can make powwow our own selves, huh?"

"Get me away from here, and I'll pay you well," promised Matoon.

"You'll pay me fifty thousand, same as you would him." Kinner leered drunkenly. "I sure could live like a king over in Mexico with fifty thousand bucks in my pants pocket."

"It's yours," agreed the lawyer. "I can trust you, Jess. Get me back to La Cruz, and the money is yours."

"I've got to do some figgerin'," Kinner said. "I got to figger some hideout for you while you get the cash from Deming. Ain't trustin' you till the cash is in my hands." He drew out the Colt .45 Curly had handed over with the whisky flask, examined it with the eye of an expert, and placed it on the table.

"You're wasting valuable time," fumed Matoon.

The whisky was taking hold of Kinner. He had been through a lot of grief and he was irritable, fearful of the consequences of taking a chance with a man he knew would not hesitate to make a fool of him. He grabbed the gun, got unsteadily to his feet.

"Shut your mouth!" he yelled. "I'm runnin' this show!"

Too late he heard the creak of the opening door behind him. He whirled the .45 in his hand blazing at the man etched against the bright sunlight. The man pitched forward, lay sprawled inside the door, and as he fell his own gun lifted, belched smoke and flame.

Kinner sagged against the table, the gun slipped from suddenly limp fingers, and he slid slowly in a sideways motion that landed him face down across the bench. Matoon struggled furiously against the binding ropes, craned his head in a horrified look.

A long silence followed the double crash of gunfire. A shadow darkened the doorway, and Mark was suddenly in the cabin. Rafael followed, and they stood there, wordless, eyes wary, guns ready.

Matoon said in a faint voice, "Thank God you got here in time, Destin."

Mark did not answer. He bent down, examined the man in the doorway. "Louie Renn's dead," he said to Rafael. "Kinner's bullet took him between the eyes." He moved on to where Kinner lay like a bag of meal across the bench.

"Still breathing," he muttered. He pulled the man over, laid him out on the floor.

"Never mind *him,* Destin," called Matoon from the cot. "Cut me loose, damn it."

Mark continued to ignore him. It was in his mind that Kinner could tell him things if not too weak to talk. The flutter of eyelids indicated that consciousness was returning.

He wasted no time, asked the question uppermost in his mind. "Where's Janet Dunbar?"

Recognition dawned in Kinner's glazing eyes. His answer came—a hoarse, painful whisper. "Benton got her away—took her to his ranch." The whisper grew more faint. "Wellerton and the bunch was here . . . They . . . they . . ." His head rolled sideways, and Mark realized that he was dead.

He had no time to waste pity on him. Making sure that Rafael was watching the door, he went quickly to Matoon, jabbed his gun against the lawyer's soft paunch.

"What about Wellerton and the bunch?" he asked.

Instant death stared at him from the tenderfoot's eyes, and Matoon made no attempt to evade. "Kinner was trying to tell you that Wellerton and his killers are riding for the Benton ranch in chase."

Mark was silent for a moment, unable to understand why Matoon was so obviously a prisoner.

"Did you know that Wellerton had made away with Miss Dunbar?" he asked.

"Ray said he had to get rid of her because she suspected him of the murder of her father. He was going to get rid of me too, for the same reason." Perspiration streamed down the lawyer's face. "For God's sake take that gun from my stomach."

Mark jabbed harder. "Have you proof that Wellerton killed Rick Dunbar?"

"Plenty," gasped Matoon. "Teel Furner saw the shooting, only Ray doesn't know it."

"Why has Wellerton left you tied up here instead of killing you?" Mark asked. "It doesn't make good sense."

"He wants ransom money," Matoon told him. "Doesn't mean a thing. I'm a dead man the moment he gets his hands on the cash."

Mark loosened the knots, and the lawyer got stiffly to his feet, stood there, rubbing chafed wrists. "How did you manage to find me here?" He gazed curiously at the dead man sprawled in the doorway. "Louie didn't know where I was."

"Louie Renn was bringing you bad news," Mark informed him, his voice grim. "We followed his trail to the abandoned buggy and across the flats up to the cabin."

"Bad news?" Matoon spoke faintly. "What do you mean, Destin?"

"We've got Teel Furner and Pegleg in gaol." Mark watched him intently. "It means you're out of the frying pan and right in the fire, Matoon."

Matoon was breathing hard, the look of a cornered wolf in his eyes. He saw the whisky flask on the table, seized it with shaking hands, and took a drink.

"I—I'm a respectable citizen," he spluttered. "You can't accuse me of any crime."

"We're riding," Mark said curtly. "No time to talk about it now." He pushed the lawyer towards the door. "I'll tell you this much—you're going to gaol and you'll stand trial for forgery, attempted fraud, and for willfully concealing knowledge of a murder. That makes you an accessory after the fact, and it's possible that Furner's testimony will make you accessory *before* the fact. In which case you'll hang."

They left the dead renegades lying on the cabin floor and rushed their horrified prisoner down the sunlit trail to the horses left concealed in the bushes.

"Lucky we have Renn's horse," Mark commented. "All right, Matoon. Climb into that saddle."

The lawyer offered no protest, meekly scrambled into the saddle. Rafael knotted his wrists securely to the horn.

"How long has Wellerton been gone from here?" Mark asked him.

"About an hour," mumbled the lawyer. His voice was suddenly shrill. "You're crazy, Destin. Wellerton had a dozen men with him. Going after him is signing your death warrant—and mine too."

Mark made no answer, swung into his saddle, and they rode down the slope, with the prisoner's horse following on a lead-rope.

They crossed the willow brakes and turned up the road. Rafael's keen eyes studied the fresh hoofprints.

"These men we follow ride fast," he said in Spanish to Mark.

Mark halted his horse, gave the Mexican a worried look. "I wish we could get word to Romero." His voice choked. "We can't overtake them in time. I'm afraid, Rafael. No telling what will happen."

Rafael was silent, his face lifted in a look at the cloudless sky, and suddenly he was down from his horse and untying the *serape* rolled tight on the back of his saddle. He saw the surprise in Mark's eyes, gave him a faint, encouraging smile.

"There is a way to send word," he explained in Spanish. "A fire—a little smoke. It is a language we Mexicans understand."

Excitement surged through Mark. He slid from his horse, set to work helping build the fire. Dry bits of brush to start the flame, which Rafael expertly covered with greener brush that finally sent up dark smoke.

"Now," said the Mexican. He shook out the gay-colored blanket, wet it with water from his canteen, and each took an end. Mark carefully followed Rafael's low-voiced instructions, and they lowered and raised the blanket over the smoldering brush. Puffs of smoke lifted high into the windless sky.

"Now we wait," Rafael said, and they stood there silent, alert eyes scanning the blue distance.

"Not much chance," Mark fretted. "Romero won't be looking for smoke-talk."

Rafael smiled, shook his head. "When there is trouble the eyes of Señor Romero never sleep, nor the eyes of Felipe and Chato and the others who ride to the Dunbar ranch." He gestured. "Come, we will try again."

They worked patiently with the blanket, and suddenly Mark saw answering puffs of smoke in the far distance. He looked inquiringly at Rafael.

"They see our talk," the Mexican said in a satisfied voice.

"What does their smoke-talk say?" Mark continued to watch the distant puffs lifting, clear against the blue sky.

"They ride to meet us." Rafael shook out the wet, smoke-grimed *serape*, hastily rolled and secured it to his saddle.

Mark said simply, "I won't forget this, Rafael." He swung up to his horse, spoke grimly to his prisoner, "Hold on tight, Matoon. You're due for a fast ride."

Chapter 19

The windmill had developed an unearthly screech that worried Tildy Hogan. She made annoyed comments about it while puffing up Mrs. Benton's pillow.

"Sounds like a lot of cats squawlin'," she complained. "Plague take the pesky thing. I should have had that nice young man use the oilcan on it when he was up the tower fixin' the rope."

"You can turn it out of the wind," Mrs. Benton suggested. "Or has the rope broken again?"

"It's that wore-out old tank," explained Tildy. "Leaks like a sieve, but I'm thinkin' there's been enough water pumped for now, so I'll go stop it. Them banshee shrieks is more than a body can stand." She stood by the bed, big and competent, hands on hips. "There now, me darlin', and as quick as I've stopped that yelpin' old windmill I'll bring you a dish of the rice puddin' I've fixed for your lunch."

An anxious frown replaced the reassuring smile on her rugged face as she hurried into the kitchen and down the back-porch steps. No further word yet from Bill Benton, and it was hard not to worry, and no man on the place to turn a hand to anything. Also she was aware of a growing uneasiness about Mark Destin ever since his hurried departure after repairing the broken windmill rope. He had seen something when up on the tower platform with the brass telescope. She had used the telescope herself, seen him riding fast for the willows, and later had heard gunshots. It was all very disturbing and frightening, and fears grew in her that perhaps the young man was lying dead down some place below the creek.

Tildy reached the tower and gazed up at the screeching wheel. More than an oilcan was needed. One of the big wooden planes was loose and rattled and banged ominously. Something would have to be done about it, or they would soon be without a windmill.

She seized the rope, her face upturned as she watched the big wheel swing out of the wind and slow its revolutions. Something caught her eyes, kept her face uplifted. A speck of black cloud in the blue noonday sky.

Tildy mechanically made the rope fast on its cleat, a wondering look on her upturned face. More little black clouds came puffing up against the blue sky, and of a sudden she realized that they were not clouds, but puffs of smoke.

She was the widow of the late Corporal Pat Hogan, veteran of many an Indian campaign, and she knew Indian smoke-talk. She could hardly believe her eyes as she absorbed the meaning of those quick, black puffs.

Tildy continued to watch, presently saw answering signals from the low hills west of the Dunbar ranch. No more signals came from the south, and, satisfied that the brief exchange of smoke-talk was finished, she went thoughtfully back to her kitchen. She was completely puzzled, could only make wild guesses. Somebody had sent an urgent warning, and, if she had correctly interpreted the answering signals, it seemed that help was on the way. Having no knowledge of what had happened to Janet Dunbar, she was unable to make sense of the mysterious affair. She only knew that Bill Benton had fled for his life to the Sinks and vaguely surmised that the smoke-talk might possibly concern him. She also knew that Bill Benton was not familiar with the use of smoke signals. It was hardly probable the warning had come from him.

She smoothed the worry from her face and carried the promised rice pudding to Mrs. Benton's room. "It's the way you like it, me darlin'," she said. "All nice and creamy, and don't you let me find a lick of it left when I come for the dish."

Back in the kitchen Tildy snatched up her long brass telescope, tucked the Colt .45 in a capacious apron pocket, and hurried out to the yard. The lack of life there was getting more and more on her nerves. It hurt her to see the once prosperous ranch visibly falling apart. She could hardly force herself to look at the empty barn and corrals.

"May the black curse ride that schemin' Matoon," she thought unhappily. "It fair breaks me heart to see me poor lamb lay there and Benton not able to raise a copper cent for the operation she needs. And her worried with fears that Benton will leave his bones in them Sinks."

She longed to climb to the platform high on the windmill tower, abandoned the idea. She dare not risk a fall, find herself crippled and unable to care for the helpless invalid. Her best vantage point was the flat roof of the henhouse.

She placed a short ladder and climbed up, the telescope clenched under an arm. Clouds were pushing over the mountains, threatening black masses that promised one of the violent thunderstorms that came so quickly at this time of the year. The clouds were moving fast to overtake the sun. She would have to hurry before the light was gone.

She leveled the telescope and carefully studied the distant landscape, choosing the general direction of the Sinks country.

She was about to give up when the lens fastened on a faint dust haze. She focused on it, and now she saw something that moved—a horse, she guessed.

"Sure is a horse," she murmured, "and movin'

awful slow, and maybe 'tis Bill Benton in the saddle, praise be."

She continued to gaze through the telescope, a puzzled expression creasing her face. "Sure and there's two of 'em on the horse," she said aloud. She moved the telescope, and now she saw more dust—rapid swirls that she knew meant horsemen riding fast, although yet too far distant for the glass to pick up.

Tildy's heart quickened. She lowered the telescope, annoyed at her suddenly trembling hands. Horsemen riding fast could mean only one thing. They were in pursuit of the lone horse with its double burden, and it was in her mind that one of the riders of the lone horse was Bill Benton.

She tried again, and her unsteady hands jerked the telescope beyond the second dust cloud, fastened on a third distant haze, a much smaller drift of dust.

She studied it frowningly, her agile mind working on the confusing problem, and of a sudden she felt that she had the answer. It was the horsemen making the third drift of dust who had used Indian smoke-talk to summon help. It also meant they knew it was possible to get help from the Dunbar ranch. There seemed no other solution that explained the approaching banners of dust. She prayed that the help promised by the answering smoke-talk from the western hills would arrive in time.

She turned her telescope in the direction of the Dunbar range, and warming hope surged through her. Only fast-riding horsemen could make the trailing banner of dust that rose sluggishly from the canyon.

She was about to take another look at the horse, with its double burden, when she heard the pound of rapidly approaching hoofbeats. Her head turned in a startled look at the rider drawing rein in the yard. She reached frantically for the gun in her apron pocket, stood there, on the henhouse roof, legs planted wide apart, leveled .45 in her clenched fingers. Surprise and relief widened her eyes, and she lowered the gun.

"Doggone you, Buck Salten!" She spoke happily. "You scared me most out of my skin!"

Buck gazed up at her. He had the haggard look of a man from whom all hope was forever gone, and his voice when he finally spoke was dull, lifeless. "Janet here, Tildy?" He asked the question as if he already knew the answer, but his eyes mutely begged her to tell him that Janet *was* there.

Tildy gazed down at him, aware of a dreadful chill in her bones. She slowly pushed the big Colt into her apron pocket, shook her head. "Janet ain't here, Buck."

Buck's long frame sagged more deeply in his saddle. "Ray Wellerton has made away with her," he said. "It's worse than livin' in hell,

Tildy—not knowin' what's happened to her."

Tildy was thinking fast. The smoke-talk was making more sense now. She said sharply, "Climb down from your saddle, Buck, and scramble up here. I reckon this telescope can tell you more than it tells me."

The urgency in her voice drew him from the saddle and up to the roof. He seized the telescope and, obeying her gesture, fixed it on the lone horse. She watched him, saw him stiffen, heard the quick intake of his breath.

"Some closer now," she said. "The horse is ridin' double, but I couldn't make out who was on him."

Buck lowered the telescope, looked at her, his eyes suddenly bright. "Benton," he said, "and—and Janet." Emotion choked his voice, and he lifted the glass for another look.

Tildy said quietly, "Point the glass back of 'em, Buck. Looks like trouble is ridin' hard on their trail."

The Diamond D man obeyed, stiffened again as he studied the larger dust cloud. "Don't savvy," he muttered. "Looks like they're bein' chased, but I sure don't savvy how Janet got away and how come she's with Benton." He thrust the telescope at her, frantic now to get back to his horse.

Tildy pushed the glass aside. "Look again," she said. "There's another outfit making dust yonder."

Buck leveled the telescope. "That's right," he muttered. "Ain't more than two or three riders, and sure comin' fast."

She gestured silently for him to point the telescope in the direction of the Dunbar range. He obeyed, and said wonderingly, "I don't savvy just how come, but I reckon it's Romero's outfit making that dust."

Tildy told him about the smoke-talk, and something like awe looked from the Diamond D man's eyes. "I reckon I *do* savvy," he said softly. "It's Mark Destin's work. It was him that sent them smoke signals for Romero to head this way instead of to Diamond D. It's the answer, Tildy, and I'm sayin' out loud that Mark is sure one smart tenderfoot."

"Tenderfoot your own self," retorted Tildy. "I'm thinkin' this La Cruz country could use a few more of *his* kind of tenderfoot."

Buck was studying the slow-moving lone horse with its double burden. "The bronc has give out," he muttered. "Janet and Benton are leavin' him and comin' on foot." He again hurriedly thrust the telescope at Tildy. "I've got to get fresh horses to 'em." He went scrambling down the ladder.

Tildy's voice stopped him. "No horses in the barn, Buck," she said unhappily.

Buck gazed up at her in silent consternation, then he was in his saddle and spurring from the yard. She watched until the tall sagebrush hid horse and rider from view. There seemed little chance now for Janet and Benton to escape capture or worse at the hands of the pursuers fast overtaking them.

The sun was gone, the heavens dark and foreboding, and sickening despair rolled over Tildy. She could have wept, only weeping never helped anybody. She prayed instead, as she went awkwardly down the short ladder. Prayer was the help in her power at that dreadful moment.

Janet was praying too as she stumbled across the chaparral, a wordless appeal for strength to keep going. The double burden and fast pace had been too much for the horse, and Benton had realized their best chance was to continue on foot, seek temporary safety in the rugged canyon, where horses could not follow. It was possible their pursuers would fail to notice the abandoned horse and keep going. A futile hope, Janet told herself. Pima the half-breed, was a skillful tracker and would quickly guess the truth and pick up the trail, only now the pack would be on foot, and every minute gained meant a minute longer to live. She knew that, once overtaken, Ray Wellerton would make a quick finish of the business.

She kept her mind cool, ran with swift, sure steps that avoided the boulders. It was harder to escape the clawing branches, and she was sickeningly aware that the torn fragments of her blouse would soon betray their direction to Pima's alert eyes.

They reached the rimrock, and Benton halted under an upthrust of rust-colored granite. She felt his anxious eyes on her, shook her head at him and forced a smile.

"I can keep this up for miles," she reassured. "Don't worry, Mr. Benton. I'm tough."

"You've got your dad's spirit," the tall ranchman said.

Her lips trembled, and she looked with tear-misted eyes at the blur of horsemen approaching up the trail they had just left. She was suddenly tense, and her hand lifted in a quick gesture. "Look! More riders—away down there?"

Benton gazed for a long moment. The darkening sky made visibility poor, but he knew those moving shapes were horsemen.

Janet said, faintly, as if afraid her voice might betray the feeble flicker of hope in her, "Do you think they—they might be friends?"

"I shouldn't wonder." Benton gazed at her thoughtfully. "There'll be a lot of people looking for you, Janet. I saw smoke signals in the sky some time back. Don't know how to read Indian smoke-talk and I kept quiet about it, not wanting to raise your hopes too much."

"Dear God," she prayed aloud, "make them *friends* and *not* enemies!"

Benton's gaze swept the upper trail, saw that

for the moment a ridge hid them from chance view of their pursuers. Once round the ridge, sharp eyes would discover the abandoned horse and men would soon be combing the chaparral.

Janet, watching him, waited his decision for their next move, saw excitement suddenly fire his eyes. He said quickly. "We'll fool them, Janet—head back the way we came, only we've got to keep out of sight. If those riders down there *are* friends we'll get to them a lot sooner."

She nodded mute assent, followed the quiet-moving ranchman along the boulder-strewn rim-rock. The pound of hoofs came to them clearly, and any moment would bring the riders round the bend of the ridge.

An angry shout warned them their horse had been discovered. The pounding of hoofs hushed. The sudden stillness was very frightening, and gooseflesh prickled Janet as she continued to creep stealthily from boulder to boulder. Pima would soon pick up the trail.

Benton's long strides forced her to run. Every moment was precious, drew them closer to the other horsemen she prayed were friends. A dry piñon branch snapped under her foot. She heard Benton's low, warning voice and slowed her pace, hoped fervently that the pistol-like report had not carried too far.

She began to doubt the wisdom of this back-tracking flight to meet the other riders. Even if they proved friends, searching for her, they would be pitifully outnumbered by her stepbrother's half score and more desperadoes. There would be a fight, bloodshed—dead men. Ray Wellerton had gone too far to give up his purpose.

The boulder-covered ground began a sharp downward slope, and Benton quickened his long stride, anxious for the concealment offered by the escarpment. Janet broke into another run, and he halted, waited for her to overtake him. She was breathless, leaned against a great slab of rock and looked up at the black clouds.

"It's going to storm," she said worriedly.

"I hope it *does* storm," Benton was examining his Winchester carbine. "They won't pick up our trail so easy."

Lightning flared in the distance; thunder muttered. Janet's nervousness grew. "Shouldn't we get closer to the trail?" she asked. "If those men *are* friends we mustn't let them miss seeing us."

Benton gazed at the approaching horsemen, his expression grave. He was not sure yet whether they were friend or foe. He hesitated to betray their presence unless certain of their identity. Janet's fears, though, were justifiable, and it was necessary to get closer to the trail before the unknown riders passed.

The stillness on the higher flats continued, and Janet wondered if, all unknown to them, the desperadoes were stealthily closing in. She checked the impulse to run, followed Benton quietly from boulder to boulder, and soon they were crouched behind a low-growing piñon scrub within a few yards of the trail.

Again the lightning flared, low on the dark horizon. Janet thought the thunder would never stop. The deafening reverberations quite covered the quick thud of horses' hoofs, and suddenly the first rider surged into view. Janet frantically clutched her companion's arm. She could hardly believe her senses.

She ran forward, calling his name, and Mark saw her, swung from the trail to her side. He was down in an instant from the saddle, gazed at her, speechless, put his arms round her in a brief, warm hug that said more than any words at that moment. He released her, found his voice. "I was afraid we wouldn't overtake you in time."

"I don't know how you managed it," Benton said. "It's a miracle." He gestured uptrail. "Our horse played out. We had to run for it on foot. I reckon they're searching the chaparral now, and no telling how close they are." He shook his head. "Only four of us, Mark, not counting Janet, and Wellerton has a big crowd with him."

"Only three of us," Mark said, a bit grimly. He spoke low words to Rafael, who nodded, hurriedly led the three horses behind a huge upthrust of rock. Surprise widened Janet's eyes as she recognized the third rider, still in his saddle.

Benton exclaimed savagely, “Matoon! What’s he doing here, Mark?”

“He’s my prisoner,” Mark told him.

“He’ll start yelling, bring the pack down on us,” worried Benton.

“Matoon knows he’s safer with us than with Wellerton,” Mark said. He saw their bewilderment, added hurriedly, “No time now to explain, and I think we’d better get on the other side of that butte.”

Janet and Benton followed him round great masses of slab-rock tumbled from the butte by countless years of erosion. The blocks of stone ridged out on both sides, formed a natural rampart twice the height of a tall man.

Benton’s quick look took in the possibilities. He said in a satisfied voice, “We can stand ’em off here, Mark.” A new worry creased his face, and he added gloomily, “As long as our ammunition holds out.”

Mark said, “Listen! I heard sounds up there on the rimrock.” He gave Benton an approving look. “You’ve got them puzzled, doubling back on them.”

“I figured they’d lose some time pickin’ up the trail,” growled Benton. “I reckon they don’t guess you’re so close, Mark. The thunder smothered your broncs’ hoofbeats, and dust wasn’t showin’ good with the sky so dark.”

"We'll surprise them," Mark said. He gave Janet a reassuring grin.

"I don't understand how you knew what had happened to me."

"You hadn't been gone long when Buck and I got there." Mark shook his head at her. "We'll talk about it some other time—when we have *more* time. I'll tell you this much. I went back to town in a hurry and got Plácido Romero and his men riding for the ranch to help Buck start the search. Then I picked up a trail that led Rafael and me to the Sinks, and that's how we got here."

"I saw smoke-talk," Benton told him. "I don't savvy smoke-talk but figured something was up."

Mark smiled at the Mexican, who was alertly watching the rimrock. "It was Rafael's idea," he explained, and gave Janet another reassuring smile. "Romero is on the way. It's up to us to hold the fort until he gets here."

Matoon broke his dejected silence. "Get me down from this horse. I'm as raw as a skinned rabbit."

Janet and Benton looked at him, and there was no pity in their eyes. Benton said curtly, "You'd be a *dead* rabbit if I had my way."

No more words came from Matoon. He sagged miserably in the saddle, head bowed.

Rafael spoke softly, "*Señor*—men come!"

They stood silent, tense. The crackle in the dry underbrush was plainly audible. The searchers were getting impatient, eager to end the chase. The victims they sought were only two—and one of them a girl.

Rough voices reached them. "These here pieces of flannel sure come from the girl's shirt," one of them said. "They cain't have got fur."

Janet recognized Pima's voice. The half-breed had picked up the trail. She could not repress a shiver of fear. They were so few, the others so many.

Ray Wellerton's voice came, impatient, furious. "Scatter out, fellers. We've got to finish this business before the storm breaks."

The trampling in the brush grew louder. Hurrying bootheels clattered on the rimrock. A man appeared, stood motionless, vaguely outlined against the dark sky. Before Mark could stop him, Benton boiling with rage, and always impatient, raised his carbine and fired. Crackling thunder drowned the sound of the shot. They saw the man stagger, pitch headlong down the steep slope.

Chapter 20

Buck Salten reined his horse from the trail. The gunshots came from somewhere down on the lower mesa. He was familiar with the country and suspected that Benton and Janet were trapped in the tumbled masses of rock that ridged the crumbled remains of the ancient butte.

The storm was shifting over from the mountains, and the dense black clouds spread a somber pall over the rugged landscape. Lightning intermittently ripped the blackness overhead, drew reverberating crashes of thunder that made the horse flinch.

Buck got down from the saddle, tied the horse to a piñon, examined the Winchester he slid from leather boot, and turned in the direction of the rimrock. It meant an extra hundred yards, but he had a hunch that the trail was vulnerable to watchful eyes.

Sounds halted him—the stamp of hoofs, the creak of saddle leather. The outfit's horses, he guessed, and restless because of the incessant thunder. He peered through the bushes, got a look at them, and the count told him that some fifteen men were somewhere between him and Janet. He was about to move on when he saw something else—a man, sitting on his heels, eyes intent on the cigarette he was making.

Buck shifted the Winchester to his left hand, slid his Colt .45 from holster, and soft-footed as a stalking panther, he crept close. Too late the man sensed his danger and made a quick sideways roll. The heavy barrel of the gun caught him across the temple. It was a bone-crushing blow that Buck made no attempt to soften. He knew without a second look that the horse-guard would be senseless for a long time.

He stood for a moment, gaze on the horses. He would have liked to turn them loose. Moments were too precious, and the attempt might draw fatal attention.

A vivid flare of lightning outlined the shape of another man crouched under a ledge, warned him that lookouts were posted there. He changed his course, and, desperate now, ran swiftly from bush to bush across the mesa, found himself close to the trail again.

He halted and scrutinized the trail, which at this point ran under an overhanging bluff. A quick dash under the bluff would carry him to the downslope and close to the old butte. It was risky. Even in that vague light he would make a visible target. He hesitated, although his fears were not for himself. He was thinking of Janet. He would be of no use to her—*dead.*

He was thankful he had resisted the impulse when suddenly his probing gaze fastened on the shape of a man sprawled between two boulders under the low branches of a piñon. His spine prickled. The attempt to run under the bluff would have meant a quick finish. The lookout would not have missed so close a target.

Buck slid the .45 from its holster again, crept nearer the unsuspecting man, heard his drawling voice. "That you, Shack? The boss said for you to stick close to the broncs."

Buck muttered an unintelligible grunt. It was plain the lookout took it for granted he was a member of the outfit. The man had no reason to expect a surprise attack from the rear.

"Benton sure picked hisself a good place to hole up in," continued the lazy drawl. "No way to git at him and the gal from this end."

Buck grunted again, crept closer, lifted his gun. He withheld the blow, curious to hear more from the loquacious lookout.

"Sure is queer about them fellers that holed up with 'em down thar," the man went on. "Looks like they must have trailed up from the Sinks and we never seen 'em. One of 'em killed Turkey Jones first shot."

Buck risked a question, his voice a hoarse whisper. "Where's the boss?"

"Him and Curly went up the bluff acrost the trail. They figger they can overlook them rocks and do some good shootin'—" The lookout man was suddenly silent, aware now of something suspiciously wrong about the hoarse whisper of the man behind him. Buck gave him no time to think about it, struck quick and hard.

He left the senseless man, hurried across the trail, and began the climb up the steep bluff. He had gained valuable information, felt reasonably certain that one of the riders who had joined Benton and Janet down in the rocks was Mark Destin. The last bit of information was not so good. Wellerton and Curly were up on the bluff, where they could get a good view of their human targets.

Fear put speed and strength into Buck's legs. He went up the steep cliff with the agility of a mountain goat.

He reached the last ledge for a final pull to the top, paused to regain his breath and for a cautious look. There was a stillness now, a momentary lull after the last reverberating roll of thunder, and above the beat of his laboring heart he fancied he heard the distant thud of fast-running horses. The sound recharged flagging muscles. *Romero and his vaqueros.*

He swung his legs over the ledge, got to his feet. He had left the rifle at the foot of the bluff, concealed in a crevice. It would be close quarters, and the only weapon he wanted was his short gun. He pulled the .45 from its holster and ran silently towards the pinnacle. It was on the far side he would find the two men he sought.

The sharp report of a rifle shocked his ears,

and then a crash of thunder blotted out all other sound, including the pounding of his boots as fear drove his legs into long, leaping strides.

Gunfire crackled under the overtones of thunder as he turned sharply round the pinnacle. He glimpsed Curly, rifle raised for another shot at the helpless targets below. Buck fired. The rifle dropped from Curly's hand. He half rose from his crouch. Suddenly his lifeless body was following his rifle down the cliff.

Wellerton saw Buck now and swung his rifle at him. The bullet struck the barrel of Buck's gun, knocked it from his hand. He kept on running, and panic showed stark on Wellerton's face. He dropped the rifle, clawed frantically at the gun in his holster. Buck's hand cut edgewise on his wrist. The gun spun from his fingers, and suddenly the men were locked in an embrace that both knew only death for one of them could break.

Wellerton was heavier than Buck, and sheer terror gave him berserk strength. Twice he came close to pushing his adversary over the cliff. Buck kept his footing, relentlessly battled the heavier man away from the precipice. His rage was under control now. He fought coolly, used all the tricks he knew; but the fear of death was in Wellerton, and again he slowly forced Buck nearer and nearer the cliff.

The fight was plainly visible to Janet. She had

seen Curly's body hurtling down the sheer side of the bluff and knew that the men struggling so desperately up there were Buck and her stepbrother. She knew, too, that Buck had arrived just in time to save them all from massacre. The first rifle bullet had broken Benton's gun arm, and she guessed from the blood-stained shirt that Mark had been hit somewhere, evidently not a serious wound. He and Rafael were still firing at anything that moved up on the mesa.

Her heart stood still. Ray was forcing Buck close to the edge again, only this time it was where the bluff fell less steeply, and there were shelves of rock, almost like a broad stairway.

A startled exclamation from Benton distracted her attention. The tall ranchman was looking curiously at Matoon, who was hanging sideways from his saddle.

"He's dead," Benton said. "One of those bullets got him in the head."

Mark heard him, left Rafael to watch the barricade, and hurried to help Benton free the lawyer's lifeless body from the saddle.

Janet felt no particular emotion about it. She was more concerned with what was happening up on the bluff. Watching Buck being slowly pushed to the edge of the cliff was more than she could bear. She was only vaguely conscious of excited Spanish words from Rafael.

"Look—Romero comes!" And he added contentedly in English for her benefit, "Thees fight ees finish. Those *bandidos* run like dogs."

Guns were popping on the mesa. Janet heard dismayed yells, the pounding hoofs of running horses. *Rafael was wrong.* It was not yet finished, this nightmare of horror, not while Buck Salten still fought his lone desperate fight with the madman who was her stepbrother.

She felt Mark close at her side, said piteously, without looking at him, her gaze intent on the struggling men, "Can't we do something? Oh, please, Mark, do something. I can't bear it!"

His arm went round her waist. It seemed good to lean against its strength. There was a gentleness there, a reassurance that he could not put into words. She recalled a favorite quotation of her father's, from the old prophet Isaiah: *In quietness and in confidence shall be our strength.* It was the strength that made Buck Salten and Mark Destin both so fine. She had been slow to really understand these men.

She was deaf to the gunfire on the mesa, the shrill yells as the *desperados* scattered and fled. She had eyes only for that life-and-death struggle on the brink of the cliff. She was unaware of her scream when the two men pitched over the edge. She saw Buck twist free and catch hold of a ledge. He hung there for a precarious moment, then pulled himself to safety.

Fascinated, horrified, Janet's gaze followed

her stepbrother's falling body as it went bouncing from ledge to ledge with ever-gaining momentum. It hit the trail, and three riders in frantic flight from the vaqueros spurred past at the moment. The horses did their best to leap over the tumbling body. Janet turned her head away, and it was against Mark's shoulder that she hid her eyes.

Now it really was finished.

She never quite knew how she got to the Benton ranch. She was too exhausted, drained of strength, to care much about what was happening. She had confused recollections of a courtly, grey-haired Mexican on a big cream-colored horse, and that he carried her across his saddle, and then Tildy Hogan was tucking her into bed, and, oddly enough, Dr. Bralen was at the bedside.

The doctor was in the dining room, talking to Bill Benton, when she came down to breakfast the next morning. She wondered at the look on the tall ranchman's face. Something had made Benton very happy.

"I was on my way to pay Red O'Malley my promised visit when I ran into Romero," Dr. Bralen explained. "It seemed a good idea to come here instead." He glanced contentedly at Benton's bandaged arm. "Lucky I did, what with gunshot wounds to patch up and a very tired young lady to look after."

Tildy Hogan, also extraordinarily happy, placed

a cup of hot coffee in front of her. "You're lookin' fine, lass," she said. "I'll bring your breakfast right in. You'll be wantin' to be on your way to Diamond D."

Dr. Bralen pushed out of his chair, said patients were waiting for him in town. Benton followed him from the room. Janet's gaze trailed after the tall, gaunt doctor. Something had happened to him. He was changed, the look of hopelessness and defeat gone from him. His eyes were clear, his shoulders erect, and his bearing that of a man unafraid.

"A grand man," Tildy said happily. " 'Tis heaven he's brought to this house."

Janet understood, and excitement made her voice breathless. "You mean Mrs. Benton?"

Tildy beamed at her. "Sure and I do mean it, child. He's goin' to operate on her. She'll be as good as ever in a couple of months, he says, bless the dear lamb."

"Oh, Tildy!"

" 'Twas Mark Destin got Benton to let him have a look at her," Tildy said. "A smart young man, for all he's a tenderfoot, they say. Got nicked in the side by one of them bullets. The doc patched him up."

Janet diffidently asked the question that had been vexing her mind. "Where is Mr. Destin? Has he gone back to La Cruz?"

"I'm thinkin' that right now he's roundin' up

the horse herd and pickin' out a team he can hitch to the buckboard." Tildy watched her with shrewd eyes. "He's drivin' you to Diamond D, he says."

"Oh!" Janet looked down at her coffee cup. "He—he says *that,* does he?"

"He's a young man you can't stop from gettin' what he wants," asserted Tildy. "He just goes right after it and no bones about it." She sighed comfortably. "You should have seen the way he fixed that pesky old windmill."

Janet slowly drank her coffee, her expression thoughtful. "Where's Buck?" she inquired.

"Sure and Buck kept on goin' to your ranch soon as the doctor patched up his scratches. Took some of Romero's vaqueros along with him."

Thinking of the ranch filled Janet with impatience to get back to the old house. Juana and Red O'Malley would be wanting to see her, reassure themselves that she was all right. She was anxious to see Buck, too. There were things she wanted to tell him—an important decision.

She made a hasty breakfast, paid Mrs. Benton a brief visit to congratulate her on the good news, and hurried out to the ranch yard.

Mark was waiting with the buckboard. They exchanged grave little smiles, and she climbed into the seat.

They drove in silence through a country washed clean by the storm. Another kind of storm had washed away a lot of blight and misery from the country's soul.

Mark broke the silence. "Things are going to be different," he said.

"Yes." She spoke thoughtfully. "It's been a horrible nightmare—weeks of horrible nightmares. It's hard to believe it is all finished."

"It's finished," Mark said. "You can forget it."

"I've been a little fool, Mark. You saved me in spite of—you and Buck."

"Forget it," he repeated.

"Not *that* part of it, Mark." Her low voice was not quite steady. "You came to La Cruz to buy a cow-ranch and bought only a lot of trouble."

"I'd do it again," Mark told her simply.

"I'm giving Buck an interest in Diamond D," she continued. "He's more than earned it, and the Borrego Creek strip is well worth a half-interest. I'm telling him the moment I get home."

"I'm glad for Buck—and for you," Mark said. He gave her a faint smile. "As Jim Ball says, they don't come finer than Buck."

She turned her head in a curious look at him. "What will you do, now that you can't buy Diamond D for your cow-ranch?"

He was silent, his thoughts on the brief talk he had just had with Bill Benton. It had been a satisfying talk, and Benton had readily agreed to sell Mark a half-interest in the ranch. He was bankrupt, and money was needed to put the ranch on its feet. Mark believed he could not do better with his twenty thousand dollars. He would learn the cow-business from the ground up.

"I'll be taking Emma to live in Santa Fe in two or three years," Benton had said. "Bar B will be all yours, Mark."

Mark thought of certain boundary lines. Bar B and Diamond D were neighbors across miles of range. Perhaps those boundary lines would be gone someday, the two ranches one vast range.

Janet's voice recalled her question. "I was asking about your own plans," she reminded. "You see—" She hesitated, a soft, shy note in her voice. "Well—I mean, it's a shame for you to give up your plans."

"I'm not giving up my plans." Laughter, a certain triumph, were in his voice. "I've just bought a half-interest in the Benton ranch, and that makes us neighbors."

Janet's mouth opened, but no words came. She could only gaze at him, her eyes bright with pleasure.

"I came out west to go into the cow-business," Mark said, a hint of hardness in his voice. "I made up my mind years ago I'd be a cowman someday, and now I *am* a cowman."

Janet came out of her trance. "Tildy Hogan said you couldn't be stopped from getting what you wanted," she said, and added sedately, "Now we're neighbors you must come and see me—and Buck—when you're not too busy."

"I'll be using this road a lot of times," Mark promised. "I'll get to know every chuckhole in the dark."

They both laughed, and then a silence fell between them, a sweet silence that neither wanted to break. So much had happened since the evening only some seventy-six hours earlier when they had met face to face for the first time on the dingy hotel porch. Hours of violence and bloodshed and death, a dreadful furnace of hate and greed and murder to temper the good steel of their courage. It was all over now, and the world seemed very beautiful in their eyes, the future beckoning—full of promise.

They turned into the ranch avenue. Mark halted the team. "Listen," he said.

It was Red O'Malley's accordion they heard, and his lilting tenor voice, and the words came softly through the trees:

> Sugar in the gourd and honey in the
>   horn,
> I was never so happy since the hour
>   I was born.

About the Author

Arthur Henry Gooden (October 23, 1879–July 22, 1971) was born in England and emigrated to the United States around the turn of the 20th century. He worked on a ranch in the San Joaquin Valley in California before turning his talents to writing. He wrote short stories for magazines, fifty-three Hollywood screenplays, and, combining his first-hand knowledge of cowboy life with compelling dialogue amongst his characters, Gooden authored several Western novels, including six books under the pen name Brett Rider. He died in Los Angeles, California.

Center Point Large Print
600 Brooks Road / PO Box 1
Thorndike, ME 04986-0001 USA

(207) 568-3717

US & Canada:
1 800 929-9108
www.centerpointlargeprint.com